DEADLY EXPERIMENT

When Fallows came to, he was seated in a heavy chair. His arms had been attached to the arms of the chair and his legs to its legs by yards of elastic bandage, wound round and round. Two men were watching him. Both were in their shirt sleeves, wearing surgical gloves.

"I think our patient is coming round."

"What the bloody hell are you playing at?" said Fallows.

"First, I'm going to give you these pills. They're ordinary sleeping pills. I think four should be sufficient. We don't want you actually to go to sleep. Just to feel drowsy.... We'll give them five minutes to start working. What we're trying is an experiment which has often been suggested but never, I think, actually performed. We're going to give you successive doses of scopalamine dextrin to inhale, while we ask you some questions.... The snag about this method," he continued, in the same level tones of a professor addressing a class of students, "is that the interreaction of the sedative and the stimulant would be so sharp that it might, if persisted with, affect the subject's heart. You'll appreciate, therefore, that by prolonging our dialogue you may be risking your own life. Now then, let's start..."

THE JOHN CREASEY CRIME COLLECTION

VOLUME 1

Edited by HERBERT HARRIS

ST. MARTIN'S PRESS/NEW YORK

Published in hardcover as *John Creasey's Crime Collection 1985*

THE JOHN CREASEY CRIME COLLECTION VOLUME 1

ISBN: 0-312-90128-3

Printed in the United States of America

First St. Martin's Press mass market edition/April 1987

10 9 8 7 6 5 4 3 2 1

CONTENTS

ACKNOWLEDGEMENTS

Acknowledgements are due to the author and Elaine Greene Ltd for "Great Aunt Allie's Flypapers" by P. D. James; to *Ellery Queen's Mystery Magazine* for "Arabella's Answer" by Peter Lovesey, "Bluebeard's Key" by Celia Fremlin, and "Love Affair" by Julian Symons; to *The Gourmet Crook Book* (Everest) for "The Whispering" by Christianna Brand; to *Weekend* for "Skeleton in the Cupboard" by Tony Wilmot; to *Mr Calder and Mr Behrens* (Harper & Row) for "The Killing of Michael Finnegan" by Michael Gilbert; to *Fiction Magazine* for "Boots" by Antonia Fraser; to *Winter's Crimes 7* (Macmillan) for "Inspector Ghote and the Noted British Author" by H. R. F. Keating; to *A Touch of Chill* (Gollancz) for "Time to Laugh" by Joan Aiken; to *Alfred Hitchcock's Mystery Magazine* for "Joe" by Penelope Wallace; to *John Creasey's Mystery Magazine* for "Detective's Wife" by Herbert Harris; to *Crime Wave* (Collins) for "Little Knives" by Madelaine Duke. "Business Lunch" by Celia Dale and "To Have and To Hold" by Clare Dawson are original stories.

INTRODUCTION

When members of the Crime Writers' Association gathered in Salisbury last year for their annual conference, the locale on this occasion was particularly apt, for in Salisbury's City Library is housed the John Creasey Literary Museum, a permanent memorial to the man who founded the Crime Writers' Association in 1953.

Few writers have been commemorated in this way, but Creasey (whose funeral I attended as the CWA's representative when he was laid to rest in a country churchyard near his home at Bodenham in 1973) was certainly Britain's most prolific author. He wrote not only some 560 novels, but numerous short stories as well.

Short story writing always fascinated him, and he provided outlets for short story writers by founding the *John Creasey Mystery Magazine* in 1956 and the *John Creasey Mystery Bedside Book*, a hardback anthology, in 1960.

The magazine, alas, ceased publication after nine years, but the *Bedside Book* continued until 1976, Creasey himself editing the first six editions, the last ten editions being edited by myself under the auspices of the CWA.

Although Creasey had been dead for four years when *Bedside Book* became *Crime Collection* in 1977, under the Gollancz imprint, it was decided to keep the name of John Creasey in the title, for, after all, the anthology was—and still is—under CWA patronage and Creasey was the Association's begetter.

It gives me great pleasure to continue his work in winning a wider readership for the brilliantly inventive short stories appearing under the label of "crime". For Creasey, selecting the stories was a labour of love, as it is for me.

HERBERT HARRIS

GREAT AUNT ALLIE'S FLYPAPERS

P. D. James

"YOU SEE MY dear Adam," explained the Canon gently as he walked with Chief Superintendent Dalgliesh under the Vicarage elms, "useful as the legacy would be to us, I wouldn't feel happy in accepting it if Great Aunt Allie came by her money in the first place by wrongful means."

What the Canon meant was that he and his wife wouldn't be happy to inherit Great Aunt Allie's £50,000 if, sixty-seven years earlier, she had poisoned her elderly husband with arsenic in order to get it. As Great Aunt Allie had been accused and acquitted of just that charge in a 1902 trial which, for her Hampshire neighbours, had rivalled the Coronation as a public spectacle, the Canon's scruples were not altogether irrelevant. Admittedly, thought Dalgliesh, most people faced with the prospect of £50,000 would be happy to subscribe to the commonly held convention that once an English Court has pronounced its verdict the final truth of the matter has been established once and for all. There may possibly be a higher judicature in the next world, but hardly in this. And so Hubert Boxdale might normally be happy to believe. But, faced with the prospect of an unexpected fortune, his scrupulous conscience was troubled. The gentle but obstinate voice went on:

"Apart from the moral principle of accepting tainted money, it wouldn't bring us happiness. I often think of that poor woman, driven restlessly around Europe in her search for peace, of that lonely life and unhappy death."

Dalgliesh recalled that Great Aunt Allie had moved in a predictable progress with her retinue of servants, current lover and general hangers-on from one luxury Riviera hotel to the next, with stays in Paris or Rome as the mood suited her. He was not sure that this orderly programme of comfort and entertainment could be described as being restlessly driven around Europe, or that the old lady had been primarily in search of peace. She had died, he recalled, by falling overboard from a millionaire's yacht during a rather wild party given by him to celebrate her eighty-eighth birthday. It was perhaps not an edifying death by the Canon's standards but he doubted whether she had, in fact, been unhappy at the time. Great Aunt Allie (it was impossible to think of her by any other name), if she had been capable of coherent thought, would probably have pronounced it a very good way to go. But this was hardly a point of view he could put to his companion.

Canon Hubert Boxdale was Superintendent Adam Dalgliesh's godfather. Dalgliesh's father had been his Oxford contemporary and life-long friend. He had been an admirable godfather, affectionate, uncensorious, genuinely concerned. In Dalgliesh's childhood he had been mindful of birthdays and imaginative about a small boy's preoccupations and desires. Dalgliesh was very fond of him and privately thought him one of the few really good men he had known. It was only surprising that the Canon had managed to live to seventy-one in a carnivorous world in which gentleness, humility and unworldliness are hardly conducive to survival let alone success. But his goodness had in some sense protected him. Faced with such manifest innocence, even those who exploited him, and they were not a few, extended some of the protection and compassion they might show to the slightly subnormal.

"Poor old darling", his daily woman would say, pocketing pay for six hours when she had worked five and helping herself to a couple of eggs from his refrigerator. "He's really not fit to be let out alone." It had surprised the then young and slightly priggish Detective Constable Dalgliesh to realise that the Canon knew perfectly well about the hours and the eggs but thought that Mrs Copthorne with five children and an indolent husband needed both more than he did. He also knew that if he started paying for five hours she would promptly work only four and extract another two eggs and that this small and only dishonesty was somehow necessary to her self-esteem. He was good. But he was not a fool.

He and his wife were, of course, poor. But they were not unhappy; indeed it was a word impossible to associate with the

Canon. The death of his two sons in the 1939 war had saddened but not destroyed him. But he had anxieties. His wife was suffering from disseminated sclerosis and was finding it increasingly hard to manage. There were comforts and appliances which she would need. He was now, belatedly, about to retire and his pension would be small. A legacy of £50,000 would enable them both to live in comfort for the rest of their lives and would also, Dalgliesh had no doubt, give them the pleasure of doing more for their various lame dogs. Really, he thought, the Canon was an almost embarrassingly deserving candidate for a modest fortune. Why couldn't the dear silly old noodle take the cash and stop worrying? He said cunningly:

"She was found not guilty, you know, by an English jury. And it all happened nearly seventy years ago. Couldn't you bring yourself to accept their verdict?"

But the Canon's scrupulous mind was impervious to such sly innuendoes. Dalgliesh told himself that he should have remembered what, as a small boy, he had discovered about Uncle Hubert's conscience; that it operated as a warning bell and that, unlike most people, he never pretended that it hadn't sounded or that he hadn't heard it or that, having heard it, something must be wrong with the mechanism.

"Oh, I did, while she was alive. We never met, you know. I didn't wish to force myself on her. After all, she was a wealthy woman. My grandfather made a new will on his marriage and left her all he possessed. Our ways of life were very different. But I usually wrote briefly at Christmas and she sent a card in reply. I wanted to keep some contact in case, one day, she might want someone to turn to and would remember that I am a priest."

And why should she want that, thought Dalgliesh. To clear her conscience? Was that what the dear old boy had in mind? So he must have had doubts from the beginning. But of course he had! Dalgliesh knew something of the story and the general feeling of the family and friends was that Great Aunt Allie had been extremely lucky to escape the gallows. His own father's view, expressed with reticence, reluctance and compassion had not in essentials differed from that given by a local reporter at the time.

"How on earth did she expect to get away with it? Damn lucky to escape topping if you ask me."

"The news of the legacy came as a complete surprise?" asked Dalgliesh.

"Indeed yes. I only saw her once at that first and only Christmas six weeks after her marriage when my grandfather died. We always talk of her as Great Aunt Allie but in fact, as you know, she married my grandfather. But it seemed impossible to think of her as a step-grandmother. There was the usual family gathering at Colebrook Croft at the time and I was there with my parents and my twin sisters. I was barely four and the twins were just eight months old. I can remember nothing of my grandfather or of his wife. After the murder—if one has to use that dreadful word—my mother returned home with us children leaving my father to cope with the police, the solicitors and the newsmen. It was a terrible time for him. I don't think I was even told that grandfather was dead until about a year later. My old nurse, who had been given Christmas as a holiday to visit her own family, told me that soon after my return home I asked her if grandfather was now young and beautiful for always. She, poor woman, took it as a sign of infant prognostication and piety. Poor Nellie was sadly superstitious and sentimental, I'm afraid. But I knew nothing of grandfather's death at the time and certainly can recall nothing of that Christmas visit or of my new step-grandmother. Mercifully, I was little more than a baby when the murder was done."

"She was a music hall artiste, wasn't she?" asked Dalgliesh.

"Yes and a very talented one. My grandfather met her when she was working with a partner in a hall in Cannes. He had gone to the south of France with a manservant for his health. I understand that she extracted a gold watch from his chain and, when he claimed it, told him that he was English, had recently suffered from a stomach ailment, had two sons and a daughter and was about to have a wonderful surprise. It was all correct except that his only daughter had died in childbirth leaving him a granddaughter, Marguerite Goddard."

"And all easily guessable from his voice and appearance," said Dalgliesh. "I suppose the surprise was the marriage?"

"It was certainly a surprise, and a most unpleasant one for

the family. It is easy to deplore the snobbishness and the conventions of another age and, indeed, there was much in Edwardian England to deplore. But it was not a propitious marriage. I think of the difference in background, education and way of life, the lack of common interest. And there was this great disparity of age. My grandfather had married a girl just three months younger than his own granddaughter. I cannot wonder that the family were concerned; that they felt that the union could not, in the end, contribute to the contentment or happiness of either party."

"And that was putting it charitably," thought Dalgliesh. The marriage certainly hadn't contributed to their happiness. From the point of view of the family it had been a disaster. He recalled hearing of an incident when the local vicar and his wife, a couple who had actually dined at Colebrook Croft on the night of the murder, first called on the bride. Apparently old Augustus Boxdale had introduced her by saying:

"Meet the prettiest little variety artiste in the business. Took a gold watch and notecase off me without any trouble. Would have had the elastic out of my pants if I hadn't watched out. Anyway she stole my heart, didn't you, sweetheart?" All this accompanied by a hearty slap on the rump and a squeal of delight from the lady who had promptly demonstrated her skill by extracting the Reverend Arthur Venables' bunch of keys from his left ear.

Dalgliesh thought it tactful not to remind the Canon of this story.

"What do you wish me to do, Sir?" he enquired.

"It's asking a great deal, I know, when you're so busy. But if I had your assurance that you believed in Aunt Allie's innocence I should feel happy about accepting the bequest. I wondered if it would be possible for you to see the records of the trial. Perhaps it would give you a clue. You're so clever at this sort of thing."

He spoke without flattery but with an innocent wonder at the strange avocations of men. Dalgliesh was, indeed, very clever at this sort of thing. A dozen or so men at present occupying security wings in H.M. prisons could testify to Chief Superintendent Dalgliesh's cleverness; as, indeed, could a handful of others walking free whose defending Counsel had been, in their own way, as clever as Chief Superintendent Dalgliesh. But to re-examine a case over sixty years old seemed to require clairvoyance rather than cleverness. The trial judge and both learned Counsel had been dead for over fifty years. Two world wars had taken their toll. Four reigns had passed. It was highly probable that, of those who had slept under the roof of Colbrook Croft on that fateful Boxing Day night of 1901, only the Canon still survived. But the old man was troubled and had sought his help and Dalgliesh, with a day or two's leave due to him, had the time to give it.

"I'll do what I can," he promised.

The transcript of a trial which had taken place sixty-seven years ago took time and trouble to obtain, even for a Chief Superintendent of the Metropolitan Police. It provided little potential comfort for the Canon. Mr Justice Bellow had summed up with that avuncular simplicity with which he was wont to address juries, regarding them apparently as a panel of well-intentioned but cretinous children. And the facts could have been comprehended by any intelligent child. Part of the summing up set them out with admirable lucidity:

"And so, gentlemen of the jury, we come to the night of December 26th. Mr Augustus Boxdale, who had perhaps indulged a little unwisely on Christmas Day, had retired to bed in his dressing-room after luncheon suffering from a recurrence of the slight indigestive trouble which had afflicted him for most of his life. You have heard that he had taken luncheon with the members of his family and ate nothing which they too did not eat. You may feel you can acquit luncheon of anything worse than overrichness.

"Dinner was served at eight p.m. promptly, as was the custom at Colebrook Croft. There were present at that meal, Mrs Augustus Boxdale the deceased's bride; his elder son Captain Maurice Boxdale with his wife; his younger son the Reverend Henry Boxdale with his wife; his granddaughter Miss Marguerite Goddard; and two neighbours, the Reverend and Mrs Arthur Venables.

"You have heard how the accused took only the first course at dinner which was ragoût of beef and then, at about eight-twenty, left the dining-room to sit with her husband. Shortly after nine o'clock she rang for the parlour-maid, Mary Huddy, and ordered a basin of gruel to be brought up to Mr Boxdale. You have heard that the deceased was fond of gruel, and, indeed, as prepared by Mrs Muncie the cook, it sounds a most nourishing and comforting dish for an elderly gentleman of weak digestion.

"You have heard Mrs Muncie describe how she prepared the gruel according to Mrs Beaton's admirable recipe and in the presence of Mary Huddy in case, as she said, 'the master should take a fancy to it when I'm not at hand and you have to make it'. After the gruel had been prepared, Mrs Muncie tasted it with a spoon and Mary Huddy carried it upstairs to the main bedroom, together with a jug of water to thin the gruel if it were too strong. As she reached the door, Mrs Boxdale came out, her hands full of stockings and underclothes. She has told you that she was on her way to the bathroom to wash them through. She asked the girl to put the basin of gruel on the washstand by the window and Mary Huddy did so in her presence. Miss Huddy has told you that, at the time, she noticed the bowl of flypapers soaking in water and she knew that this solution was one used by Mrs Boxdale as a cosmetic wash. Indeed, all the women who spent that evening in the house, with the exception of Mrs Venables, have told you that they knew it was Mrs Boxdale's practice to prepare this solution of flypapers.

"Mary Huddy and the accused left the bedroom together and you have heard the evidence of Mrs Muncie that Miss Huddy returned to the kitchen after an absence of only a few minutes. Shortly after nine o'clock the ladies left the dining-room and entered the drawing-room to take coffee. At nine-fifteen p.m. Miss Goddard excused herself to the company and said that she would go to see if her grandfather needed anything. The time is established precisely because the clock struck the quarter-hour as she left and Mrs Venables commented on the sweetness of its chime. You have also heard Mrs Venables' evidence and the evidence of Mrs Maurice Boxdale and Mrs Henry Boxdale that none of the ladies left the drawing-room during the evening; and Mr Venables has testified that the three gentlemen remained together until Miss Goddard appeared about three-quarters of an hour later to inform them that her grandfather had become very ill and to request that the doctor be sent for immediately.

"Miss Goddard has told you that, when she entered her grandfather's room, he was just finishing his gruel and was grumbling about its taste. She got the impression that this was merely a protest at being deprived of his dinner rather than that he genuinely considered that there was something wrong with the gruel. At any rate, he finished most of it and appeared to enjoy it despite his grumbles.

"You have heard Miss Goddard describe how, after her grandfather had had as much as he wanted of the gruel, she took the bowl next door and left it on the washstand. She then returned to her grandfather's bedroom and Mr Boxdale, his wife and his granddaughter played three-handed whist for about three-quarters of an hour.

"At ten o'clock Mr Augustus Boxdale complained of feeling very ill. He suffered from griping pains in the stomach, from sickness, and from looseness of the bowel. As soon as the symptoms began Miss Goddard went downstairs to let her uncles know that her grandfather was worse and to ask that Doctor Eversley should be sent for urgently. Doctor Eversley has given you his evidence. He arrived at Colebrook Croft at ten-thirty p.m. when he found his patient very distressed and weak. He treated the symptoms and gave what relief he could, but Mr Augustus Boxdale died shortly before midnight.

"Gentlemen of the jury, you have heard Marguerite Goddard describe how, as her grandfather's paroxysms increased in intensity, she remembered the gruel and wondered whether it could have disagreed with him in some way. She mentioned this possibility to her elder uncle, Captain Maurice Boxdale. Captain Boxdale has told you how he at once handed the bowl, with its residue of gruel, to Doctor Eversley with the request that the Doctor should lock it in a cupboard in the library, seal the lock, and himself keep the key. You have heard how the contents of the bowl were later analysed and with what result."

An extraordinary precaution for the gallant Captain to have taken, thought Dalgliesh, and a most perspicacious young woman. Was it by chance or by design that the bowl hadn't been taken down to be washed up as soon as the old man had finished with it? Why was it, he wondered, that Marguerite Goddard hadn't rung for the parlour-maid and requested her to remove it? Miss Goddard appeared the only other suspect. He wished he knew more about her.

But, except for the main protagonists, the characters in the drama did not emerge very clearly from the trial report. Why, indeed, should they? The British accusatorial system of trial is designed to answer one question: is the accused guilty, beyond reasonable doubt, of the crime charged? Exploration of the nuances of personality, speculation and gossip have no place in the witness-box. The two Boxdale brothers came out as very dull fellows indeed. They and their estimable, respectable, sloping-bosomed wives had sat at dinner in full view of each other from eight until after nine o'clock (a substantial meal that dinner) and had said so in the witness-box more or less in identical words. The ladies' bosoms might have been heaving with far from estimable emotions of dislike, envy, embarrassment, or resentment of the interloper. If so, they didn't tell the Court.

But the two brothers and their wives were clearly innocent, even if a detective of that time could have conceived of the guilt of gentlefolk so well respected, so eminently respectable. Even their impeccable alibis had a nice touch of social and sexual distinction. The Reverend Arthur Venables had vouched for the gentlemen, his good wife for the ladies. Besides, what motive had they? They could no longer gain financially by the old man's death. If anything, it was in their interests to keep him alive in the hope that disillusion with his marriage, or a return to sanity, might occur to cause him to change his will. So far Dalgliesh had learned nothing that could cause him to give the Canon the assurance for which he hoped.

It was then that he remembered Aubrey Glatt. Glatt was a wealthy amateur criminologist who had made a study of all the notable Victorian and Edwardian poison cases. He was not interested in anything earlier or later, being as obsessively wedded to his period as any serious historian, which, indeed, he had some claim to call himself. He lived in a Georgian house in Winchester—his affection for the Victorian and Edwardian age did not extend to its architecture—and was only three miles from Colebrook Croft. A visit to the London Library disclosed that he hadn't written a book on the case, but it was improbable that he had totally neglected a crime so close at hand and so in period. Dalgliesh had occasionally helped him with technical details of police procedure. Glatt, in response to a telephone call, was happy to return the favour with the offer of afternoon tea and information.

Tea was served in his elegant drawing-room by a parlour-maid in goffered cap with streamers. Dalgliesh wondered what wage Glatt paid her to persuade her to wear it. She looked as if she could have played a role in any of his favourite Victorian dramas, and Dalgliesh had an uncomfortable thought that arsenic might be dispensed with the cucumber sandwiches.

Glatt nibbled away and was expansive.

"It's interesting that you should have taken this sudden and, if I may say so, somewhat inexplicable interest in the Boxdale murder. I got out my notebook on the case only yesterday. Colebrook Croft is being demolished to make way for a new housing estate and I thought I would visit it for the last time. The family, of course, haven't lived there since the 1914–18 war. Architecturally it's completely undistinguished but one grieves to see it go. We might drive over after tea if you are agreeable.

"I never wrote my book on the case, you know. I planned a work entitled 'The Colebrook Croft Mystery' or 'Who Killed Augustus Boxdale?' But the answer was all too obvious."

"No real mystery?" suggested Dalgliesh.

"Who else could it have been but Allegra Boxdale? She was born Allegra Porter, you know. Do you think her mother could have been thinking of Byron? I imagine not. There's a picture of her on page two of the notebook, by the way, taken by a photographer in Cannes on her wedding day. I call it beauty and the beast."

The photograph had scarcely faded and Great Aunt Allie smiled clearly at Dalgliesh across nearly seventy years. Her broad face, with its wide mouth and rather snub nose, was framed by two wings of dark hair swept high and topped in the fashion of the day by an immense flowered hat. The features were too coarse for real beauty, but the eyes were magnificent, deep-set and well-spaced, and the chin round and determined.

Beside this vital young Amazon, poor Augustus Boxdale, smiling fatuously at the camera and clutching his bride as if for support, was but a frail and undersized beast. Their pose was unfortunate. She looked as if she were about to fling him over her shoulder.

Glatt shrugged. "The face of a murderess? I've known less likely ones. Her Counsel suggested, of course, that the old man had poisoned his own gruel during the short time she left it on the washstand to cool while she visited the bathroom. But why should he? All the evidence suggests that he was in a state of post-nuptial euphoria, poor senile old booby. Our Augustus was in no hurry to leave this world, particularly by such an agonizing means. Besides, I doubt whether he even knew the gruel was there. He was in bed next door in his dressing-room, remember."

Dalgliesh asked:

"What about Marguerite Goddard? There's no evidence about the exact time when she entered the bedroom."

"I thought you'd get on to that. She could have arrived while her step-grandmother was in the bathroom, poisoned the gruel, hidden herself either in the main bedroom or elsewhere until it had been taken in to Augustus, then joined her grandfather and his bride as if she had just come upstairs. It's possible, I admit. But is it likely? She was less inconvenienced than any of the family by her grandfather's second marriage. Her mother was Augustus Boxdale's eldest child and married, very young, a wealthy patent-medicine manufacturer. She died in childbirth and the husband only survived her by a year. Marguerite Goddard was an heiress. She was also most advantageously engaged to Captain the Honourable John Brize-Lacey. It was quite a catch for a Boxdale—or a Goddard. Marguerite Goddard, young, beautiful, secure in her possession of the Goddard fortune, not to mention the Goddard emeralds and the eldest son of a Lord, was hardly a serious suspect. In my view, Defence Counsel, that was Roland Gort Lloyd remember, was wise to leave her strictly alone."

"It was a memorable defence, I believe."

"Magnificent. There's no doubt Allegra Boxdale owed her life to Gort Lloyd. I know that concluding speech by heart.

"'Gentlemen of the jury, I beseech you, in the sacred name

of Justice, to consider what you are at. It is your responsibility, and yours alone, to decide the fate of this young woman. She stands before you now, young, vibrant, glowing with health, the years stretching before her with their promise and their hopes. It is in your power to cut off all this as you might top a nettle with one swish of your cane. To condemn her to the slow torture of those last waiting weeks; to that last dreadful walk; to heap calumny on her name; to desecrate those few happy weeks of marriage with the man who loved her so greatly; to cast her into the final darkness of an ignominious grave.'

"Pause for dramatic effect. Then the crescendo in that magnificent voice. 'And on what evidence, gentlemen? I ask you.' Another pause. Then the thunder. 'On what evidence?'"

"A powerful defence," said Dalgliesh. "But I wonder how it would go down with a modern judge and jury."

"Well, it went down very effectively with that 1902 Jury. Of course the abolition of capital punishment has rather cramped the more histrionic style. I'm not sure that the reference to topping nettles was in the best of taste. But the jury got the message. They decided that, on the whole, they preferred not to have the responsibility of sending the accused to the gallows. They were out six hours reaching their verdict and it was greeted with some applause. If any of those worthy citizens had been asked to wager five pounds of their own good money on her innocence, I suspect that it would have been a different matter. Allegra Boxdale had helped him, of course. The Criminal Evidence Act, passed three years earlier, enabled him to put her in the witness-box. She wasn't an actress of a kind for nothing. Somehow she managed to persuade the jury that she had genuinely loved the old man."

"Perhaps she had," suggested Dalgliesh. "I don't suppose there had been much kindness in her life. And he was kind."

"No doubt. No doubt. But love!" Glatt was impatient. "My dear Dalgliesh! He was a singularly ugly old man of sixty-nine. She was an attractive girl of twenty-one!"

Dalgliesh doubted whether love, that iconoclastic passion, was susceptible to this kind of simple arithmetic but he didn't argue. Glatt went on:

"And the prosecution couldn't suggest any other romantic

attachment. The police got in touch with her previous partner, of course. He was discovered to be a bald, uxorious little man sharp as a weasel, with a buxom wife and five children. He had moved down the coast after the partnership broke up and was now working with a new girl. He said, regretfully, that she was coming along nicely, thank you, gentlemen, but would never be a patch on Allie and that, if Allie got her neck out of the noose and ever wanted a job, she knew where to come. It was obvious even to the most suspicious policeman that his interest was purely professional. As he said: 'What was a grain or two of arsenic between friends?'

"The Boxdales had no luck after the trial. Captain Maurice Boxdale was killed in 1916, leaving no children, and the Reverend Henry lost his wife and their twin daughters in the 1918 influenza epidemic. He survived until 1932. The boy Hubert may still be alive, but I doubt it. That family were a sickly lot.

"My greatest achievement, incidentally, was in tracing Marguerite Goddard. I hadn't realised that she was still alive. She never married Brize-Lacey or, indeed, anyone else. He distinguished himself in the 1914–18 war, came successfully through, and eventually married an eminently suitable young woman, the sister of a brother officer. He inherited the title in 1925 and died in 1953. But Marguerite Goddard may be alive now for all I know. She may even be living in the same modest Bournemouth hotel where I found her. Not that my efforts in tracing her were rewarded. She absolutely refused to see me. That's the note that she sent out to me by the way."

It was meticulously pasted into the notebook in its chronological order and carefully annotated. Aubrey Glatt was a natural researcher; Dalgliesh couldn't help wondering whether this passion for accuracy might not have been more rewardingly spent than in the careful documentation of murder.

The note was written in an elegant upright hand, the strokes black and very thin but unwavering.

"Miss Goddard presents her compliments to Mr Aubrey Glatt. She did not murder her grandfather and has neither the time nor inclination to gratify his curiosity by discussing the person who did."

Aubrey Glatt said: "After that extremely disobliging note, I felt there was really no point in going on with the book."

Glatt's passion for Edwardian England extended to more than its murders and they drove to Colebrook Croft through the green Hampshire lanes, perched high in an elegant 1910 Daimler. Aubrey wore a thin tweed coat and deerstalker hat and looked, Dalgliesh thought, rather like a Sherlock Holmes with himself as attendant Watson.

"We are only just in time, my dear Dalgliesh," he said when they arrived. "The engines of destruction are assembled. That ball on a chain looks like the eyeball of God, ready to strike. Let us make our number with the attendant artisans. You, as a guardian of the law, will have no wish to trespass."

The work of demolition had not yet begun, but the inside of the house had been stripped and plundered, and the great rooms echoed to their footsteps like gaunt and deserted barracks after the final retreat. They moved from room to room, Glatt mourning the forgotten glories of an age he had been born thirty years too late to enjoy, Dalgliesh with his mind on more immediate and practical concerns.

The design of the house was simple and formalized. The first floor, on which were most of the main bedrooms, had a long corridor running the whole length of the façade. The master bedroom was at the southern end with two large windows giving a distant view of Winchester Cathedral tower. A communicating door led to a small dressing-room.

The main corridor had a row of four identical large windows. The brass curtain-rods and wooden rings had been removed (they were collectors' items now) but the ornate carved pelmets were still in place. Here must have hung pairs of heavy curtains giving cover to anyone who wished to slip out of view. And Dalgliesh noted with interest that one of the windows was exactly opposite the door of the main bedroom. By the time they had left Colebrook Croft and Glatt had dropped him at Winchester Station, Dalgliesh was beginning to formulate a theory.

His next move was to trace Marguerite Goddard, if she were still alive. It took him nearly a week of weary searching, a frustrating trail along the south coast from hotel to hotel. Almost everywhere, his enquiries were met with defensive hostility. It was the usual story of a very old lady who had become more demanding, arrogant and eccentric as her health and fortune waned; an unwelcome embarrassment to manager and fellow guests alike. The hotels were all modest, a few almost sordid. What, he wondered, had become of the Goddard fortune?

From the last landlady he learned that Miss Goddard had become ill, really very sick indeed, and had been removed six months previously to the local district general hospital. And it was there that he found her.

The Ward Sister was surprisingly young, a petite, dark-haired girl with a tired face and challenging eyes.

"Miss Goddard is very ill. We've put her in one of the side wards. Are you a relative? If so, you're the first one who has bothered to call and you're lucky to be in time. When she is delirious she seems to expect a Captain Brize-Lacey to call. You're not he by any chance?"

"Captain Brize-Lacey will not be calling. No, I'm not a relative. She doesn't even know me. But I would like to visit her if she's well enough and is willing to see me. Could you please give her this note?"

He couldn't force himself on a defenceless and dying woman. She still had the right to say no. He was afraid she would refuse him. And if she did, he might never learn the truth. He thought for a second and then wrote four words on the back page of his diary, signed them, tore out the page, folded it and handed it to the Sister.

She was back very shortly.

"She'll see you. She's weak, of course, and very old, but she's perfectly lucid now. Only please don't tire her."

"I'll try not to stay too long."

The girl laughed:

"Don't worry. She'll throw you out soon enough if she gets bored. The Chaplain and the Red Cross librarian have a terrible time with her. Third door on the left. There's a stool to sit on under the bed. We ring a bell at the end of visiting time."

She bustled off, leaving him to find his own way. The corridor was very quiet. At the far end he could glimpse through the open door of the main ward the regimented rows of beds, each with its pale blue coverlet; the bright flow of flowers on the over-bed tables and the laden visitors making their way in pairs to each bedside. There was a faint buzz of welcome, a hum of conversation. But no one was visiting the side wards. Here in the silence of the aseptic corridor Dalgliesh could smell death.

The woman propped high against the pillows in the third room on the left no longer looked human. She lay rigidly, her long arms disposed like sticks on the coverlet. This was a skeleton, clothed with a thin membrane of flesh, beneath whose yellow transparency the tendons and veins were plainly visible as if in an anatomist's model. She was nearly bald, and the high-domed skull under its spare down of hair was as brittle and vulnerable as a child's. Only the eyes still held life, burning in their deep sockets with an animal vitality. But when she spoke, her voice was distinctive and unwavering, evoking, as her appearance never could, the memory of imperious youth.

She took up his note and read aloud four words:

"'It was the child'. You are right, of course. The four-year-old Hubert Boxdale killed his grandfather. You signed this note Adam Dalgliesh. There was no Dalgliesh connected with the case."

"I am a detective of the Metropolitan Police. But I'm not here in any official capacity. I have known about this case for a number of years from a dear friend. I have a natural curiosity to learn the truth. And I have formed a theory."

"And now, like that poseur Aubrey Glatt, you want to write a book?"

"No. I shall tell no one. You have my promise."

Her voice was ironic.

"Thank you. I am a dying woman, Mr Dalgliesh. I tell you that not to invite your sympathy, which it would be an impertinence for you to offer and which I neither want nor require, but to explain why it no longer matters to me what you say or do. But I too have a natural curiosity. Your note, cleverly, was intended to provoke it. I should like to know how you discovered the truth."

Dalgliesh drew the visitors' stool from under the bed and sat down beside her. She did not look at him. The skeleton hands still holding his note did not move.

"Everyone in Colebrook Croft who could have killed Augustus Boxdale was accounted for, except the one person whom nobody considered, the small boy. He was an intelligent, articulate and lonely child. He was almost certainly left to his own devices. His nurse did not accompany the family to Colebrook Croft, and the servants who were there had the extra work of Christmas and the care of the delicate twin girls. The boy probably spent much time with his grandfather and the new bride. She too was lonely and disregarded. He could have trotted around with her as she went about her various activities. He could have watched her making her arsenical face wash and when he asked, as a child will, what it was for, could have been told 'to make me young and beautiful'. He loved his grandfather, but he must have known that the old man was neither young nor beautiful. Suppose he woke up on that Boxing Day night, overfed and excited after the Christmas festivities. Suppose he went to Allegra Boxdale's room in search of comfort and companionship, and saw the basin of gruel and the arsenical mixture together on the washstand. Suppose he decided that here was something he could do for his grandfather."

The voice from the bed said quietly:

"And suppose someone stood unnoticed in the doorway and watched him."

"So you were behind the window curtains on the landing looking through the open door?"

"Of course. He knelt on the chair, two chubby hands clasping the bowl of poison, pouring it with infinite care into his grandfather's gruel. I watched while he replaced the linen cloth over the basin, got down from his chair, replaced it with careful art against the wall and trotted out into the corridor and back to the nursery. About three seconds later Allegra came out of the bathroom, and I watched while she carried the gruel into my grandfather. A second later I went into the main bedroom. The bowl of poison had been a little heavy for Hubert's small hands to manage, and I saw that a small pool had been spilt on the polished top of the washstand. I mopped it up with my handkerchief. Then I poured some of the water from the jug into the poison bowl to bring up the level. It only took a couple of seconds, and I was ready to join Allegra and my grandfather in the bedroom and sit with him while he ate his gruel. I watched him die without pity and without remorse. I think I hated them both equally. The grandfather who had adored, petted and indulged me all through my childhood had deteriorated into this disgusting old lecher, unable to keep his hands off his woman even when I was in the room. He had rejected me and his family, jeopardised my engagement, made our name a laughing-stock in the County—and for a woman my grandmother wouldn't have employed as a kitchen-maid. I wanted them both dead. And they were both going to die. But it would be by other hands than mine. I could deceive myself that it wasn't my doing."

Dalgliesh asked: "When did she find out?"

"She knew that evening. When my grandfather's agony began, she went outside for the jug of water. She wanted a cool cloth for his head. It was then that she noticed that the level of water in the jug had fallen and that a small pool of liquid on the washstand had been mopped up. I should have realised that she would have seen that pool. She had been trained to register every detail; it was almost subconscious with her. She thought at the time that Mary Huddy had spilt some of the water when she set down the tray and the gruel. But who but I could have mopped it up? And why?"

"And when did she face you with the truth?"

"Not until after the trial. Allegra had magnificent courage. She knew what was at stake. But she also knew what she stood to gain. She gambled with her life for a fortune."

And then Dalgliesh understood what had happened to the Goddard inheritance.

"So she made you pay?"

"Of course. Every penny. The Goddard fortune, the Goddard emeralds. She lived in luxury for sixty-seven years on my money. She ate and dressed on my money. When she moved with her lovers from hotel to hotel, it was on my money. She paid them with my money. And if she has left anything, which I doubt, it is my money. My grandfather left very little. He had been senile and had let money run through his fingers like sand."

"And your engagement?"

"It was broken, you could say by mutual consent. A marriage, Mr Dalgliesh, is like any other legal contract. It is most successful when both parties are convinced they have a bargain. Captain Brize-Lacey was sufficiently discouraged by the scandal of a murder in the family. He was a proud and highly conventional man. But that alone might have been accepted with the Goddard fortune and the Goddard emeralds to deodorize the bad smell. But the marriage couldn't have succeeded if he had discovered that he had married socially beneath him, into a family with a major scandal and no compensating fortune."

Dalgliesh said: "Once you had begun to pay you had no choice but to go on. I see that. But why did you pay? She could hardly have told her story. It would have meant involving the child."

"Oh no! That wasn't her plan at all. She never meant to involve the child. She was a sentimental woman and she was fond of Hubert. No, she intended to accuse me of murder outright. Then, if I decided to tell the truth, how would it help me? How could I admit that I had watched Hubert, actually watched a child barely four years old preparing an agonizing death for his grandfather without speaking a word to stop him? I could hardly claim that I hadn't understood the implication of what I had seen. After all, I wiped up the spilled liquid, I topped up the bowl. She had nothing to lose, remember, neither life nor reputation. They couldn't try her twice. That's why she waited until after the trial. It made her secure for ever. But what of me? In the circles in which I moved reputation was everything. She needed only to breathe the story in the ears of a few servants and I was finished. The truth can be remarkably tenacious. But it wasn't only reputation. I paid in the shadow of the gallows."

Dalgliesh asked, "But could she ever prove it?"

Suddenly she looked at him and gave an eerie screech of laughter. It tore at her throat until he thought the taut tendons would snap.

"Of course she could! You fool! Don't you understand? She took my handkerchief, the one I used to mop up the arsenic mixture. That was her profession, remember. Some time during that evening, perhaps when we were all crowding around the bed, two soft plump fingers insinuated themselves between the satin of my evening dress and my flesh and extracted that stained and damning piece of linen."

She stretched out feebly towards the bedside locker. Dalgliesh saw what she wanted and pulled open the drawer. There on the top was a small square of very fine linen with a border of hand-stitched lace. He took it up. In the corner was her monogram delicately embroidered. And half of the handkerchief was still stiff and stained with brown.

She said: "She left instructions with her solicitors that this was to be returned to me after her death. She always knew where I was. She made it her business to know. You see, it could be said that she had a life interest in me. But now she's dead. And I shall soon follow. You may have the handkerchief, Mr Dalgliesh. It can be of no further use to either of us now."

Dalgliesh put it in his pocket without speaking. As soon as possible, he would see that it was burnt. But there was something else he had to say. "Is there anything you would wish me to do? Is there anyone you want told, or to tell? Would you care to see a priest?"

Again there was that uncanny screech of laughter, but it was softer now:

"There's nothing I can say to a priest. I only regret what I did because it wasn't successful. That is hardly the proper frame of mind for a good confession. But I bear her no ill will. No envy, malice or uncharitableness. She won; I lost. One should be a good loser. But I don't want any priest telling me about penance. I've paid, Mr Dalgliesh. For sixty-seven years I've paid. And in this world, young man, the rich only pay once."

She lay back as if suddenly exhausted. There was silence for a moment. Then she said with sudden vigour:

"I believe your visit has done me good. I would be obliged if you would make it convenient to return each afternoon for the next three days. I shan't trouble you after that."

Dalgliesh extended his leave with some difficulty and stayed at a local inn. He saw her each afternoon. They never spoke again of the murder. And when he came punctually at 2 p.m. on the fourth day it was to be told that Miss Goddard had died peacefully in the night with apparently no trouble to anyone. She was, as she had said, a good loser.

A week later Dalgliesh reported to the Canon.

"I was able to see a man who has made a detailed study of the case. He had already done most of the work for me. I have read the transcript of the trial and visited Colebrook Croft. And I have seen one other person, closely connected with the case but who is now dead. I know you will want me to respect confidences and to say no more than I need."

It sounded pompous and minatory but he couldn't help that. The Canon murmured his quiet assurance. Thank God he wasn't a man to question. Where he trusted, he trusted absolutely. If Dalgliesh gave his word there would be no more questioning. But he was anxious. Suspense hung around them. Dalgliesh went on quickly:

"As a result I can give you my word that the verdict was a just verdict and that not one penny of your grandfather's fortune is coming to you through anyone's wrong-doing."

He turned his face away and gazed out of the vicarage window at the sweet green coolness of the summer's day, so that he did not have to watch the Canon's happiness and relief. There was a silence. The old man was probably giving thanks in his own way. Then he was aware that his godfather was speaking. Something was being said about gratitude, about the time he had given up to the investigation.

"Please don't misunderstand me, Adam. But when the formalities have been completed, I should like to denote something to a charity named by you, one close to your heart."

Dalgliesh smiled. His contributions to charity were impersonal; a quarterly obligation discharged by banker's order. The Canon obviously regarded charities as so many old clothes; all were friends, but some fitted better and were more affectionately regarded than others.

But inspiration came:

"It's good of you to think of it, Sir. I rather liked what I learned about Great Aunt Allie. It would be pleasant to give something in her name. Isn't there a society for the assistance of retired and indigent variety artists, conjurers and so on?"

The Canon, predictably, knew that there was and could name it.

Dalgliesh said: "Then I think, Canon, that Great Aunt Allie would agree that a donation in her name would be entirely appropriate."

ARABELLA'S ANSWER

Peter Lovesey

ANSWERS TO CORRESPONDENTS

January, 1878

ARABELLA. If you are serious in aspiring to elicit a reply from a reputable journal such as ours, you should take the elementary trouble to express yourself in legible handwriting.

March, 1878

ARABELLA. Your Papa is perfectly right. A young girl of fifteen should not be seen at a dinner party at which unmarried gentlemen are guests. Your protestations at being, as you express it, "confined" to your room do you no credit. A wiser girl would be content to occupy herself in some profitably quiet pastime, such as sewing, for the duration of the party. So long as you childishly persist in questioning decorum, you reveal your utter unreadiness for adult society.

October, 1879

ARABELLA. No gentleman sends flowers or any other presents to a young lady to whom he has not been introduced. Let him learn some manners and present his card to your parents if he entertains a notion of making your acquaintance. We doubt whether his conduct thus far will commend itself to your Papa.

December, 1879

ARABELLA. In common civility you are bound to receive the young gentleman if he has called on your Papa and satisfied him that his intentions are honourable. The "misgivings" that you instance in your letter are of no consequence. A gentleman should be judged by his conduct, not his outward imperfections. The protruding teeth and shortness of stature are no fault of his, any more than your tallness is of your making. We expect to hear that you have set aside these absurd objections and obeyed your parents, who clearly have a more enlightened apprehension of this young gentleman than yourself.

February, 1880

ARABELLA. We suspect that your anxieties are prompted by the shyness which is natural in a young girl, but which properly must grow into the self-possession of a lady. How can you possibly say that the gentleman's blandishments are unwelcome when you have met him only once in your parents' home?

June, 1880

ARABELLA. She who finds difficulty in making conversation with her escort should not despair. There are many talkers, but few who know how to converse agreeably. The art of conversation may be learned. Mark how the most accomplished of conversationalists avoid conceit and affectation. Their speech is characterized by naturalness and sincerity which may be spiced with humour, but never oversteps the limits of propriety.

August, 1880

ARABELLA. We are surprised by your inquiry. Kissing is not a subject that we care to give advice upon, particularly to members of the sex that may receive such tokens of affection, in certain circumstances, but ought never to initiate them.

January, 1881

ARABELLA. To give no answer if the young man proposes to marry you would not only be discourteous; it would not achieve the outcome you apparently expect. When the lady is so ill advised as to say nothing, the gentleman is entitled to publish the banns at once, for "silence gives consent". Have you really considered how the gentleman is placed? Making a declaration of love is one of the most trying ordeals he will experience in his life. We counsel you to give the most earnest consideration to the question, if you are so fortunate as to be asked it. Many are not, and live to regret it. Some have been known to say "No" when they meant "Yes".

March, 1881

ARABELLA. Your letter reaffirms our faith in the innate wisdom of womankind. In conveying our felicities on your forthcoming marriage, we would advise you that a gown of ivory satin trimmed with lace and orange blossoms is *de rigueur*.

August, 1881

ARABELLA. We see no reason why you should object to cleaning your husband's boots, as you have no servant, but we cannot comprehend your meaning when you state that he "leaves them outside his bedroom door at night." Are we to gather from this that you occupy a different bedroom from your husband? If so, is this at your behest, or his?

October, 1881

ARABELLA. As we have frequently reiterated in this column, the joys of marriage grow out of duty, honesty and fidelity. If, as you assure us, you have not been negligent in any of these, you must ask yourself if there is not some other impediment in your behaviour, which, when remedied, will allow a happier intimacy to ripen. Have you considered whether your choice of clothes and the way you dress your hair are pleasing to your husband?

November, 1881

ARABELLA. As a rule we deprecate the recourse to powder and rouge as an enhancement to good looks. It is possible, however, that ill-health or the anxiety sometimes experienced in the first months of marriage may deprive the skin of its colour and complexion, and in such cases art may be called in as an aid to nature.

January, 1882

ARABELLA. We condemn in the strongest possible terms the practice of using drops of belladonna in the eyes. Belladonna is the extract from that noxious plant, the deadly nightshade (*atropa belladonna*). To keep it on one's dressing table would be dangerous and foolish. A pinch of boracic powder dissolved in warm water and used with an eye-cup is a safe and beneficial tonic that may be relied upon to bring a brightness to the eyes.

A little vaseline or cocoa-butter well rubbed into the eyebrows and lashes at night will promote their growth. Frequent brushing with a small brow-brush is also efficacious.

March, 1882
ARABELLA. Your difficulties are more common among newly-married wives than probably you realise.

May, 1882
ARABELLA. We think it most injudicious for a wife to listen to tale-bearing neighbours. The company a husband keeps is usually dictated by the duties and obligations of his professional and business life. To expect a man to pursue his manifold interests without ever communicating with the sex who make up half of humanity is to expect the impossible. Shut your ears to gossip. If you have genuine cause for concern, it will manifest itself in other ways. Hold fast to our previous advice. Endeavour to be as pleasant and engaging as possible, to keep your husband at home. Propagate the first shoots of affection as soon as they appear.

July, 1882
ARABELLA. The experience you describe is both regrettable and deplorable, and we trust that there has been no recurrence of the incident since you wrote your letter. If the gentleman concerned was a Frenchman, as you suppose, he may be unused to our British code of decorum. He may, to be as charitable as we can to our cousins from across the Channel, have been under a misapprehension as to your married state. Yet we are bound to observe that a gentleman who attempts to ingratiate himself with a lady, whether married or not, *in a public street*, is a disgrace to his nation. If he should importune you again, look straight onwards, ignore his addresses and tell your husband as soon as you get home. We assume, of course, that the Frenchman's conduct was not encouraged by any light manner on your part.

September, 1882
ARABELLA. We sympathise with your position. It is true that in a previous issue we gave our approval to the judicious use of

rouge and powder to enhance your pale complexion in the expectation that it would please your husband. Now that he appears to blame the rouge-box for the excessive behaviour of the foreign gentleman who pesters you, we think you are bound to give up using it.

January, 1883
ARABELLA. We seem to remember cautioning you last year of the dangers attendant upon the use of belladonna drops and we are surprised that you should waste our time with a further enquiry. For the benefit of other readers we repeat that belladonna is a deadly poison and ought never to be used for cosmetic purposes.

March, 1883
ARABELLA. A bereavement such as you have so tragically and so suddenly suffered will strike a chord of sympathy in every young wife who has known that dread fear of impending tragedy when her husband is unwell. You may console yourself with the knowledge that you did all that was possible to comfort your brave consort in the throes of his delirium and convulsion. To have abandoned him even for a short time to summon a physician was unthinkable, and, from your account of the severity of the onset, would not have made a jot of difference. The proper dress materials for deep mourning are crape and silk. We can recommend Messrs Jay of Regent Street, the London General Mourning Warehouse, for the most sympathetic assistance and advice on suitable costumes, mantles and millinery. Their advertisement will be found elsewhere on these pages.

July, 1883
ARABELLA. We are surprised that you should ask such a question. Velvet is utterly inadmissible for a widow in deep mourning.

September, 1883
ARABELLA. Certainly not. In the first year of mourning, a jersey would be unseemly in the extreme.

October, 1883

ARABELLA. Any person who has the temerity to address a
widow of less than one year in familiar terms forfeits the right
to the title of gentleman. The fact that he is French is no
mitigation of the offence. Indeed, if he is the same person of
whom you had cause to complain on a previous occasion, he
must be a blackguard of the deepest dye. On no account
should you permit him to engage you in conversation. Avoid
the possibility of meeting him again by varying the route you
are accustomed to taking when walking to the shops. As the
proverb wisely cautions us, better go round than fall into the
ditch.

March, 1884

ARABELLA. Black beads are permissible in the second year of
mourning, but gold or silver or pearls would be disrespectful.
We cannot understand how any widow could consider adorning
herself in jewellery so soon after the loss of the one to whom
she pledged her entire life. We are shocked at your enquiry,
and we can only ascribe it to an aberration consequent upon
your grief. Set aside all thoughts of gratifying yourself by such
vanities.

May, 1884

ARABELLA. It would be in the worst possible taste for a widow
of fifteen months to "walk out" with a gentleman, whatever he
professes in the name of sympathy for you and respect for the
one you mourn. Let him show his sympathy and respect by
leaving you to your private grief until at least two years have
passed since your bereavement. As to the "restlessness" that
you admit to feeling, this may be subdued by turning your
energy to some useful occupation in the house or garden.
Many a widow has found solace in the later stages of mourning
by cultivating flowers.

July, 1884

ARABELLA. How can we proffer advice if you do not fully
acquaint us with the circumstances in which you live? Of course
you cannot employ your time in the garden if you live in a
second-floor apartment without a garden, but there is no reason

why you should not cultivate plants of the indoor variety. Contrary to a widely held belief, it is not necessary to have a conservatory for the successful rearing of plants in the home. Certain varieties of fern may be cultivated with gratifying success in, say, a drawing room or dining room. All that they require is a little water regularly given. We have seen some most attractive species growing under glass domes, and some prefer them to wax flowers.

September, 1884
ARABELLA. The variety known as maidenhair is in our opinion the prettiest. Perhaps you over-watered the lady fern.

November, 1884
ARABELLA. Since you seem unable to care adequately for the ferns we recommend, we suggest you try a hardier indoor plant of the palm variety, such as an aspidistra. The aspidistra will grow best in a pot of sufficient size to allow for the roots to develop. A brass plant-pot of the largest size supplied by Messrs Pugh & Martindale would be ideal. Their shop is not far from where you live. The address may be found in the advertisement on the back page of this issue.

January, 1885
ARABELLA. We are gratified to hear that you purchased a large brass pot for your aspidistra, as we suggested in our November issue, and that it is thriving. With regard to another matter that you mention, we wish it to be known that your letters until the latest did not make it clear that the French gentleman whose attentions to you appeared so importunate, is, in fact, the owner of the art gallery over which you live. Had we been privy to this information before, we might have taken a different view of his conduct. It is only civil for a neighbour to raise his hat and pass the time of day to a lady, and his invitation to "walk out", while still unthinkable, may now be seen in a more favourable light, with allowance for alien customs. Your own sentiments towards this gentleman must remain irreproachable.

February, 1885

ARABELLA. We did not expect that our altruistic comments in the last issue would encourage an effusion of such unseemliness. No man, however "handsome, immaculately tailored and charmingly civil towards the fair sex", be he from France or Timbuktu, ought to be described in such unbecoming terms by one who, not two years since, buried her dear departed husband. If you have a vestige of propriety left, dismiss him from your thoughts.

March, 1885

ARABELLA. Your latest communication unhappily confirms what we have for some time suspected: that you are suffering from the delusions of a foolish, infatuated female. How can you otherwise suppose that a lady who has chanced to stand below your window in the vicinity of the art gallery on one or two occasions has "designs" on the owner, even if he were "the most eligible man in London"? Clear your mind of such nonsense and attend to the horticultural interests we have been at such pains to foster.

April, 1885

It is with profound regret and a deep sense of shock that we announce the death of Miss Gertrude Smyth, who edited our *Answers to Correspondents* since this journal was founded six years ago. Miss Smyth was the victim last month of a singularly unfortunate and distressing accident in Chelsea, when she was struck on the head by a brass flower-pot that fell from an upper window ledge. Miss Smyth's sagacious and authoritative advice was of the greatest service to myriads of our readers. Out of respect for her memory, we are publishing no *Answers to Correspondents* this month. The column will be resumed in our next issue.

May, 1885

ARABELLA. We can see no impediment to your being married in September in Paris.

THE WHISPERING

Christianna Brand

SHE LEANED AGAINST the counter and the empty glass made a tiny chattering against the mahogany with the shaking of her ringless left hand. They were whispering about her over there in the corner. She said so to the barman. "They're whispering about me over there."

"Oh, for Pete's sake!" he said. "You always think people are whispering."

"Why do they whisper? Why don't they just talk to me straight out?"

"Perhaps they don't wish to talk to you straight out," he said, "or any other way. And I'll be frank with you—neither do I."

Tears welled up into her large blue eyes. She said with maudlin dignity: "In future I'll go to some other bar."

"You do that," he said. "God knows we're fed up with you in here."

But she stayed. She always stayed. Wherever else she went, it would be the same. "It was all such a long time ago," she said to the man. "Why should they whisper still?"

But they whispered: and the whispering grew and grew.

Such a long time ago . . .

Of course, Simon should never have taken her there in the first place. But she'd begged and pleaded and he never could resist her. "You know I'd take you if I could, Daffy. I'd do anything for you, you know I would, I'd die for you . . ."

And so would they all, all the others, all the boys—they'd lie down and die for Daffy Jones. And not only the young ones. "My Pa," Daffy used to say, "he'd go out and get himself run over if it would do me any good. No, honestly he would—he'd die for me." His Daffodil, he called her, his Golden Daffodil.

Talk about daffy, Simon thought—but there it was, she did remind one of a daffodil, so slender and fresh in the light narrow green frocks she so often wore, with that bell of bright yellow hair.

"All the same, Daffy, I couldn't take you to the Blue Bar. It's just what it says, it's off-colour, it's an awful place. I couldn't."

But it sounded thrilling and the other girls at school would have fits when they heard she'd been there. "Oh, Simon, don't be so stuffy! Please."

"Honestly, I couldn't. What would your father say? He'd have a heart attack."

"My father has heart attacks the whole time," she said.

"Well, I didn't mean that. I mean he'd do hand-springs."

"If my father did hand-springs he'd have a heart attack," she said laughing, "so it comes to the same thing."

"I just meant that he wouldn't like it. He'd murder me!"

Daffy was his cousin, her father was his Uncle John.

"It's a dreadful, sordid place, sailors and tarts and people like that, everybody drunk or hashed up, some of them even on the hard stuff." He had, in fact, been there only once himself, taken by two much older boys who had left school—his own school. He went to boarding school; not Daffy's. It had shocked and scared him; scared him even more to think it might ever come out that he had been there.

And she recognised that. She was a fly one, little Daffy Jones.

She said: "But *you* go there," and added with the smallest, slyest of meaningful glances, "what would *your* Pa say?"

So he took her. Never mind the threat implicit, he loved her, he had always loved her, always, since they'd been small children together: Daffy so fresh and dewy-eyed, Daffy irresistible.

"Gosh!" she said when they got there, "isn't it frightful? Fancy you!"

"Oh, well," he said, casually sophisticate, "one grows up."

But when his neighbour on the close-packed bench against

the greasy wall offered him a drag, he said at once: "No thanks."

"Oh, do!" said Daffy. "I'd love to have a try." Not for nothing was she known at school, with double meaning, as the Sex-Pot, but he was not to know that. "Only I don't like sharing," she said to the man.

"Plenty more where that came from," said the man, producing a handful of ready-rolled untidy cigarettes. He suggested to Simon, "Only it'll cost you bread, man, bread."

Of all the phoneys! But poor Simon fell for it all like a ton of bricks and forked out twice as much for the stuff as Daffy could have got it for, any day, from the school gardener.

"Do let me have a—a drag, do they call it?—Simon. I'd love to try it."

The stuff takes you different ways. Simon it wafted into a beautiful dream, sitting huddled on the bench gazing before him into a brilliance where beautiful people danced and hugged and did beautiful things, right out there in the open before everyone. He awoke to the sound of her screeching. She was shaking him, screaming at him.

"Look at me! Look what he did to me."

She looked beautiful, he thought, standing there with her dress half ripped off her body, showing the lovely white nakedness underneath, her hair all torn and tousled, her eyes so strangely bright—she must have been having a beautiful, beautiful time.

"You look beautiful, Daffy," he said. "Did you have a good time?"

"Good? It was horrible. Look what he did to me!"

But she had liked it. For most of the time. She had never before been with a real, grown-up man. But then . . .

"He wanted it all wrong," she said. "I thought he was going mad. I didn't know what he was up to." She went into details. "So I tried to make him stop because, after all, there are limits, and he went berserk—it was absolutely frightful."

And indeed when he looked at her again, fighting his way up out of his euphoric self-absorption, she did perhaps look rather a mess.

"I'd better take you home. We'd better both go home." Lovely, blissful home, warm bed, comfortable dreams . . .

She was hugging together her ripped dress, trying to comb out her torn and tangled hair, scrabbling in her handbag for lipstick and little tubes of shiny eye make-up: spitting into an oblong box of mascara, thickening her lashes with great blobs of it, with some vague idea of getting back to normal, making herself "look good".

"What'll I tell them? How'll I explain to Mummy and Daddy? They'll go mad."

"Tell them what happened," he said comfortably. "You couldn't help it. Say he made a pass at you and, of course, you wouldn't and he beat you up."

"They'll say what was I doing here?" Out of her anxiety, grew belligerence. "You should never have brought me to a place like this."

He protested: "You made me bring you."

"You, my own cousin! What will my Pa say?" Her father was a simple man: simple and gentle. But when he saw her like this, his little pet, his innocent flower . . . "He'll murder you," she said.

"*You* went with the man. I told you not to."

"You should have stopped me."

"How could I?" he said, simply. "I was stoned."

"Well, you shouldn't have got stoned and let me." She sat hunched up beside him on the bench. Now and again, vaguely curious glances swept over them and swept on. She looked a bit young for the Blue Bar—too young and too—well, different—to have been outside, having it rough with that sailor chap they called The Butcher; for that matter, *both* of them looked much too young, two silly kids out of place, from another world. Still, that was their affair. She, in her turn, looked back at them: dirty, raddled women, too remote from long-past youth and beauty to be of use to anyone but the rough, drunken, drug-soaked degenerates that would come to such a place.

"Simon, if my father knew! Swear you won't ever tell him I was here."

"What shall we say to them, then?"

"Say that we—say we were walking along, say we were coming home from the Singing Café, that's harmless enough, along the river path. And just by that bench, the bench in front of Mardon's hotel, say it was there; we must stick to the same story exactly—say there were these three boys and they jumped up and started making passes at me. And you fought them off—I'll say you were terribly brave—but it was three to one and one of them got me away. Here, pull out your tie, mess up your clothes, look as if you'd been in a fight." But he'd have no scratches and bruises, no black eye, he wouldn't look a bit as if he'd been in a fight; and what was more, he didn't look as though he were taking in a word she said. Anyone would see that he was stoned, even her innocent father would recognize that much. He'll be at the zombie stage, she said to herself, he'll never stick to anything. She said: "No, after all, skip it. I'd better go alone."

Her light summer coat covered her ripped clothes. She got home at last, going the direct way, not along the river path. It was late, but the later she got home, the more likely it was that her father would be anxiously waiting to see that she was safe. And, sure enough, at the first scrape of her key in the lock, the landing light went on and he was creeping downstairs so as not to wake her mother, wrapped in his old brown checked dressing-gown, the tassel of his cord following him with tiny muffled bumps from step to step.

"Daffy? Where've you been? You're awfully late."

The coat covered her clothes but the pale, bruised face told its own story and the torn, tousled yellow hair. She had been thinking all the way home what best to say. His face, always so thin and worn, now turning to a bad colour she too well knew, gave her her cue. She tumbled into his arms. "Oh, Daddy!"

"What is it, darling, what's happened? Oh, my God—you haven't been . . . ? They haven't . . . ?" He led her, as she sobbed and shuddered, into the sitting-room, lowered her on to the sofa, fell on his knees before the electric fire to switch it on, as though offering a prayer to it for warmth and comfort for her, and came back to sit beside her on the sofa, circling her shoulders with a trembling arm.

"Don't cry, sweetheart. You're safe now, sweetheart. Tell Daddy, darling, it'll be better when you've told." But he left her again for a moment, ran to the door, called up the stairs: "Hester!", darted back to the cupboard, found brandy and a glass. "Here, darling, try, just a sip. Then you can tell me."

His hand was shaking as he held the glass, his face was a terrible colour, that ugly blue-grey, rather frighteningly patched with a dusky red. He fumbled almost surreptitiously in the breast pocket of his pyjamas, shook a small pill into his hand and swallowed it.

She sobbed and shivered and at last burst out with it all. "Oh, Daddy! It was Simon."

"Simon?" he said; stupefied at the sound of that name.

"On that bench by the river, Daddy. You know, the bench in front of Mardon's Hotel—"

"Mardon's?" he said. "That's not on your way home."

"No, but he—he wanted to go there. So we went and then we stopped and sat on the bench and we were just looking at the river and talking—at least I was just talking; and then . . . ." She buried her face against his shoulder. "Don't make me tell!"

"Oh, my God, Daffy!" he said, and you could sense his reaction to her plea, humble and gentle: it's her mother she needs, not me. He left her again for a moment and went out into the hall, calling more urgently up from the foot of the stairs. "Hester! Wake up, come down! Hester, it's Daphne. Come down."

And she came, hurry-scurrying, anxious, trembling, her dressing-gown clutched with a shaking hand tight up against her throat as though to shut out some bitter cold wind in that well-warmed house.

"What is it, my darling, what's happened? Oh, God, darling! —your face, all those marks—your hands, your hair." And she cried out, as the father cried out, voicing the nameless fear never far from their hearts: "You haven't . . . ? They haven't . . . ?"

"It was Simon," she said dully.

"Simon? What Simon? Which Simon?"

"Simon, our Simon."

"You did mean your cousin Simon, Daffy?"

"Mummy, I *tried* not to let him."

The mother could not—would not—take it in. "Simon? He's only a boy, he's only seventeen."

"Boys of seventeen nowadays . . ." said her husband.

"But Simon?—he's her own cousin, he's like her brother."

"No, Mum," said Daphne. "He isn't. He's never been." But how would she, innocent blossom, have recognised that? "I mean, he was always sort of—sloppy, sort of lovey-dovey, you know." And she searched in her keen little mind for a phrase from her mother's own courting days. "I mean he's always sort of carried the torch for me."

"But Daffy, what happened?"

What had happened? He hadn't taken her to that place, no; for any investigation might produce someone who had observed her, going off outside, so flirtatious and willing, with the sailor. Butch. But Simon would soon admit that they had been there: would confess to having taken her there—to having given way to her entreaties and taken her there. And to having smoked that wicked pot and so been unable to control her when she had insisted upon leaving him. Simon in his silly innocence would give it all away. Well, then, Simon must be discredited in advance. "He was stoned, Daddy. He didn't know what he was doing. He was stoned out of his mind."

They picked up these dreadful expressions from the television. "You mean he'd been drinking?"

"He was on hash. On hashish. Of course, I didn't know. I couldn't understand him. He kept talking about some awful place, some sort of dance place, you know, where sailors went with women, awful women, and everyone was on hash or something, even on the hard stuff; Simon told me that, he said lots of them were 'on the hard stuff'. He said he'd take me there, he wanted to take me there. I believe in the end," said Daffy carefully, "he almost thought he *had* taken me there, he was in a sort of dream, a sort of nightmare, he thought he was there, he thought I was one of those—those women . . ." She broke off, shuddering and whimpering; looking into their white, stricken faces, searching for any sign of doubt. But there was none. Simon could protest and deny but would be obliged to admit that he had been under the influence of an unfamiliar drug—he was far too stupid and honest not to tell the truth; and might, in the end, even be brought to half believe in her story himself. No one in that place was likely to have taken any notice of them; let alone to admit to having stood by and watched her, so young and obviously unaccustomed, being taken out to be raped and beaten up by the man even they called The Butcher.

"We were going to the folk-singing café—you know, you all sit round and have coffee and listen to the singing. Well, we did go and we were sitting at the back of the café, away from the stage, and suddenly the man next to Simon passed him a cigarette and Simon said 'Thank you' and smoked it and then he said had the man got any more that he wouldn't mind selling him, because he'd run out; and the man said, 'It'll cost you bread, man,' but, of course, that can mean only 'you'll have to pay for them'. At least, that's what I thought; but anyway, he sold Simon a few loose ones and Simon was smoking away and he seemed to go a bit dreamy, not to say zombie, but of course I thought it was only the music. But on the way home, we went and sat on the bench like I told you, Daddy . . ."

"She didn't want to go," he said quickly to her mother.

"It wouldn't matter, darling, if you did," said her mother, gently. "I mean, just sitting on a bench in the moonlight just . . ." You could see her thinking that one mustn't be square and narrow-minded, things had changed these days. "Just doing a bit of necking, darling."

Honestly, thought Daffy, they were so naive it was almost sickening. She said: "Oh, yes, I know, Mummy; but actually I was tired. I wanted to come home. And then he—he was so strange and insistent and then he started trying to kiss me and then—then . . ."

"Oh, Daphne, he didn't—?" Her mother sat staring at her, one hand fisted against her mouth as though to plug in the little moaning, whimpering sounds that would force their way out. Her father was silent and his silence was worse than the whimpering.

Into that frightening silence, she began to gabble; and with the gabbling, memories came flooding back. "Then he . . . I fought and struggled . . ." Real memories, genuinely terrifying, genuinely vile, the shock and horror of that onslaught by a man savage with drink and frustration of a perverted passion. The earlier passages of her acquiescence were passed over: the rest, with genuine sobbings and bleatings, blurted out in a genuine sickness of frightened and disgusted recollection. The thin summer coat had all this time remained wrapped about her. Now she stood up and let it fall.

That slender white body like a lily, swaying within its ragged enfolding leaf of the little green dress: livid weals scoring the delicate skin, throat, arms, breast, great patches of red which tomorrow would be purple bruises, dried blood where filthy nails had scratched: marks of teeth on a soft round shoulder . . . The mother gave one horror-stricken glance and fell back, half fainting, into her corner of the sofa. The father said in a high, harsh, scraping voice: "Daffy. You must answer. Did he? Did Simon—"

If any investigation arose, it could be proved all too surely that here was no dear little virgo intacta. She collapsed, sobbing afresh. "Oh, Daddy, please! Don't ask me."

But he repeated it, sick, dull, with that horrible grey-blue look on his face, though now, thanks to the medicine, the flush had died down. "I must ask you, Daffy. Did he . . .? Dear God!—Daffy, did Simon succeed in—raping you?"

She lifted her head and looked back into his face; the small flower-face looking back into the haggard thin face with that blue-grey, ash-grey skin. She bit on an already bleeding lip and turned away her head.

A simple man, with a serious heart condition, perhaps with but little time left to live. A man with one passion, with one hope, one idea, one total, blinding perfection of happiness in his life—so young, so fresh, untouched by the dirty world about her, so starry innocent—his golden girl, his golden Daffodil . . . A gentle man who for the rest of his life had retained the symbol of the hideous years of enforced ungentleness: his old Army revolver. He went to it now, went with a sort of automatism, turned back to that symbol of the red rage that had in those bad days consumed him at the sight of friends and comrades lying shattered into hideous stillness at the hands of the enemy; the red rage that then—as now again it must—had borne him on the only wings that would carry him to the duty that must be done: the wings of an unthinking, revengeful fury. Like an automaton, he loaded the gun with a single shot, left the house, walked the short distance to his brother's home: stood in the darkness outside the white painted door and called out, sharp and harsh, hardly knowing that he lifted his voice: "Simon! Come out here!"

The front door opened. Framed in the light from the hall,

still reeling a little, shocked, sickened by the memories which, with a terrifying clarity, were now returning, the boy stood there and looked out into the night. Looked out and saw where the stream of light caught the barrel of the revolver in a black gleam: and cried out: "It wasn't my fault, Uncle John! She *made* me take her there."

Like a man deaf and dumb, he lifted the gun, took aim at the boy's left breast and fired; and stood quietly aside through the ensuing uproar till the police came to take him away.

And so the Golden Daffodil—the press had latched on to her pet name in one minute flat—was on all the front pages. Only Mummy—true to form—had fought off the reporters and photographers and there was always the same photograph and it was an awful thing—taken quite early on the following morning when she was still drenched in tears about poor Simon being dead and poor Daddy being in prison; no make-up, hair in the most frightful mess because, of course, there'd been no time to go to Freesia's to get it done; face patched with bruises, and still in one's dressing-gown, though, fortunately the lovely new one that had been Mummy's last birthday present. And things were slightly dicey. Policemen kept coming and asking her questions—or policewomen, rather: it was all so delicately handled that really it almost made Daffy giggle—though of course it was too awful about Daddy and Simon. Mummy made her stay in bed and she lay propped up on pillows and wanly lived again through the recital of Simon's attack and Daddy's reaction to what she had told him about it. That all went all right, went fine, and after all now at least Simon could never contradict her. But after that . . .

First Maureen and Lindy turned up. Allowed to visit her after anxious telephone calls between the Mums.

"You won't—well, tell them anything about all *that*, darling? They might not understand. Of course they're older than you are, but still . . ."

So it all had to be told in whispers; not about the Blue Bar, of course, best to keep that entirely to oneself—it was quite rivetting enough just pinned on to poor Simon (who ever would have thought that a proper little cousin of Daffy's would have had such kinky ideas?). But when she mentioned Mardon's bench, Maureen responded immediately: "You can't have been on that bench, because *we* were. We were there half the night with the Frazer boys."

She didn't think of the come-back quick enough. She drew a red herring. "I didn't know you even knew the Frazer boys."

"Good lord, Daffy, Maureen and Roddy Frazer have been having it off for weeks. Haven't you, Maureen?"

"He's terrific," said Maureen.

"Eddie's not too bad," said Lindy. "But inexperienced." She wouldn't have bothered with him, she added, but they wanted to make up a foursome.

"I went with him once and I thought he was absolutely dreary."

"Oh, well, we know your standards, Daffy," said Lindy laughing. "But, anyway, why all this drama with your cousin, Simon? Why not just let him?" And she laughed again and said that heaven knew, kinky or not, Daffy hadn't exactly had anything to lose by it.

"He happens to be dead," said Daphne stiffly; drawing the subject ever further from the bench by the river.

"Oh, well, yes we know that, darling; and of course it's too frightful. And about your father and all that. My God, it's frightful!"

"Why on earth did you have to go and tell your father, Daph?"

"He caught me sneaking in. I was in such a mess, I had to say something. And anyway, I was pretty steamed up. I did have an awful time. I mean, look at these bruises."

"I can't see why you should struggle? Why not just let him get on with it?"

"Well, good heavens, he was like a sex maniac! He'd been smoking all evening and heaven knows what this pusher at the bar, well I mean in the café, had sold him. He was stoned clean, he just did his nut. Of course I couldn't tell my parents I'd let him. I had to say he'd forced me."

"Good lord—poor Simon."

"Yes, but he did knock me about. Of course it's awful about Daddy shooting him, but still he did knock me about."

"All the same, Daphne, it wasn't on that bench outside Mardon's," said Maureen, coming back to cases. "Because we were there ourselves."

"I didn't say the bench outside Mardon's. I said it wasn't the one outside Mardon's. The one we went to was the one further down, by the warehouse. You know I always go to the warehouse one, at least I always used to with Tom."

"What's Tom going to say about all this poor-little-raped-virgin stuff, when it comes out?"

"For that matter, Daffy, what's everyone going to say? I mean, everyone knows about *you*."

"Well, then everyone will just have to shut up, won't they?" said Daffy. She gave them that sly little sideways glance of hers, the meaningful glance that had finally blackmailed poor Simon into giving way and taking her to the Blue Bar. "Otherwise I might start talking in self-defence. I mean, if they knew how everyone at school was doing it, not to mention the pot and all the rest of it—if they knew the temptations I'd had and the example that had been set me by—by older girls than me: well, I wouldn't be so much to blame, would I? So everyone had better just shut up, hadn't they? And I didn't say I was down by the river near Mardon's, I said 'we were on that bench, not the Mardon's one but the other bench'. Or would you like to get up in court when they're trying my father for murder and say that you know I wasn't at the Mardon's bench because you were there yourselves all night having it off with a couple of boys?"

"My God, that young Daphne, she's a cool one!" said Maureen to Linda as they hastily went away. (All the same, she *had* said she'd been outside Mardon's.)

Daphne herself was not too pleased with the way she had handled it. She should have thought of that threat earlier. Because one day she was going to have to face Daddy and she'd definitely told Daddy that she'd been by the Mardon's bench; and he'd commented that that wasn't on the way home—he wouldn't forget that, you couldn't just slur it over with *him*. Had Mummy heard? No, she hadn't come downstairs by then. So only Daddy would know. A thought flicked through her mind and flicked out again. If Daddy knew she'd told one lie, would he begin to wonder if, after all, Simon had been innocent?

If Daddy should give her away! If everyone got to know that she'd gone to that place, that she'd been with that sailor, that she'd lied about poor Simon and lied and lied and lied . . . If all the newspapers, cooing now about poor little innocent-injured Golden Daffodil—if they knew that she was just a sexy trollop who could give lessons to any of the boys at school and *had* given lessons to most of them! If they knew that she'd let Daddy go off and murder Simon—murder him!—was letting Daddy now face the rest of his life in prison, all because of her lies . . . And Mummy, poor Mummy, having to live on, with all the family knowing that Daddy had killed Simon, her own cousin, his own nephew, his own brother's son—had actually shot and killed him: because of her lies . . .! If Daddy were ever to give her away!

But he wouldn't. How could he ever harm her, his Golden Daffodil? He'd die to protect her. Daddy would *die* for her.

And it wasn't only Maureen and Lindy. Now a man came forward and told the police that he'd recognized her picture in the paper as that of a girl he'd seen that night at the Blue Bar, a disreputable haunt of sailors in the bad part of town.

The police had informed the solicitor who was looking after Daddy's defence and he came to see her. Could this man's story possibly be true?

"Of course not," said Daffy, opening the large blue eyes. "I never even heard of such a place."

"You were at the folk-singing café all through the evening?"

"Yes, till we went home by the river. Of course we were."

"Did you see anyone who might confirm that?"

"What, you mean at the café? No, we didn't see anyone we knew. We were near the back and they keep the lights very low because of the singing."

"One man did speak to you?"

"Yes, but he was a pusher. *He* wouldn't come forward, would he?"

No flies on little Miss Jones, reflected the solicitor. He suggested: "Your cousin, however, had wanted to take you to some place like this bar? You told your father so."

"Oh, yes, but . . . " She thought it all out rapidly. It was getting rather scary. "Perhaps the man saw Simon there on some other night," she suggested, "and just mixed up the nights. He used to take other girls there—or anyway to some place."

"It was your picture the man recognized."

"He couldn't from the papers, that was the most awful thing. He probably recognized Simon's and remembered seeing him there on some other night with some other girl and then associated the other girl with me." It sounded pretty good, but it wouldn't deceive Daddy; Daddy would think it too much of a coincidence, after all she'd told him about Simon wanting to take her to just such a place. And the thought flicked in and out again. If Daddy realized that all along Simon had been innocent of any assault on her—would he really stand by her still? Would he let Simon be blamed for the rest of his life—well, for the rest of his death, then: wouldn't that seem even worse to Daddy?—that Simon was dead and unable to defend himself, that all Simon's family, Daddy's own family, his brothers and sisters and Granny and everyone—should live on, believing that dead Simon had been so vile, when all the time he'd been innocent? Of course she could admit to having been to the Blue Bar—to having allowed Simon to inveigle her to that awful place and then been ashamed to admit it; it need make no difference to the story of his subsequent attack on the river bank. But then if more people came forward, if people remembered how she'd gone off with the sailor of her own accord—indeed against Simon's rather woozy protestations. Nothing to do but deny it; deny it all.

"Don't tell Daddy about it," she said. "It simply isn't true that the man could have seen me there; it would only upset him."

It upset the solicitor also. He thought to himself: "If this damn little bitch has been lying all this time!" But it was necessary to take the story to her father.

The sad, grey man caged up in the prison hospital awaiting his trial said at once: "Of course it isn't true."

"The man's very sure. He says he remarked at the time how ill-suited they were to such a place."

"No, no, he *wanted* to take her—" But that didn't make sense. A thought, a memory, came to his mind, terrifying in its intensity. But he thrust it aside. "Surely this—mistake of this man's needn't come out in court?"

"I don't think so, no. They were obliged to inform us. But

it's no good to the prosecution. You're pleading guilty, so that's all there is to it. And for the defence—"

"I don't want any defence. I've told you. I killed the boy for what he did to my child. I don't want any defence."

"It's just a matter of mitigating circumstances. But anyway," said the lawyer, "this wouldn't help us either, so I think we'll just drop the whole matter." Hardly a mitigating circumstance if the boy turned out to have been shot for something he had never done.

The lawyer went away. But the memory came back. That cry, only half heard, all unattended to. "It wasn't my fault, Uncle John. She *made* me take her there." Dear God! If Simon had been innocent after all!

Goodness, the photographers outside the court! It was like being a film star. And of course her hair was done now and Freesia, quite thrilled, had made a special job of it and it looked terrific. And the bruises on her face had faded. Pity she couldn't have used her proper make-up but it would be best, they'd said, to appear very young and fresh and innocent, not to say generally gormless: so that Daddy couldn't be blamed too much for what he'd done. And, indeed, in the witness-box she looked like a flower, the light shining down from the canopy above, on the careful halo of golden hair: the golden Golden Daffodil.

Your name is Daphne Jones? Of such and such an address? And you are sixteen years of age . . .?

Only sixteen years of age.

Only sixteen; and had been with every boy in the top form at school, with or without drugs for extra kicks.

"Yes, sixteen last birthday."

"Now, don't upset yourself, Miss Jones—or Daphne, may I call you Daphne? I just wanted to ask you to tell us very simply in your own words what happened that night, the night your cousin died."

(*It wasn't my fault, Uncle John. She made me take her there.*)

Best to cover all tracks. They weren't going to use it in court, she knew that now; but best to cover all tracks: the man might talk to the paper afterwards, one never knew.

"He wanted to take me to a dance place he knew about. He

used to go there, he used to take other girls. But it sounded like a horrible place so I wouldn't go."

"You went instead to—?"

"We went to the Singing Café and then we came home by the path along the river bank—"

"Would that be your direct way home?"

"No, he just wanted to come that way. He made me come that way." But she saw from beneath her eye-lashes the suddenly tightened grip of the two thin hands clasped on the edge of the dock and she knew that that had been a mistake. Daddy would know better; Simon had never in all his life made her do anything against her will—it had been all the other way.

"He wasn't like his usual self," she said quickly. "He'd been smoking this pot."

"And then I think you came to a certain bench—?"

"Yes," she said, quickly again, running it on into the next sentence, "and then we sat down and we were looking at the river—"

It made no difference whatever to the case against John Jones, which bench it had been. But something had to be said in the wretched man's defence and if one could spin it out a little more, Counsel felt, it would look a bit more like earning one's fee. He humped himself over, leaning on both fisted hands, looking earnestly down at a map laid out before him.

"That would be the bench outside Dent's warehouse—here?"

"Yes," she said, slurring it over quickly again, into the following words, "and we sat there—"

She saw the quick upwards jerk of the bowed head. He called out sharply from the dock, called out sharply in that high, harsh, too-well-remembered voice he had spoken in that night, just before Simon died. "You told me it was Mardon's bench."

Shushing from the Clerk of the Court and ushers; a glance of compassionate severity from the Bench. But now she knew that Daddy knew. There was nothing to be done about that—nothing. She must concentrate on convincing the court that she spoke the truth. She explained it all away in her frank little, rather charmingly garrulous way.

"I keep just saying that it wasn't the bench by Mardon's but then people seem to remember that I said the word 'Mardon's' and they think I said it *was*. But it wasn't. It was the warehouse bench. He took me to the warehouse bench."

"Very well. In fact, which bench it was doesn't really matter. But something happened there which you later told your father? Now—what did you tell him? Tell us, please, just as you told it to him."

So she told it all again: lived yet again through that horrible half hour with the sailor, Butch—lived through the last half of the time anyway: the less said about the first ten minutes the better, but the rest she lived through as she had lived through it many times already—each time ascribing her injuries, as now, to her cousin. Lived through it: poured it all out, the filth, the bestiality, the brutality, the dress half torn away, the terrible bruising . . . They listened breathlessly and, as her voice fell silent in the hushed court, she knew that she had won—had won for herself but had won for Daddy also—if only he would accept it. A father—hearing that story poured out through bruised and bleeding lips, seeing the white young face ugly with bruising, the bitten and broken skin, the torn, dishevelled hair—whatever the father had subsequently done, must be condoned to the fullest limit of the law's discretion. Poor little injured blossom, poor smirched and broken golden Daffodil! Not a man in court but knew—but hoped with all his heart—that he would have done the same. Not a man in court who did not feel sick to the pit of his stomach at the wrongs that had been done to this lovely child. Not one man.

Or only one.

He had to be helped to the witness box; and now the light shone down, not upon yellow halo and pale, uplifted face but on a bowed head whose face and hair seemed almost of a uniform grey. He fumbled his way through the oath. He said: "I have to tell. I have to say . . ."

From the body of the court where now she sat with her mother, she shot up to her feet.

She cried out, sick, faltering, terrified, hardly knowing what she was doing: "Daddy!" And on a note of pleading, again, "Daddy!"

Hushing and shushing. Throughout it he stood there looking

back into her terrified face: a long, long, searching look. If that boy had all along been innocent . . . ! He looked into her sick white face and knew that she had lied to him. He had killed—he had murdered—an innocent child.

Her mother saw the first signal: the terrible purple red flush rising up over the ashy grey; and into the silence she, also, cried out. "John! Your pills!" and besought the stern face a thousand miles away up there on the Bench: "He's going to have a heart attack. He must take his pills."

He stood there, reeling, his hand going slowly, automatically to his breast pocket, his eyes still fixed on the young, scared, pleading face across the courtroom. An usher proffered the glass of water, all eyes were riveted on the scene where he stood there in the witness box. Across the turned heads she stared back at him. Daddy would never give her away. Daddy would rather die than do harm to his golden Daffodil.

Over the turned white wigs, the averted faces—begging, beseeching, almost imperceptibly she shook her head.

The hand reaching for the life-saving drug, dropped to his side. Daddy would die for her.

And he died. Like a ruined building, slowly toppling, crumbling with horrible acceleration, tumbling at last into a crumpled heap on the floor of the witness box, out of their sight. The heart for so long a traitor to its own harbouring body, looked into the fair face of treachery and broke and bled: and beat no more.

The photographs on the front pages of the evening papers were terrific! Freesia's hair-do was wonderful, just like a halo. It made her look like an angel, honestly it did.

But by the next morning the whispering had begun. And it grew and it grew and it grew . . .

SKELETON IN THE CUPBOARD

Tony Wilmot

HE WAS WATCHING the park gates from his usual bench by the pond. The girl would soon be joining him for her midday break.

For several days now they had been sitting at the same bench and exchanged pleasantries after she had laughed at the way the ducks fought over the crusts he had thrown to them.

She was twentyish, attractive, with a pulse-quickening figure, but he didn't flatter himself that her interest was in any way sexual. He subscribed to the adage "No fool like an old fool". Besides, he was more than twice her age.

To him, it was a harmless flirtation—a fillip to his middle-aged man's morale—and he had found himself looking forward to their lunchtime "assignations".

Earlier that morning, however, events had taken a more serious turn. She had paid a visit to the Vehicle Registration Department in the Town Hall.

His secretary had come into his office. "There's a young lady here, Mr Smythe, asking if we keep records of car ownership . . . MG sports cars in particular. I said I thought not."

He had felt a twinge of unease at the mention of the car type.

"Quite so," he'd replied. "Tell her registrations are all on the national computer now. In any case, we couldn't give out that kind of information."

He had peered at the reception desk through his office's glass partition. The enquirer was the girl from the park bench. An odd coincidence, he'd thought. Or was it something more?

Now, as she entered the park gates with that long stride and purposeful expression, his unease returned.

"Hello—we meet again," she said, sitting beside him.

"Ah, yes . . . sky looks a bit overcast. Hope we aren't in for some rain." He gestured at the apple she was peeling with a penknife. "Lunch?"

"Yes, worse luck. I'm on a diet."

He smiled. "You seem to be here most days. Do you work hereabouts?"

"Oh no. In fact, I don't live here. I'm just staying in town while I'm doing some research. I'm from Elmston, actually."

"Really? I know Elmston . . ." he began. The words were out before the warning bell rang. "Well, I don't exactly know it . . . pal of mine . . . knew him years ago . . . used to live there. Is this your first visit here?"

"Yes."

"Nice place," he said. "Bit dull, though."

"Not at all. It's charming."

"What are you researching? Our town's chequered history, perhaps? Parts date from the Roman occupation."

"How interesting. But no—I'm trying to trace someone."

"Ah! Bit of detective work?"

She smiled. "In a way. I'm beginning to find out what a job it is tracing someone who may not want to be traced. No wonder the police have to spend so much time on investigations."

"And the 'trail' has led from Elmston to here?"

"Indirectly, yes. But I've had to spend time in several places first. I'm hoping this will be the last."

"Sounds very intriguing," he said, hoping to entice her to reveal more without seeming to be prying into her private life.

"I suppose it is, in a way. I'm going back more than 20 years, though." She made a wry face. "Which is setting myself a difficult task."

"I don't suppose you were even born then?" he said.

"I was—just! Anyway, I've managed to unearth a few clues. The person I'm looking for had an MG sports car then and got married during the same period. I know it's a bit of a long shot but it might just pay off."

His unease became a shiver which set him on edge even more. He was like the rabbit hypnotised by the snake, wanting to get away but unable to move. "But I mustn't bore you with my personal affairs," she went on. "What about you? What line of business are you in?"

"Oh, nothing much. Civil servant, actually. Quite dull, I'm afraid. I wish I could be an 007 like you but . . . I'm just a nine-to-five chap."

"Don't be so modest. There's nothing wrong with being a civil servant."

He made a deprecating gesture but inwardly he was thrilled that a pretty girl was finding him interesting enough to want to flirt with him.

"Married, of course?" He was on the point of saying no when he noticed her glance at the ring on his left hand. He nodded. "The dishy men always are! Lived here long, have you?"

He didn't like the turn the conversation was taking. "Oh, quite some time." He made a show of checking his wristwatch. "Well, I must be getting back. The grindstone waits for no man! I, er . . . that is, perhaps we might see each other again tomorrow?"

"Yes, let's. About one o'clock?"

He said that would be fine.

As he walked back to the Town Hall, doubts and fears scurried around his head like cornered rats. It was just too damned close to be coincidence any more. For *he* used to run an MG. And *he* had married twenty years ago.

He couldn't concentrate at the office. An hour before finishing time, he got his car from the staff car-park and drove to his semi in a leafy suburb on the outskirts of town.

Margaret, his wife, was doing some work in the garden. "Robert, is that you? You're early. Nothing wrong at the office, is there?"

"No, of course not." Why did women always think the worst? "I thought I'd finish off that lampstand in the shed while there's still some daylight."

"Right-o! I'll call you when dinner's ready."

He put the inside catch on the shed door and made sure his wife was still in the front garden. Then he got a metal box from behind his workbench.

The key to the box was hidden under a bottle of weedkiller. Inside the box were two yellowing clippings from the *Elmston Observer*.

One was headlined: *Girl, 10, killed in hit-and-run*.

For the umpteenth time he read how the girl had been knocked down on a zebra crossing while on her way home from a schoolfriend's house.

The details were embedded in his memory. He had driven over to Margaret's parents' house in the MG that evening. They had lived just outside Elmston then.

Because of some road works, the traffic had been diverted.

He had been exceeding the speed limit, too. It was an unfamiliar route and the crossing had taken him by surprise.

The car's brakes were slack because he'd skipped a service to save money—and a shower had made the road surface slippery. . .

Even though it was twenty years ago, he could still remember the sickening thud . . . the scream . . . the crumpled body on the side of the road.

Of course he should have stopped, but he'd panicked. He'd been short-listed for a new job for which a clean driving licence was a condition of employment, and he had been only days away from his wedding. Reporting the accident would have ruined everything.

The second clipping, headed *Police appeal for witnesses*, said several people had heard the screech of brakes but none had seen the accident.

A police spokesman was quoted as saying they were "pursuing several lines of enquiry".

He locked the clippings away again and returned the box to its hiding place. He had never fully understood why he had kept them all those years. What, he wondered, would the psychologists make of that? A guilt complex, perhaps? A subconscious desire to punish himself for his crime?

It was his favourite tuna-fish salad for dinner but the memory of the accident had dulled his appetite. He pecked away at it, nodding absently as Margaret related the events of her day.

All through the meal the thought kept hammering in his brain: how long before the girl found out that *he* was the hit-and-run driver?

More than likely she was a former schoolfriend wanting to see justice done. Or a relative . . . the dead girl's sister, even.

The police enquiries had no doubt fizzled out years

ago—they would have had far more pressing cases on their plate—but the little girl's family and friends wouldn't have given up the search.

That night he hardly slept. At the office next day he clockwatched until it was time to go to the park. The girl was there when he arrived.

"I was hoping I'd see you today," she said. "You see, I'm certain I've come to the right town. You know I mentioned an MG . . . well, how's this for amateur sleuthing? . . . there's the car's number."

A muscle in his cheek began to twitch rapidly as he read what was on her notebook. *His* MG's number. But how had she . . . ? The newspaper report said there had been no eyewitnesses.

"I'm missing the middle one or two digits in the number-plate—but it's enough."

"Very cloak and daggerish," he said, forcing a smile. "Have you tried the local Vehicle Registration Department? Perhaps they can help."

"Oh yes. No luck, though. But guess what—I've got a photograph of the car."

The park seemed to spin. He gripped the bench with both hands.

"You all right?" she asked.

"What? Oh yes. Just a twinge of indigestion."

"Well, I haven't actually got the photograph," she went on. "I've only seen the negative. I'm having a ten-by-eight print done from it."

"You have been busy!" His voice sounded unreal. "Look, that friend of mine from Elmston. I've just remembered. *He* had an MG. He could be the one who you are looking for . . . I might still have an address for him at home . . .

"Have you got a phone number where I can contact you? Better still, an address in case I miss you here tomorrow."

She wrote down both in her note-book and tore the page out for him. "Now I must be off," she said. "I've got more sleuthing to do. I'll look out for you here again tomorrow."

He gave her a minute or two's start, then began to follow her.

Her first stop was at a photographic shop near the main square. She came out carrying a large buff-coloured envelope.

That would be the MG print, he thought as he observed her getting her bearings.

He kept about fifty yards behind as she crossed the town centre to the offices of the *Evening Gazette*.

He followed her through the revolving doors, keeping the public newspaper stands in the foyer between himself and the point where she was talking at the enquiry counter.

Pretending to leaf through the week's back numbers, he could hear snatches of conversation above the din of typewriters and telephones.

". . . wedding report 21 years ago . . . would it be possible to . . ."

". . . archives are on the fourth floor . . . first door on the right as you come out of the lift . . ."

He watched the girl take the lift. Time passed. People came and went. He felt clammy and conspicuous.

Eventually she reappeared out of the lift. The receptionist smiled. Had she found what she'd been looking for?

Yes, she had.

He was in a cold sweat now, but he had no difficulty keeping her in sight, for he knew the town like the back of his hand. Where would she head next? Oh God, he thought, don't let it be the police station.

"Robert! Long time no see!" He started. It was a man he knew from the Parks Department. He felt like a schoolboy caught playing truant. "Stretching your legs, eh, Robert?"

"Oh, er, yes." He could see the girl disappearing down a side turning. "Popped out for cigarettes."

The man grinned. "Some looker, eh?"

"What?"

"That girl you were staring at."

"Oh." He forced a smile. "Look, can't stop now. Let's have a drink next week. I'll ring you."

When he finally got away, the girl was nowhere to be seen. He spent the rest of the afternoon fretting at his desk. Whose wedding had she looked up? And why?

It wasn't until he and Margaret were watching TV that

evening that the answer came to him; in fact, it was staring him in the face . . .

On the piano was an ornately framed picture of him and Margaret on their wedding day. Of course! Why hadn't he thought of it sooner? The other photos in the family album: *there was one of the MG*.

He found the album and flicked through it. There it was—the pair of them snapped in the MG as they were leaving the reception to go off on honeymoon.

He stared at himself from twenty years ago: thin face, unlined, thick curling hair. Now he had a double chin, was balding, wore a moustache and bifocals. Unrecognisable!

On the back of the MG was a "Just Married" placard which obscured the middle two digits on the rear number-plate.

The girl must have gone to every photographer in the district until she found the one who had taken their wedding pictures. The negatives would have been on file, probably in a storeroom.

The girl had got a print. Then she had searched the *Evening Gazette*'s back issues for the paper's own picture of the same couple in the MG . . . which would tell her the names and parents' addresses.

And there the search would stop, for Margaret's parents had emigrated long ago and his own parents were dead. He was safe.

Then it struck him like a blow. "The electoral roll," he said out loud. "She simply goes through it, street by street, until she finds my name . . ."

"Did you say something, Robert?" Margaret called.

"What? No, nothing."

It would be only a matter of time now before his skeleton was out of its cupboard. He'd be branded a child-killer, all the more heinous because he had covered his tracks (he'd sold the MG immediately they had got back from honeymoon).

He'd get at least five years for manslaughter. He'd lose his job; his reputation would be ruined; everything he'd built up over the years . . . down the drain!

He knew he hadn't got the strength of character to begin all over again; he was too set in his ways . . .

"I think I'll go to The Swan for a pint, love. Don't wait up. I might be late."

"Oh, all right. I'll leave something out for your supper."

At times like this, he mused, it was positively an advantage having a conventionally predictable spouse.

It was a fifteen-minute drive to the block of service flats where the girl was staying; hers was on the ground floor.

She came to the door in a dressing-gown with a towel wrapped round her hair.

He was sorry to barge in on her unannounced, he blurted; but he'd found himself in the neighbourhood, so he'd thought he'd give her that information about his friend.

"Oh, well, come in. You'll have to forgive my appearance—I'm in the middle of washing my hair. Can I get you a drink?"

"I won't, thanks—I'm driving."

"Ah yes . . . the old breathalyser!"

He tried to smile but couldn't move his face muscles. "That friend," he began, swallowing. "His name's . . . Smythe . . . Robert Smythe."

"That's it," she cried. "The same one I've been looking for! I found his address this afternoon, in the electoral roll at the Town Hall."

So it was true, he thought; she *was* tracking him down.

"Perhaps I will have that drink," he said, slipping a hand into his jacket pocket.

She was at the drinks cabinet, her back to him. "Gin and tonic all right?"

"Fine." He pulled out a length of cord. It went round her neck so easily. He didn't make a sound as he pulled it tight. Nor did she . . .

At the breakfast table next morning, Margaret thought Robert looked pale and drawn; there were dark rings round his eyes and he seemed unusually preoccupied. Clearly he needed a holiday; he was working far too hard at that office.

She knew it probably wouldn't be much good urging him to take the day off but she decided to try; and, to her surprise, he agreed.

"I do have a bit of a migraine, love," he said.

"The rest will do you good. I'll ring the office and say you're not well."

The "plop" on the mat inside the front door told her the post had arrived. "I'll go," she said.

Two letters. One was Robert's bank statement, the other was for her. An unfamiliar handwriting.

She tore it open on her way back to the kitchen. It was a three-page letter, with a snapshot. The sudden shock, as she began to read, made her giddy.

". . . *all I had to go on was your maiden name . . . you'd be surprised how many Margarets with that surname have got married since I was born . . . it meant checking each one to find if it was the right Margaret . . .*"

She stared at the attractive, fair-haired girl in the snap. Could it be . . . after all these years? It was something she had buried in her memory, something she had thought would remain buried; but, deep down, hadn't she always known she would never be able to escape from her past?

". . . *when I first learned the truth about myself, I was hurt and angry . . . but now that I'm grown up myself, I'm able to understand why you did what you did . . .*"

She sat at the table and rested her hands on the scrubbed pine to stop them from trembling. She glanced at Robert but he seemed unaware of her agitation.

". . . *finally traced you through your marriage to Robert Smythe . . . and now I feel I must meet you . . . of course, my adoptive parents will always be 'Mum' and 'Dad' to me but . . .*"

Blinking back the tears, she heard Robert asking if the letter was bad news.

"Bad? Oh no . . ." Quite the contrary, she thought. But how would her husband take it?

The guilt she had borne all those years suddenly overwhelmed her and she pushed the snapshot across the table.

"Robert, I don't quite know how to . . . there's something I've got to tell you . . . something that happened before I met you . . ."

THE KILLING OF MICHAEL FINNEGAN

Michael Gilbert

"THEY BURIED HIM to death," said Elfe. He said it without any attempt to soften the meaning of what he was saying. "He was almost certainly alive when they dumped him in the car and set fire to it."

Deputy Assistant Commissioner Elfe had a long, sad face and grey hair. In the twenty years that he had been head of the Special Branch he had seen more brutality, more treachery, more fanaticism, more hatred than had any of his predecessors in war or in peace. Twice he had tried to retire, and twice had been persuaded to stay.

"He couldn't have put up much of a fight," said Mr Calder, "only having one arm and one and a half legs."

They were talking about Michael Finnegan, whose charred carcass had been found in a burnt-out stolen car in one of the lonelier parts of Hampstead Heath. Finnegan had been a lieutenant in the Marines until he had blown off his right arm and parts of his right leg whilst defusing a new type of anti-personnel mine. During his long convalescence his wife Sheilagh had held the home together, supplementing Michael's disability pension by working as a secretary. Then Finnegan had taught himself to write left-handed, and had gained a reputation, and a reasonable amount of cash for his articles; first only in service journals, but later in the national press, where he had constituted himself a commentator on men and affairs.

"It's odd," as Mr Behrens once observed, "you'd think that he'd be a militant chauvinist. Actually he seems to be a moderate and a pacifist. It was Finnegan who started arguing that we ought to withdraw our troops from Ireland. That was long before the IRA made it one of the main planks in their platform."

"You can never tell how a serious injury will affect a man," said Mr Calder. This was, of course, before he had become professionally involved with Michael Finnegan.

"For the last year you've been acting as his runner, haven't you?" said Elfe. "You must have got to know him well."

"Him and his wife," said Mr Calder. "They were a great couple." He thought about the unremarkable house at Banstead with its tiny flower garden in front and its rather larger kitchen garden at the back, both of which Michael Finnegan tended one-armed, hobbling down between whiles for a pint at the local. A respected man with many friends, and acquaintances, none of whom knew that he was playing a lonely, patient, dangerous game. His articles in the papers, his casual contacts, letters to old friends in Ireland, conversations with new friends in the pub, all had been slanted towards a predetermined end.

The fact was that the shape of the IRA's activities in England was changing, a change which had been forced on them by the systematic penetration of their English groups. Now, when an act of terrorism was planned, the operators came from Ireland to carry it out, departing as soon as it was done. They travelled a roundabout route, via Morocco or Tunis, entering England from France or Belgium and returning by the same way. Explosives, detonators and other material for the job came separately, and in advance. Their one essential requirement was an operational base where materials could be stored and the operators could lodge for the few days needed for the job.

It was to hold out his house as such a safe base that every move in Michael Finnegan's life had been planned.

"We agreed," said Mr Calder, "that as far as possible, Michael should have no direct contacts of any sort with the security forces. What the Department did was to lease a house which had a good view, from its front windows, of Michael's back gate. They installed one of their pensioners in it, old Mrs Lovelock—"

"Minnie Lovelock?" said Elfe. "She used to type for me forty years ago. I was terrified of her, even then."

"All she had to do was to keep Michael's kitchen window sill under observation at certain hours. There was a simple code of signals. A flower pot meant the arrival of explosives or arms.

One or more milk bottles signalled the arrival of that number of operators. And the house gave us one further advantage. Minnie put it about that she had sublet a room on the ground floor to a commercial gentleman who kept his samples there, and occasionally put up there for the night. For the last year the commercial gent was me. I was able to slip out, after dark, up the garden path and in at the back door. I tried to go at least once a month. My ostensible job was to collect any information Michael might have for us. In fact, I believe my visits kept him sane. We used to talk for hours. He liked to hear the gossip, all about the inter-departmental feuds, and funny stories about the Minister."

"And about the head of the Special Branch?"

"Oh, certainly. He particularly enjoyed the story of how two of your men tried to arrest each other."

Elfe grunted and said, "Go on."

"And there was one further advantage. Michael had a key of this room. In a serious emergency he could deposit a message—after dark, of course—or even use it as an escape hatch for Sheilagh and himself."

"Did his wife know what he was up to?"

"She had to be told something, if only to explain my visits. Our cover story was that Michael was gathering information about subversion in the docks. This was plausible, as he'd done an Intelligence job in the Marines. She may have suspected that it was more than that. She never interfered. She's a grand girl."

Elfe said, "Yes." And after a pause, "Yes. That's really what I wanted to tell you. I've had a word with your chief. He agrees with me. This is a job we can't use you in."

"Oh," said Mr Calder coldly. "Why not?"

"Because you'd feel yourself personally involved. You'd be unable to be sufficiently dispassionate about it. You knew Finnegan and his wife far too well."

Mr Calder thought about that. If Fortescue had backed the prohibition it would be little use kicking. He said, "I suppose we *are* doing something about it."

"Of course. Superintendent Outram and Sergeant Fallows are handling it. They're both members of the AT squad, and very capable operators."

"I know Tom Outram," said Mr Calder. "He's a sound man. I'll promise not to get under his feet. But I'm already marginally involved. If he wants to question Sheilagh he'll have to do it at my cottage. I moved her straight down there as soon as I heard the news. Gave her a strong sleeping pill and put her to bed."

"They wondered where she'd disappeared to. I'll tell them she's living with you."

"If you put it quite like that," said Mr Calder, "it might be misunderstood. She's being chaperoned, by my dog Rasselas."

"I think," said Superintendent Outram, "that we'd better see Mrs Finnegan alone. That is, if you don't mind."

He and Sergeant Fallows had driven out to Mr Calder's cottage, which was built on a shoulder of the North Downs above Lamperdown in Kent.

"I don't mind," said Mr Calder. "But you'll have to look out for Rasselas."

"Your dog?"

"Yes. Mrs Finnegan's still in a state of shock, and Rasselas is very worried about it. The postman said something sharp to her—not meaning any harm at all—and he went for him. Luckily I was there and I was able to stop him."

"Couldn't we see her without Rasselas?"

"I wouldn't care to try and shift him."

Outram thought about it. Then he said, "Then I think you'd better sit in with us."

"I think that might be wise," said Mr Calder gravely.

Sheilagh Finnegan had black hair and a white face out of which looked eyes of startling Irish blue. Her mouth was thin and tight and angry. It was clear that she was under stress. When Outram and Fallows came in she took one look at them and jerked as though an electric shock had gone through her.

Rasselas, who was stretched out on the floor beside her, raised his head and regarded the two men thoughtfully.

"Just like he was measuring us for a coffin," said Fallows afterwards.

Mr Calder sat on the sofa, and put one hand on the dog's head.

It took Outram fifteen minutes of patient, low-keyed questioning to discover that Mrs Finnegan could tell him very little. Her husband, she said, had suggested that she needed a break, and had arranged for her to spend a week in a small private hotel at Folkestone. She wasn't sorry to agree because she hadn't had a real holiday in the last three or four years.

Outram nodded sympathetically. Had the holiday been fixed suddenly? Out of the blue, like? Sheilagh gave more attention to this than she had to some of the earlier questions. She said, "We'd often talked about it before. Michael knew I had friends at Folkestone."

"But on this occasion it was your husband who suggested it? How long before you left?"

"Two or three days."

"Then it *was* fairly sudden."

"Fairly sudden, yes."

"Did he give any particular reason? Had he had an unexpected message? Something like that."

"He didn't say anything about a message. I wouldn't have known about it, anyway. I was out at work all day."

Outram said, "Yes, of course."

There was nothing much more she could tell them. A quarter of an hour later the two men drove off. As their car turned down the hill they passed Mr Behrens, who was walking up from Lamperdown. Mr Behrens waved to the superintendent.

"Looks a genial old cove," said Sergeant Fallows.

"That's what he looks like," agreed Outram.

When Mr Behrens reached the cottage he found Mr Calder and Sheilagh making coffee in the kitchen. They added a third cup to the tray and carried it back to the sitting room where Rasselas was apparently asleep. By contrast with what had gone before it was a relaxed and peaceful scene.

Mr Calder tried the coffee, found it still too hot, put the cup carefully back on its saucer, and said, "Why were you holding out on the superintendent?"

"How did you know I was holding out?"

"Rasselas and I both knew it."

Hearing his name the great dog opened one brown eye, as though to confirm what Mr Calder had said, and then shut it again.

"If I tell you about it," said Sheilagh, "you'll understand why I was holding out."

"Then tell us at once," said Mr Behrens.

"Of course I knew something was in the wind. I didn't know exactly what Michael was up to. He was careful not to tell me any details. But whatever it was he was doing, I realised it was coming to a head. That was why he sent me away. He said it shouldn't be more than two or three days. He'd get word to me as soon as he could. That was on the Friday. I had a miserable weekend, you can imagine. Monday came, and Tuesday, and still no word. By Wednesday I couldn't take it any longer. What I did was wrong, I know, but I couldn't help myself."

"You went back," said Mr Calder. He said it sympathetically.

"That's just what I did. I planned it carefully. I wasn't going to barge in and upset all Michael's plans. I just wanted to see he was all right and go away again. He'd given me a key of that room in Mrs Lovelock's house. I got there after dark. There's a clear view from the window straight into our kitchen. The light was on and the curtains weren't drawn."

As she talked she was living the scene. Mr Behrens pictured her, crouched in the dark, like an eager theatre-goer in the gallery staring down on to the lighted stage.

She said, "I could see Michael. He was boiling a kettle on the stove and moving about, setting out cups and plates. There were two other people in the room. I could see the legs of a man who was sitting at the kitchen table. Once, when he leant forward, I got a glimpse of him. All I could tell you was that he was young and had black hair. The other was a girl. I saw her quite plainly. She was dark, too. Medium height and rather thin. The sort of girl who could dress as a man and get away with it. I got the impression, somehow, that they'd just arrived, and Michael was bustling about making them at home. The girl still had her outdoor coat on. Maybe that's what gave me the idea. Just then I saw another man coming. He was walking along the road which runs behind our kitchen garden, and when he stopped, he was right under the window where I was sitting. When he opened the gate I could see that he was taking a lot of trouble not to make any noise. He shut the gate very gently, and stood there for a moment, looking at the lighted kitchen window. Then he tip-toed up the garden path and stood, to one side of the kitchen window, looking in. That's when I saw his face clearly for the first time."

Sheilagh was speaking more slowly now. Mr Calder was leaning forward with his hands on his knees. Rasselas was no longer pretending to be asleep. Mr Behrens could feel the tension without understanding it.

"Then he seemed to make up his mind. He went across to the kitchen door, opened it, without knocking, and went in quickly, as though he was planning to surprise the people inside. Next moment, someone had dragged the curtains across. From the moment I first saw that man I knew that he meant harm to Michael. But once the curtains were shut I couldn't see what was happening."

"You couldn't see," said Mr Calder. "But could you hear?"

"Nothing. On account of Mrs Lovelock's television set in the room just above me. She's deaf and keeps it on full strength. All I could do was sit and wait. It must have been nearly an hour later when I saw the back door open. All the lights in the house had been turned out and it was difficult to see but Michael was between the two men. They seemed to be supporting him. The girl was walking behind. They came out and turned up the road. Then I noticed there was a car parked about twenty yards further up. They all got into it. And I went on sitting there. I couldn't think what to do."

There was a moment of silence. Neither of the men wanted to break it. Sheilagh said, "I do realise now that I should have done something. I should have run down, screamed, made a fuss. Anything to stop them taking Michael away like that. But I didn't know what was happening. Going with them might all have been part of his plan."

"It was an impossible situation," said Mr Calder.

"When you thought about it afterwards," said Mr Behrens, "am I right about this?—you got the impression that things had been going smoothly until that other man arrived, and that he was the one who upset things?"

"He was the one who gave Michael away," said Sheilagh. "I'm sure of it." There was a different note in her voice now. Something hard and very cold.

"I agree with Calder," said Mr Behrens. "You couldn't have

done anything else at the time. But as soon as you knew that things had gone wrong for Michael why didn't you tell the police everything that you've just told us. Time was vital. You could give a good description of two of the people involved. Surely there wasn't a moment to lose."

Sheilagh said, "I didn't go to the police because I recognised the man, the one who arrived on foot. I'd seen his photograph. Michael had pointed it out to me in the paper. I only saw him clearly as he stood outside the lighted window, but I was fairly certain I was right." She paused, then added, "Now I'm quite certain."

Both men looked at her.

She said, "It was Sergeant Fallows."

The silence that followed was broken unexpectedly. Rasselas gave a growl at the back of his throat, got up, stalked to the door, pushed it open with his nose, and went out. They heard him settling down again outside.

"That's where he goes when he's on guard," said Mr Calder.

There was another silence.

"I know what you're thinking," said Sheilagh. "You both think I'm crazy, but I'm not. It *was* Fallows."

"Not an easy face to forget," agreed Mr Calder, "and it would explain something that had been puzzling me. We'd taken such tight precautions over Michael that I didn't see how they could suddenly have known that he was a plant. He might eventually have done something, or said something, which gave him away. They might have got suspicious. But not certain. Not straight away. It could only have happened like that if he was betrayed, and the only person who could have betrayed him was someone working in the Squad."

Mr Behrens' mind had been moving on a different line. He said, "When they got into the car, and turned the lights on, you'd have been able to see the number plate at the back I take it."

"That's right. I saw it, and wrote it down. I've put it here. LKK 910 P."

"Good girl. Now think back. When you were talking about the last man to arrive you called him 'the one who came on foot'. What made you say that?"

Sheilagh said, "I'm not sure. I suppose because he came

from the opposite direction to where the car was parked. So I assumed—"

"I'm not disputing it. In fact, I'm sure you were right. Fallows wouldn't have driven up in a police car. He wouldn't even have risked taking his own car. He'd have gone by bus or train to the nearest point and walked the rest of the way."

Mr Calder said, "Then the car belonged to the Irish couple. Of course, they might have stolen it, like the one they left on the Heath."

"They might. But why risk it? It would only draw attention to them, which was the last thing they wanted. My guess is that they hired it. Just for the time they were planning to be here."

"If you're right," said Mr Calder, "there's a lot to do and not much time to do it. You'd better trace that car. And remember, we've been officially warned off, so you can't use the police computer."

"LKK's a Kent number. I've got a friend in County Hall who'll help."

"I'll look into the Fallows end of it. It'll mean leaving you alone here for a bit, Sheilagh, but if anyone should turn up and cause trouble Rasselas will attend to him."

"In case there might be two of them," said Mr Behrens, "you'd better take this. It's loaded. That's the safety catch. You push it down when you want to fire."

The girl examined the gun with interest. She said, "I've never used one, but I suppose, if I got quite close to the man, pointed it at his stomach, and pulled the trigger—"

"The results should be decisive," said Mr Behrens.

Fallows was whistling softly to himself as he walked along the carpeted corridor to the door of his flat. It was on the top floor of a new block on the Regent's Park side of Albany Street and seemed an expensive pad for a detective sergeant. He opened the door, walked down the short hall into the living room, switched on the light and stopped.

A middle-aged man, with greying hair and steel-rimmed glasses, was standing by the fireplace regarding him benevolently. Fallows recognised him, but had no time to be surprised. As he stepped forward something soft but heavy hit him on the back of the neck.

When he came round, about five minutes later, he was seated in a heavy chair. His arms had been attached to the arms of the chair and his legs to its legs by yards of elastic bandage, wound round and round. Mr Behrens was examining the contents of an attaché case which he had brought with him. Mr Calder was watching him. Both men were in their shirt sleeves and were wearing surgical gloves.

"I think our patient is coming round," said Mr Calder.

"What the bloody hell are you playing at?" said Fallows.

Mr Behrens said, "First, I'm going to give you these pills. They're ordinary sleeping pills. I think four should be sufficient. We don't want him actually to go to sleep. Just to feel drowsy."

"Bloody hell you will."

"If you want me to wedge your mouth open, hold your nose and hit you on the throat each time until you swallow, I'm quite prepared to do it, but it'd be undignified and rather painful."

Fallows glared at him, but there was an implacable look behind the steel spectacles which silenced him. He swallowed the pills.

Mr Behrens looked at his watch, and said, "We'll give them five minutes to start working. What we're trying"—he turned courteously back to Fallows—"is an experiment which has often been suggested but never, I think, actually performed. We're going to give you successive doses of scopalamine dextrin to inhale, whilst we ask you some questions. In the ordinary way I have no doubt you would be strong enough to resist the scopalamine until you became unconscious. There are men who have sufficient resources of will power to do that. That's why we first weaken your resistance with a strong sedative. Provided we strike exactly the right balance, the results should be satisfactory. About ready now, I think."

He took a capsule from a box on the table and broke it under Fallows' nose.

"The snag about this method," he continued, in the same level tones of a professor addressing a class of students, "is that the interreaction of the sedative and the stimulant would be so sharp that it might, if persisted with, affect the subject's heart. You'll appreciate therefore—head up, Sergeant—that by prolonging our dialogue you may be risking your own life. Now then. Let's start with your visit to Banstead—"

This produced a single, sharp obscenity.

Fifty minutes later Mr Behrens switched off his tape recorder. He said, "I think he's gone. I did warn him that it might happen if he fought too hard."

"And my God, did he fight," said Mr Calder. He was sweating. "We'd better set the scene. I think he'd look more convincing if we put him on his bed."

He was unwinding the elastic bandages and was glad to see that, in spite of Fallows' struggles, they had left no mark. The nearly empty bottle of sleeping pills, a half empty bottle of whisky and a tumbler were arranged on the bedside table. Mr Behrens closed Fallows' flaccid hand round the tumbler, and then knocked it onto the floor.

"Leave the bedside light on," said Mr Calder. "No one commits suicide in the dark."

"I've done a transcript of the tape for you," said Sheilagh. "I've cut out some of the swearing, but otherwise it's all there. There's no doubt, now, that he betrayed Michael, is there?"

"None at all," said Mr Behrens. "That was something he seemed almost proud of. The trouble was that when we edged up to one of the things we really wanted to know, an automatic defence mechanism seemed to take over and when we fed him a little more scopalamine to break through it, he started to ramble."

"All the same," said Mr Calder, "we know a good deal. We know what they're planning to do, and roughly when. But not how."

Mr Behrens was studying the neatly typed paper. He said, "J.J. That's clear enough. Jumping Judas. It's their name for Mr Justice Jellicoe. That's their target all right. They've been gunning for him ever since he sent down the Manchester bombers. I've traced their car. It was hired in Dover last Friday, for ten days. The man they hired it from told them he had another customer who wanted it on the Monday afternoon. They said that suited them because they were planning to let him have it back by one o'clock that day. Which means that whatever they're going to do is timed to be done sometime on

Monday morning, and they aim to be boarding a cross-Channel ferry by the time it happens."

"They might have been lying to the man," said Sheilagh.

"Yes. They might have been. But bear in mind that if they brought the car back on Saturday afternoon or Sunday the hire firm would be shut for the weekend and they'd have to leave the car standing about in the street, which would call attention to it. No. I think they've got a timetable, and they're sticking to it."

"Which gives us three days to find out what it is," said Mr Calder. "If the pay-off is on Monday there are two main possibilities. Jellicoe spends his weekends at his country house at Witham, in Essex. He's pretty safe there. He's got a permanent police guard and three boxer dogs who are devoted to him. He comes up to court on Monday by car, with a police driver. All right. That's once chance. They could arrange some sort of ambush. Detonate one of their favourite long distance mines. Not easy, though, because there are different routes the car can take. This isn't the Ulster border. They can't go round laying minefields all over Essex."

"The alternative," said Behrens, "is to try something in or around the Law Courts. We'll have to split this. You take the Witham end. Have a word with the bodyguard. They may not know that we've been warned off, so they'll probably co-operate. I'll tackle the London end."

"Isn't there something I could do?" said Sheilagh.

"Yes," said Mr Calder. "There is. Play that tape over again and again. Twenty times. Until you know it by heart. There was something, inside Fallows' muddled brain, trying to get out. It may be a couple of words. Even a single word. If you can interpret it, it could be the key to the whole thing."

So Friday was spent by Mr Calder at Witham, making friends with a police sergeant and a police constable; by Sheilagh Finnegan listening to the drug-induced ramblings of the man who had been responsible for her husband's death; and by Mr Behrens investigating the possibility of blowing up a judge in court.

As a first step he introduced himself to Major Baines. The major, after service in the Royal Marines, had been given the job of looking after security at the Law Courts. He had known Michael Finnegan, and was more than willing to help.

He said, "It's a rambling great building. I think the chap who designed it had a Ruritanian palace in mind. Narrow windows, heavy doors, battlements and turrets, and iron gratings. The judges have a private entrance, which is inside the car park. Everyone else, barristers, solicitors, visitors, all have to use the front door in the Strand, or the back door in Carey Street. They're both guarded, of course. Teams of security officers, good men. Mostly ex-policemen."

"I was watching them for a time, first thing this morning," said Mr Behrens. "Most people had to open their bags and cases, but there were people carrying sort of blue and red washing bags. They let them through uninspected."

"They'd be barristers, or barristers' clerks, and they'd let them through because they knew their faces. But I can assure you of one thing. When Mr Justice Jellicoe is on the premises everyone opens everything."

"Which court will he be using?"

Major Baines consulted the printed list. "On Monday he's in Court Number Two. That's one of the courts at the back. I'll show you."

He led the way down the vast entrance hall. Mr Behrens saw what he meant when he described it as a palace. Marble columns, spiral staircases, interior balconies and an elaborately tessellated floor.

"Up these stairs," said Baines. "That's Number Two Court. And there's the back door, straight ahead of you. It leads out into Carey Street."

"So that anyone making for Court Number Two would be likely to come this way."

"Not if they were coming from the Strand."

"True," said Mr Behrens. "I think I'll hang around for a bit and watch the form."

He went back to the main hall and found himself a seat which commanded the front entrance.

It was now ten o'clock and the flow of people coming in was continuous. They were channelled between desks placed lengthways, and three security guards were operating. They did their job thoroughly. Occasionally, when they recognized a face, a man was waved through. Otherwise everyone opened anything they were carrying and placed it on top of the desk. Suitcases, briefcases, even women's handbags were carefully examined. The red and blue bags which, Mr Behrens decided, must contain law books were sometimes looked into, sometimes not. They would all be looked into on Monday morning.

"It looked pretty water-tight to me," said Mr Behrens to Sheilagh and Mr Calder, as they compared notes after supper. "Enough explosive to be effective would be bulky and an elaborate timing device would add to the weight and bulk. They might take a chance and put the whole thing in the bottom of one of those book bags and hope it wouldn't be looked at, but they don't seem to me to be people who take chances of that sort."

"Could the stuff have been brought in during the weekend and left somewhere in the court?"

"I put it to Baines. He said no. The building is shut on Friday evening and given a thorough going-over on Saturday."

"Sheilagh and I have worked one thing out," said Mr Behrens. "There's a reference, towards the end, to 'fields'. In the transcript it's been reproduced as 'in the fields', and the assumption was that the attempt was going to be made in the country, when Jellicoe was driving up to London. But if you listen very carefully it isn't 'in the fields'. It's 'in fields' with the emphasis on the first word, and there's a sort of crackle in the tape before it which makes it difficult to be sure, but I think what he's saying is 'Lincoln's Inn Fields'."

They listened once more to the tape.

Mr Calder said, "I think you're right."

"And it does explain one point," said Mr Behrens. "When I explored the area this morning it struck me how difficult it was to park a car. But Lincoln's Inn Fields could be ideal—there are parking spaces all down the south and east sides, and the south-east corner is less than two hundred yards from the rear entrance to the courts."

"Likely enough," said Mr Calder, "but it still doesn't explain how they're going to get the stuff in. Did you get anything else out of the tape, Sheilagh?"

"I made a list of the words and expressions he used most often. Some were just swearing, apart from that his mind seemed to be running on time. He said 'midday' and 'twelve o'clock' a dozen times at least. And he talks about a 'midday special'. That seemed to be some sort of joke. He doesn't actually use the word 'explosion', but he talks once or twice about a report, or reports."

"Report?" said Mr Calder thoughtfully. "That sounds more like a shot from a gun than a bomb."

"It's usually in the plural. Reports."

"Several guns."

"Rather elaborate, surely. Hidden rifles, trained on the Bench, and timed to go off at midday?"

"And it still doesn't explain how he gets the stuff past the guards," said Mr Behrens.

He took the problem down the hill with him to his house in Lamperdown village and carried it up to bed. He knew, from experience, that he would get little sleep until he had solved it. The irritating thing was that the answer was there. He was sure of it. He had only to remember what he had seen and connect it up with the words on the tape, and the solution would appear, as inevitably as the jackpot came out of the slot when you got three lemons in a row.

Visualise the people, pouring through the entrance into the building, carrying briefcases, book bags, handbags. One man had had a camera slung over his shoulder. The guard had called his attention to a notice prohibiting the taking of photographs in court. This little episode had held up the queue for a moment. The young man behind, a barristers' clerk, Mr Behrens guessed, had been in a hurry, and had pushed past the camera-owner. He had not been searched, because he hadn't been carrying a case. But he had been carrying *something*. When Mr Behrens reached this point he did, in fact, doze off, so that the solution must have reached him in his sleep.

Next morning, after breakfast, he telephoned his solicitor, catching him before he set out for the golf course. He said, "When you go into court, and have to tell the judge what another judge said in another case—"

"Quote a precedent, you mean."

"That's right. Well, do you take the book with you, or is it already in court?"

"Both. There's a complete set of Reports in court. Several

sets, in fact. They're for the judges. And you bring your own with you"

"That might mean lugging in a lot of books."

"A trolley-full sometimes."

"Suppose you had, say, five or six sets of Reports to carry. How would you manage?"

"I'd get my clerk to carry them."

"All right," said Mr Behrens patiently, "how would he manage?"

"If it was just half a dozen books, he's got a sort of strap affair, with a handle."

"That's what I thought I remembered seeing," said Mr Behrens. "Thank you very much."

"I suppose you've got some reason for asking all these questions?"

"An excellent reason."

His solicitor, who knew Mr Behrens, said no more.

"We'll get there early," said Mr Calder, "and park as close as we can to the south-east corner. There's plenty of cover in the garden and we can watch both lines of cars. As soon as one of us spots LKK 910 P he tips off the others using one of these pocket radios. Quite easy, Sheilagh. Just press the button and talk. Then let it go, and listen."

"That doesn't sound too difficult," said Sheilagh, "what then?"

"Then Henry gets busy."

"Who's Henry?"

"An old friend of mine who'll be coming with us. His job is to unlock the boot of their car as soon as they're clear of it. By my reckoning he'll have ten minutes for the job, which will be nine and a half minutes more than he needs."

The man and girl walked up Searle Street, not hurrying, but not wasting time, crossed Carey Street, climbed the five shallow steps and pushed through the swing doors and into the court building.

Mr Behrens had got there before them. He was standing on the far side of the barrier. A little queue had already formed and he had plenty of time to observe them.

They had dressed for the occasion with ritual care. The man in a dark suit, cream shirt and dark red tie. The girl in the uniform of a female barrister, black dress, black shoes and stockings, with a single touch of colour, the collar points of a yellow shirt showing at the throat.

As he watched them edge forward to the barrier Mr Behrens felt a prickle of superstitious dread. They may have been nervous, but they showed no sign of it. They looked serious and composed, like the young crusaders who, for the more thorough purging of the holy places, mutilated the living bodies of their pagan prisoners; like the novices who watched impassively at the *auto-da-fé* where men and women were burned to the greater glory of God.

Now they were at the barrier. The girl was carrying a book bag and a satchel. She opened them both. The search was thorough and took time. The man showed very slight signs of impatience.

Mr Behrens thought, "they've rehearsed this very carefully".

When it came to the man's turn he placed the six books, held together in a white strap, on the counter and opened the briefcase. The guard searched the briefcase, and nodded. The man picked up the books and the case and walked down the short length of corridor to where the girl was standing. He ignored her, turned the corner and made for Court Number Two. Although it was not yet ten o'clock there were already a number of people in the courtroom. Two elderly barristers were standing by the front bench discussing something. Behind them a girl was arranging a pile of books and papers. The young man placed his six books, still strapped together, on the far end of the back bench, and went out as quietly as he had come in. No one took any notice of him.

A minute later Mr Behrens appeared, picked up the books, and left. No one took any notice of him either.

When the young man came out, he had joined the girl and they moved off together. Having come in by the back entrance it was evidently their intention to leave by the front. They had gone about ten paces when a man stopped them. He said, "Excuse me, but have you got your cards?"

"Cards?" said the young man. He seemed unconcerned.

"We're issuing personal identity cards to all barristers using the court. Your clerk should have told you. If you'll come with me I'll give you yours."

The girl looked at the man, who nodded slightly, and they set off after their guide. He led the way down a long, empty passage towards the western annexe to the courts.

The young man closed up behind him. He put his hand into a side pocket, pulled out a leather cosh, moved a step closer, and hit the man on the head. Their guide went forward onto his knees and rolled over onto his face.

The young man and the girl had swung round and were moving back the way they had come.

"Walk, don't run," said the young man.

They turned a corner, and went down a spiral staircase which led to the main hall and the front entrance.

When they were outside, and circling the court building, the girl said, "That man. Did you notice?"

"Notice what?"

"When you hit him. He was expecting it."

"What do you mean?"

"He started to fall forward just before you hit him. It must have taken most of the force out of the blow."

Without checking his pace the young man said, "Do you think he was a plant? Holding us up so they could get to the car ahead of us?"

"I thought it might be."

The young man put one hand on the shoulder-holster inside his coat, and said, "If that's right, you'll see some fireworks."

There was no one waiting by the car. The nearest person to it was a small man, with a face like a friendly monkey, who was sitting on a bench inside the garden reading the *Daily Mirror*.

No one tried to stop them as they drove out of Lincoln's Inn Fields and turned south towards the Embankment. "Twenty past ten," said the young man. "Good timing." They were five miles short of Dover, on the bare escarpment above Bridge, before he spoke again. He said, "Twelve o'clock. Anytime now."

Either his watch was fast or the timing mechanism was slow. It was fully five minutes later when their car went up in a searing sheet of white flame.

BOOTS

Antonia Fraser

HER MOTHER USED to call her Little Red Riding Boots, and
eventually by degrees of use (and affection) just Boots. And
now that Emily was no longer quite so little—the smart red
plastic boots which had given rise to the joke were beginning
to pinch—she still liked being called the pet name by her
mother. It was a private matter between them.

Emily's mother, Cora, was a widow: a pretty, slight young
woman, not yet thirty, but still a widow. When Emily was a
baby, her father had gone away to somewhere hot on an
engineering project and got himself killed. That at least was
how Emily had heard Cora describing the situation on the
occasion of her first date with Mr Inch.

"And not a penny after all these years," Cora added. "Just a
load of luggage months later. Including the clothes he was
wearing! Still covered in his blood . . ."

Then Mr Inch—not Cora—got up and shut the door.

Listening from her little bedroom, which was just next to the
sitting-room, Emily imagined her father getting himself killed.
Or rather she thought of the nasty accident she had recently
witnessed on the zebra crossing opposite their house. Blood
everywhere. Rather as if the old woman had been exploded,
like you sometimes saw on the news on television. The old
woman had been hit by one of the nasty long lorries which
were always rumbling down their particular high street. Cora
felt very strongly about the lorries, and often spoke to Emily
about them, complaining about them, warning her about the
crossing.

Perhaps that was why Cora had let Emily go on watching the
scene out of the window for quite a long time when the old
woman was hit, in spite of all the blood.

Later, Cora explained her views on this kind of thing to Mr Inch and Emily listened.

"You see, you can't protect a child from life. From the first I never hid anything from Boots—Emily. It's all around us, isn't it? I mean, I want Emily to grow up knowing all about life: that's the best kind of protection, isn't it?"

"She is awfully young." Mr Inch sounded rather doubtful. "Perhaps it's just because she looks so tiny and delicate. Such a little doll. And pretty too. One wants to protect her. Pretty like her mother—"

On this occasion also, Mr Inch got up and shut the door. He was always shutting the door, thought Emily, shutting her out as if he did not like her. And yet when Mr Inch was alone with her, if her mother was cooking something smelly with the door shut, even more if Cora dashed down to the shops, Mr Inch used to take the opportunity to say that he liked Emily, that he liked Emily very much. And perhaps one day, who could say, perhaps Mr Inch might come to live with Emily and her mother all the time—would Emily like that?

At this point Mr Inch generally touched Emily's long thick curly hair, not gold but brown, otherwise hair just like a princess's in a fairy story (so Cora sometimes said, brushing it). Mr Inch also touched Emily's mother's hair in the same way: that was of course much shorter, which made it even curlier. But while Mr Inch touched Cora's hair in front of Emily, he never, Emily noticed, touched her own hair when Cora was present.

Emily paused to imagine what it would be like if Mr Inch got himself killed, like Emily's father. Would he explode like the old woman at the crossing? Sometimes Emily watched out of the window and saw Mr Inch approaching the house: he was supposed to cross by the zebra too (although sometimes he did not bother). Sometimes Emily would watch Mr Inch just running towards the house, galloping really, on his long legs. When Mr Inch visited Cora he always brought flowers, sweets for Emily, and sometimes a bottle of wine as well. After a bit Emily noticed that he began to bring food too. He still managed to run towards their house, even carrying all these things.

When Mr Inch ran, he looked like a big dog. A big old dog. Or perhaps a wolf.

By now Emily had really grown out of fairy stories, including that story which her mother fondly imagined to be her steady favourite, Little Red Riding Boots. To tell the truth, she much preferred grown-up television; even if she did not understand it all, she found she understood more and more. Besides, Cora did not object.

That too, said Cora, was a form of protection.

"The news helps you to adjust painlessly . . . A child picks and chooses," she told Mr Inch. "Knowledge is safety . . ."

"But Cora, darling, there are some things you wouldn't want your sweet little Boots to know—I mean, what have you told her about us?"

Since this time neither Cora nor Mr Inch shut the door, Emily was left to reflect scornfully that there was no need for her mother to tell her about Mr Inch, since she saw him for herself, now almost every day, kissing her mother, touching her curly hair. And hadn't Mr Inch told Emily himself that he hoped to come and live with them one day while touching her hair, Emily's much longer hair?

All the same, there was a resemblance between Mr Inch and a wolf. His big teeth. The way he smiled when alone with Emily, for example:

"All the better to eat you with—" Emily could remember the story even if she could no longer be bothered to read it. Once, in spite of herself, she got out the old book and looked at her favourite picture—or rather, what had once been her favourite picture—of Grandmother in her frilly cap, Grandmother with big teeth, smiling.

Little Red Riding Boots stood in front of Grandmother, and though you could see the boots all right, all red and shiny, just like Emily's own, standing in the corner of her bedroom, you could not see the expression on the little girl's face. Nevertheless, Emily could imagine that expression perfectly well. Definitely the little girl would not be looking afraid, in spite of everything, in spite of Grandmother's big teeth, in spite of being alone with her in the house.

This was because Emily herself was not afraid of Mr Inch, even when she was alone with him in the flat, and he called her his little girl, his little Boots (which Emily firmly ignored) and talked about all the treats he would give her "one day", a day Mr Inch strongly hoped would come soon.

The girl in the picture was standing quite still. She knew that soon the woodcutter would come rushing in, as he did in the next picture, and save her. Then he would kill the wicked wolf, and in some books (not the version which was supposed to be her favourite) the woodcutter made a great cut in the wolf's stomach and out came, tumbling, all the other people the wolf had eaten. No blood, though, which was rather silly, because everyone knew that if you cut people open or knocked them or anything like that, there was masses of blood everywhere.

You saw it all the time in films when you were allowed to sit with your supper and hold your mother's hand during the frightening bits:

"Squeeze me, Boots, squeeze my hand."

Emily loved sitting with Cora like this, to watch the films on television, and it was one of the things she really did not like about Mr Inch that when he arrived, Emily had to stop doing it.

Mr Inch watched the films with Cora instead and he held her hand; he probably squeezed it too. Sometimes he did other things. Once Emily had a bad dream and she came into the sitting-room. The television was still on but Mr Inch and Emily's mother were not watching it. Emily's mother lay on the floor all untidy and horrid, not pretty and tidy like she generally was, and Mr Inch was bending over her. His trousers were lying on the floor between Emily and the television, and Emily saw his long white hairy legs, and his white shirt tails flapping when he hastily got up from the floor.

Now that *was* frightening, not like a film or the news, and Emily did not really like to think of the incident afterwards. Instead she began to imagine, in greater detail, how Mr Inch might get himself killed, like the wolf, like her father. She did not hold out much hope of Mr Inch going somewhere hot, because he never seemed to go anywhere, and also Mr Inch had plenty of money; lack of money was the reason why Emily's father had gone somewhere hot in the first place. Nor was he likely to be killed crossing the road, like the old woman, if only because Mr Inch was always warning Cora (and Emily) to take care; even when Emily watched Mr Inch running in their direction, she noticed that he always stopped for the lorries, and allowed plenty of time for them to pass. As for the woodcutter—which was a silly idea, anyway, because where would you find a woodcutter in the city?—even if you took it seriously, you could not expect a woodcutter to rush into their flat, because Cora saw so few people.

She was far too busy caring for her little girl, Cora explained to Mr Inch when they first met. Baby-sitters were expensive, and in any case unreliable.

"I shouldn't dream of trying to take you away from this dear little person," Mr Inch had remarked on this occasion, flashing his big white teeth at Emily. "It was always one of my great regrets that I never had a daughter of my own."

No, Emily did not see how a woodcutter could be brought into the story. She wished that Mr Inch would be famous, and then he would go on television and maybe be killed. But Cora said that Mr Inch was not famous:

"Just a very good kind man, Boots, who wants to look after us."

"Now I've got two little girls to look after," said Mr Inch one day. For a moment Emily was mystified by his remark: she had a sudden hope that Mr Inch had found another little girl to look after somewhere else. It was only when Mr Inch took first Cora's hand, then Emily's, that she realized with a certain indignation that Mr Inch's other little girl was supposed to be her mother.

After that, Mr Inch's caring and looking-after of Cora and Emily grew stronger all the time.

"I'll take very good care of her," said Mr Inch, when Cora asked him to go down to the supermarket with Emily, "And I'm sure you won't object on the way back if there's just one ice cream."

"Run along, Boots," called Cora from the kitchen. "And hold Mr Inch's hand very tight. Specially crossing the road."

Actually there was no need for Cora to mention crossing the road to Mr Inch, because he held Emily's hand so terribly tight on the way to the shops that she had to stop herself squeaking. Then Mr Inch cheated. He bought Emily not one but two ice creams. He took her to the Ice Cream Parlour: Emily had never been inside before because Cora said it was too expensive.

Emily ate her ice creams in silence. She was imagining cutting open Mr Inch with the woodcutter's axe: she did not think the things inside Mr Inch would be very nice to see (certainly no exciting people had been swallowed by Mr Inch). But there would be plenty of blood.

Even when Mr Inch asked Emily to come and sit on his lap and said that he had something very exciting to tell her, that he was going to be her new Daddy, Emily still did not say anything. She let Mr Inch touch her long hair, and after a bit she laid her head on Mr Inch's chest, which is what he seemed to want, but still she was very quiet. "Poor little Boots is tired," said Mr Inch. "We'd better go home to Mummy."

So Emily and Mr Inch walked along the crowded street, the short way back to their flat from the shops. Emily did not say anything and she did not listen to what Mr Inch was saying either. When Emily and Mr Inch got to the crossing, they paused and Emily—as well as Mr Inch—looked right, left and right again, just as Cora had taught her. This time Mr Inch was not holding Emily's hand nearly so tight so it was Emily who squeezed Mr Inch's hand, his big hairy hand, and Emily who smiled at Mr Inch, with her little white pearly teeth.

It was when one of the really big lorries was approaching, the sort that Cora said shouldn't be allowed down their street, the sort which were rumbling their flats to bits, that the little red boots, shiny red plastic boots, suddenly went twinkling and skipping and flashing out into the road.

Fast, fast, went the little red boots, shining. Quick, quick, went the wicked wolf after the little red boots.

Afterwards somebody said that the child had actually cried out: "Catch me! Catch me! I bet you can't catch me!" But Cora, even in her distress, said that couldn't possibly be true, because Emily would never be so careless and silly on a zebra crossing. Hadn't Emily crossed it every day, sometimes twice a day, all her life? In spite of what the lorry driver said about the little girl dashing out, and the man running after her, Cora still blamed the driver for the accident.

As for poor Mr Inch—well, he had died trying to save Emily, save her from the dreadful heavy lorry, hadn't he? He was a hero. Even if he was now a sad sodden lump of a hero, like an old dog which had been run over on the road.

Emily said nothing. Now Boots expected to live happily ever after with her mother, watching television, as in a fairy story.

BLUEBEARD'S KEY

Celia Fremlin

"FOR GOD'S SAKE, Melanie, give the kid a chance! Can you wonder he's disturbed—just think what he's been through! Barely thirteen . . . and eight different foster-homes already . . . !"

And now Muggins for the ninth! Melanie didn't say it aloud, of course, because she understood only too well the anxiety—the panic, really—that lay behind her husband's bluster. Newly-promoted in his Social Service Department, desperately anxious to make his mark, to justify his promotion, Derek had made on his own responsibility this quixotic, this grandly compassionate decision which was fast revealing itself to have been a monumental blunder. Even she, angry though she was at having been dragged so gratuitously into so hideous a predicament—even she couldn't, in all honesty, see a way out of it. How could Derek be expected, now, to go cap-in-hand to his humiliatingly-much-younger colleagues and plead with them to get him out of this mess into which, against their unanimous advice, he had landed himself?

Oh, they would help him, no doubt: politely, with raised eyebrows, carefully refraining from actually saying "I told you so!", they would set about deploying all their bright, youthful expertise to show up the older man's bumbling sentimentality, his shameful inability to handle in a realistic manner the kind of crises which were what the new job was all about. Behind his back they would sneer, and make pitying remarks: "Doesn't know he's born!" . . . "Still wet behind his aging ears!" . . . "No fool like an old fool!" . . . All the remarks, in fact, which Derek had secretly feared people would make, right from the beginning.

For Derek had taken up social work comparatively late in life. A disillusioned school-teacher, already in his late thirties, he had embarked on a Social Science Course like a drowning man clutching at a raft, in the wild hope that here at last, in the field of individual personal problems, he would have a chance to use those gifts of compassion, of empathy, of psychological insight which he was sure he possessed, and which he had at one time fondly imagined would stand him in good stead in the vast, multiracial comprehensive school in which he found himself.

They hadn't. Such rarefied virtues stood about as much chance of survival in this environment as rare orchids on a football ground; they were trampled flat, within hours, by the sheer roaring, stampeding tumult of it all. Derek had come home from his first day like a man in shock—a shock from which, it seemed to Melanie, he never entirely recovered throughout his years of teaching. For he battled on, while Melanie, helpless, racked by anxiety for him, had stood by watching her husband's bright hopes failing, his principles collapsing, his shining ideals battered into pulp by the impact of reality. As the months and years went by, it seemed to her that his very soul was shrivelling as he found himself forced down and down, day after day, into behaving exactly like all those repressive, reactionary martinets of schoolmasters whom he had spent his bright, teacher-trained youth reviling. Day after day he would come home to her, hoarse with yelling, bitter with the shame of having had to yell, his whole body sagging under the weight of the threats, the punishments, the bawlings-out which all day long he had been administering in the very teeth of everything he had ever believed in.

The idea of switching to social work, albeit in mid-career, had been like an inspiration from Heaven, and from the moment of its taking root, Derek had been a changed man; radiant, bursting with energy, and filled once again with all the old youthful idealism, the confidence in his power to build a better world. And Melanie, although she was already pregnant with Alison, and the drop in income during his two-year training would be punishing, was one hundred percent behind him. *Any* price was worth paying to see her husband happy and fulfilled at last.

And they'd managed, somehow. Luck, as it turned out,

was on their side. Alison was a beautiful baby, healthy and uncomplicated, and with a naturally contented disposition which allowed her to be left, untraumatised, with this neighbour or that while Melanie resumed her part-time job. Derek's training grant had been upped, unexpectedly, during his second year, and at the end he sailed through his exams with flying colours. And even after qualification, his luck still held. They'd feared that, what with the unemployment situation and his relatively advanced years, it might prove difficult for Derek to find a job; but, lo and behold, almost the perfect post came his way almost at once; and now, after not much more than a year, he'd been promoted to a position of almost frightening responsibility.

No, not almost. *Totally* frightening; and this Melanie was forcing herself to remember, biting back the fury and the revulsion that half-choked her whenever she thought about the sullen, evil-tempered little creature that had been landed on her, with his sallow, near-adult face atop his undersized body, and with his unpredictable bouts of destructive malice which had already, in these few days, left their ugly mark on more than one of Melanie's treasured possessions.

"It's his deprived background—don't you understand?" Derek had reproved her when she'd confronted him this evening with Christopher's latest effort—a favourite blouse of hers streaked with shoe-polish and with all the buttons ripped off—"You have to remember what he's been through—his mother abandoning him when he was only a baby! Very likely still breast-feeding, and so it may be that, to him, that blouse symbolises . . ."

That was how the row had started; and now, at nearly midnight, with Alison in bed and Christopher still sulking in his own room—now the quarrel was taking on a second lease of life.

"Have you no compassion for the poor kid?" Derek was expostulating, "I just don't understand how you can be so hard—so unfeeling! Think about it! How would *you* feel if *you'd* been shunted from pillar to post the way he has! If *you'd* been rejected from eight different homes, one after another! *Eight!* How would *you* feel?"

"I'd feel I'd better watch my step a bit," Melanie retorted

crisply, "and refrain from smashing up my ninth happy home! I'd feel I should reflect on a few of the things it would be politic *not* to do. Like not pushing a teapot of scalding tea over the edge of the table on to the carpet only inches from where the toddler is playing! Like not throwing handfuls of gravel into my hostess's sewing-machine . . . Not going round the house with an umbrella, poking it at every electric light bulb I could reach . . . ! I'd feel I had to go easy on that sort of thing. For a while, anyway. That's what I'd feel!"

"Melanie!" His voice rasped with panicky self-righteousness, and she knew she had got him rattled. "Melanie, how can you be so—so *heartless*! So *hard*! Can't you see this destructiveness for what it is—a cry for help? Can't you see that all the poor kid needs is love? Warm, unconditional, non-judgmental, totally accepting . . ."

"Stop it! Shut up! I can't bear it . . . !" Melanie's hands were over her face as if to ward off these psychological clichés which he seemed to be using as weapons, snatched at random from an inexhaustible pile kept ready to hand for just such occasions as this. "Stop it! 'Love', indeed! It's not love the little monster needs, it's a bloody good . . . !"

"A bloody good hiding" is not a phrase that falls becomingly from the lips of a social worker's wife; she checked herself just in time, but not before Derek had got the message.

"Melanie!" he expostulated, truly shocked. "You're not to talk about the kid like that! It's wicked! After all, he *is* only a kid, he's . . ."

"And stop calling him a 'kid'!" Melanie yelled, beside herself by now. "The kid . . . the kid . . . the kid!—it's one of those slimy, Catch-22 words which extort approval for the bloody child before the argument even starts. Why can't you just call him 'the boy'? Or 'the foundling'? Or 'the bastard'? Or whatever the hell he is!"

She had gone too far, and she knew it. Remorse caught at her, checking, for a moment, the full flow of her anger. Hadn't she, right at the beginning, promised Derek her whole-hearted support in his brave new venture? Had she not resolved to back him up, to take his side, to be a true helpmeet, sharing the problems, the setbacks, the burdens, whatever they might turn out to be?

And now here she was, backing off at the first hurdle, failing him at the first real test.

But *what* a test! It was the unfairness of it—that was what rankled. To expect that she, an ordinary housewife, who just happened to be married to a social worker, should be able to shoulder single-handed, at barely a day's notice, a ghastly and intractable problem which whole teams of experts had so far found to be utterly beyond them!

Because that was the truth of the matter. It was obvious. *Nobody* had been able to cope with Christopher; not the psychiatrists; not the child-care people; not any of those eight foster-homes. And this was why, of course, Derek had been moved to make his grand, quixotic, and highly unorthodox gesture. "I'll take him!" he must have said when the committee discussing Christopher's case reached deadlock: "I'll take him home with me tonight—into my own family! My wife and I will give him what we all agree he needs—the security of a loving home."

Or words to that effect. Grand words, anyway; heroic, laying himself on the line. And the Committee, in duty bound to protest at the irregularity of such a proposal, would nevertheless have been secretly thankful at being thus let off the hook, and with due show of hesitancy would finally have acquiesced in the hare-brained proposal.

After all, if it failed he'd be the one to carry the can. And if it succeeded—why, what a break for everybody! The kid had been on the books for years—a chronic groan in everybody's in-tray. Good old Derek. Provided he made a success of it, that is.

Success. Melanie turned the word over in her mind. Success, presumably, meant turning Christopher into a pleasant, outgoing, well-adjusted boy. And how did one set about it? Why, by showing him love, compassion and tolerance, Derek had blandly assured her before rushing out of the house this morning, with a briefcase full of important papers in his hand.

Love. Compassion. Tolerance. The whole bloody trio. And who was it, in practice, who was going to have to administer them? Not Derek himself. Oh no. Safe out of the house from eight in the morning till eight or nine at night, he hardly ever saw Christopher, never mind trying to cope with him. *He* didn't have to snatch the scissors from the child's thin, swift fingers just before he sliced into the dining-room curtains; didn't have to clear up the mess when Christopher deftly up-ended the paraffin heater (fortunately not alight) all over the bathroom floor; hadn't had to search out, endlessly, all those slivers of glass from the electric light bulbs before Alison hurt herself on them.

Even as the thought passed through her mind, another of the slivers glinted up at her, this time from among the sofa cushions.

"Look!" she screamed at Derek. "Just look! Someone could have sat on it! Or Alison might've . . ."

"But she didn't, did she? Look, darling, do pull yourself together and stop getting hysterical over nothing!" The honeyed detachment of his tone would have been the last straw, had she not heard the fear behind it, the desperate pleading. His back was towards her now, he leaned on the mantelpiece, face in hands, and his voice came to her muffled.

"I'm sorry, Melanie. It's been rough on you—don't think I don't know it. But please—Oh, Melanie—don't you see? I've taken this on, and I've got to see it through! Got to! I can't fail, Melanie, I just can't!"

She heard the despair in his voice, and "Of course you won't fail!" she assured him; and hoped that he didn't hear the despair in hers.

At first, she'd thought that Christopher must be mentally defective, so pointless was the destructive behaviour in which he engaged; gouging shallow trenches in the polished table with the point of a knitting-needle; lining up all Alison's plastic farm animals as if for some nice little game with her, and then, with a brass candlestick, smashing them systematically one by one, with a speed and economy of effort that would have done credit to a factory assembly-line.

"Mentally defective?" Derek had scoffed at the idea. "Of course he isn't! He's quite bright, actually. They've done tests . . ."

"Oh, tests!" Melanie had mocked; but soon had to change her tune when she discovered for herself that indeed he was quite bright. In his quieter moods, he enjoyed doing crossword puzzles; and sometimes, just for fun, he would set himself quite awesome arithmetical tasks, filling whole sheets of paper with columns of figures to add or multiply or divide, and coming up with the correct answer at quite phenomenal speed.

The first time he'd done this, Melanie, laboriously checking the result and finding it correct, had been fulsome in praise.

"Christopher! That's marvellous!" she'd enthused. "I think you're the most wonderful . . ." But barely was she launched into her flattering speech when a wary, malevolent look came over the sallow little features; he twisted the paper from her hands and tore it across and across into tiny pieces, hurling them to the floor and then stamping on them, over and over again, as if they were tiny living creatures that he wanted to be certain he'd killed.

Derek, hearing about the incident later that evening, had looked worried at first. Then, his face clearing, he'd started talking about "rejection syndromes", and had urged Melanie —quite kindly—to try and avoid being patronising. "Treat him as an equal," he'd admonished her, before disappearing into his study to get on with some important work. "Talk to him as you would to an adult."

Well, how *do* you talk to an adult who behaves like that? And who then, when you ask him, gently, what's bothering him, gives you a glance of total loathing, and bolts upstairs to his room, his feet scuttering on the stairs like a startled rat, and his door slamming so that the whole house shakes? They were familiar sounds now, this pattering of feet and slamming of a door; and, to Melanie, very dreadful. They meant, always, that Christopher was escaping from the scene of some crime—sometimes trivial, sometimes serious, but always terrifying until she had managed to discover what it was, and where.

It was useless trying to talk to Christopher about his misdemeanours—or, indeed, about anything; and at one point she'd found herself wondering if maybe he actually couldn't talk? But he could, perfectly well, when he chose, as she discovered on the afternoon when she tried (very gently and humanely, as Derek would have wished) to dissuade him from a second assault on the electric lights; to explain to him—rationally, non-judgmentally, all the rest—about the practical problems that were liable to arise from the smashing of electric light bulbs: the expense of buying new ones; the trouble of fitting them in; the danger from the splinters of glass . . .

Christopher seemed to be listening, taking it in. His eyes never left her face, and when she had quite finished—not before—he gave his considered reply:

"Bloody fucking lights!" he observed. "Who needs the bloody fucking lights?"

Alison was enchanted.

"B'uddy fuckin yights!" she chortled, gazing up at Christopher adoringly. "B'uddy fuckin yights! B'uddy fuckin yights!"

The phrase had really grabbed her, and she went on repeating it, on and off, all the afternoon, until at last Melanie got fed up with it.

"Hush, Allie, that's—" she stopped herself in time before saying the forbidden word "naughty"—"That's a *silly* thing to say, Allie! You mustn't keep saying those words!"

Unfortunately Derek, arriving home at just this moment, had heard it all; and later he reproached Melanie for her prudish and repressive attitude.

". . . And especially since she's learned the phrase from *Christopher*," he pointed out, pronouncing the name in a hushed, holy kind of way as if it came out of the Bible—"Think how rejected the poor kid's going to feel if we don't let our own child learn from him and imitate him! You know," he added, with that exaggeratedly non-judgmental look which Melanie was learning to dread—"you know, this could be the breakthrough we've been waiting for! Don't you see?—it could be the start of a real relationship between him and Allie! He's never experienced a real relationship before, not with anyone, ever. It could be the making of him! Don't you see? The simple, uncritical love of a tiny child . . ."

Over my dead body, was Melanie's immediate thought; but she held her tongue, hoping that, if not discussed, the idea might fizzle out.

But it didn't. The very next evening Derek brought it up again; he had evidently been mulling it over all day.

"About Allie and Christopher," he began, not quite looking at her. "You know what we were saying yesterday—well, all right, what *I* was saying—about cultivating a real, meaningful relationship between them? Well, I've been thinking, and it seems to me that the first thing is to let them *play* together sometimes. Play on their own, I mean . . . unsupervised. What do you think . . . ?" And when Melanie remained obstinately silent, he continued, a certain edge coming into his voice:

"Look, Melanie, I don't want to seem to criticise, I know you're doing your best, but I do think you are making a mistake the way you keep watching them all the time, whenever they are even in the same room. You never take your eyes off them. He must notice it, you know; he must feel it. It must seem to him that you don't trust him with her!"

"Bloody right, I don't! And I never will! If you'd seen the things he does with scissors . . . with hammers . . . with knitting-needles . . . !"

"But not to *her*! He's never attacked *her*, now has he? He's fond of her, it's obvious, and if we can only get that fondness to grow . . . to blossom . . . it could be the salvation of him! Don't you see? But for this to happen, you have to *trust* him. Stop being so wary . . . so suspicious . . . always expecting the worst! Like the way you invariably lock the nursery door at night after she's in bed . . . What do you think he feels about *that*!"

"What *he* feels? What *I'd* like to understand is what *you* feel, that you're willing to put your own daughter in such awful danger! Do you see yourself as Abraham, or something, sacrificing your child's life to prove your faith in the Great God Freud . . . ?"

And so the battle raged, until both were exhausted and there were only a few more shots left on either side.

"There shouldn't *be* locked doors in a family home!" Derek pronounced virtuously. "It's a *home* we're supposed to be offering the poor kid, not a detention centre!"

"And so what about your study door?" Melanie countered sharply. "I notice you keep *that* locked firmly enough! How about trusting him in there—with all your papers . . . and the wine racks . . . and the beat-the-budget whisky . . ."

"That's different! Those papers are *important* . . . !" He stopped, quelled by his wife's icy glance.

"Well, OK, Melanie. You win. Fair's fair, and I do see your point; if I'm asking *you* to trust him, then it's only fair that *I* should trust him too. Right? So, from now on, I leave the study door unlocked, and you leave the nursery unlocked. OK?"

It wasn't OK. Never in a million years. Come what may, she would go on locking that door, clinging to the frail hope that she might, by various devious ploys, prevent Derek noticing that she was doing so.

Such hope was short-lived. Only two days later, on the Saturday, Derek found himself, for once, at home and at leisure in time to put Alison to bed himself—bathing her, telling her a story, making her Teddy-bear dance a hornpipe on the coverlet—all the things he hadn't had time for for ages, and in which Alison, of course, delighted.

"More, Daddy, more!" she squealed. Then, racking her brain for further delaying tactics: "Daddy, you haven't said goodnight to Teddy . . . ! Daddy, you haven't hung up my dressing gown . . ." and then, finally, when he had at last got himself outside the door—"Daddy! Daddy! You haven't yocked my door! Mummy always yocks my door!"

That did it. Within seconds of Derek's pounding down the stairs, the row was in full swing.

"You promised . . . !"

"I did not! Over my dead body will she be left at the mercy of that vicious little . . . !"

"Don't you dare talk about Christopher like that! It's all your fault! You've hated the poor kid ever since he set foot in the house! If you'd ever shown one spark of kindness . . . one single glimmer of . . ."

And it was then, through the noise of both their raised voices, that Melanie heard it: the pitter-patter of swift, scurrying feet . . . the slam of an upstairs door. And it was now, too, that she realised, with a lurch of horror, that this time, of course, the nursery door wouldn't have been locked.

In a flash, she was across the room . . . at the foot of the stairs; but Derek's arm dragged her back.

"See what I mean? You won't leave them alone for so much as two seconds! They're only *playing*, for God's sake— running around on the landing! If you keep interfering all the time, how do you suppose they can ever form a real, meaningful . . . !"

And it was then, both at the same time, that they smelt burning.

Derek was at the top of the stairs first, three steps ahead of her, and as he flung open the nursery door Melanie, behind him, heard his gasp of horror; smelt the first, ominous whiff of paraffin . . .

A second later he was out again, with Alison, unhurt, in his arms, while behind him, inside the room, a carefully-stacked pile of newspapers shot flames upwards and outwards all around the cot; even as she watched, the cot-cover, liberally sprinkled with paraffin, became a sheet of flame. The roar of it was in her ears, she could hardly hear the thunder of Derek's steps on the stairs as he raced the child to safety, shouting to her to follow him.

But she didn't. She just stood there, numbed with—was it shock? Or was it something else?

Christopher! She was the one who knew where he was; had heard the terrible pattering footsteps, had recognized the door that slammed as the study door. He was still in there . . .

She had thought, for a moment, that he would have locked himself in; but no, it was all right, here was the key in the door, on the outside. Someone must rescue the little fiend, push open the door, shout a warning, drag the poisonous, rat-faced little monster into safety.

Quietly, unhurriedly—for the flames had not yet crossed the landing—she turned the key in the lock, listening to be sure that the latch had clicked home. Let the pattering little feet go pattering down into the Burning Fiery Furnace, let him this time slam the door of Hell behind him.

Safely and swiftly she must have slipped down the stairs, for here she was, unnoticed, in the noise and the confusion of the garden. Neighbours—passers-by—half the world seemed to be gathering, calling to one another, rushing around, trying to help . . . one of them was already hurrying Alison to the safety of a house, two doors away . . .

And now the firemen. The clanging bells—the shouts—"Get back! Get back!"—and water, water everywhere. In the midst of all this, Derek, white-faced, came darting from the house . . . a fireman shouted at him angrily . . . and now the firemen were everywhere, swarming all over the house, outside and inside . . .

Inside. Where, before many minutes, they would find a small dead body behind a locked door: *a door with the key still in it, locked from the outside* . . .

It was some hours later before she learned that Christopher hadn't died from the fire at all (it never in fact spread to the study), nor even from the smoke. He had died from drinking a whole bottle of whisky at a sitting, on top of no one knew how many tastes of the various bottles that lay opened, higgledy-piggledy, all over the floor.

"Must've locked himself in so's not to be interrupted in the middle of his binge," someone suggested; and this was the first inkling Melanie had that the key had not, after all, been found incriminatingly on the outside of the door where she had so unthinkingly left it.

In fact, it hadn't been found on the inside, either; no doubt the unfortunate boy had hidden it somewhere, so everyone surmised: it was bound to turn up, sooner or later.

And turn up it did, very late that same evening. It turned up in Derek's jacket pocket, and it was Melanie who found it, deep down under his car-keys, handkerchiefs and the rest. She held it, for a minute, in the palm of her hand, studying it, and at first not quite getting the message.

It came to her, though, quite quickly. She recalled Derek's white face as he raced out of the house that second time. She'd wondered, momentarily, what he'd been doing: now she knew.

He'd found that door locked; and instead of instantly unlocking it, horrified at what he'd found—he'd *left it as it was*—except for taking the precaution of removing the incriminating key.

He had done, in effect, exactly what she had done; knowing—as he must have—that she had done it, too.

And now *she* knew that *he* had done it.

How could they live with this knowledge, for all the rest of their lives?

How could they face each other, ever again?

Perhaps, if neither of them spoke of it to the other—not

ever? If neither of them, ever, by hint or look or gesture, gave the smallest indication of the thing that they both knew?

Lives have been lived like this, surely? Many lives, perhaps? Who knows?

One thing at least she could do; she could get rid of this terrible key, the black, indestructible reminder of the thing that henceforth must be forgotten.

Her hands trembled as she picked it up. It felt cold as poison; and smooth, somehow, as if polished by the endless wiping off of blood. Leaning as far as she could out of the window, she flung it with all her force into the midnight garden, right to the very end, where the tangled, uncultivated bit would cover it over completely, and no one would ever find it.

And in fact no one did, at least not for a good many years. It was during one summer holiday from school that Alison, now nearly eight, came across it deep in the tangle of undergrowth that she liked to pretend was a forest. Delighted by her find, she ran indoors with it, full of excitement and announced that it was Bluebeard's key, she just knew it was!

The game caught on. The weather was beautiful that summer, and all though the long golden days she and her little friends played Bluebeard, rushing in and out of each other's houses, shutting each other in cupboards, and chopping off each other's heads with pretend scimitars.

The other mothers all seemed quite happy about the game; a quite normal, typical sort of pastime, they thought, for children of this age.

But Melanie hated it. She tried to deflect the children on to something else; but in vain. In the end, she actually confiscated the key; but at this Alison became quite frantic in her protests:

"*Mummy*! I *must* have the key! It's my Bluebeard key! It's the only key that will open the cupboard where there is the dreadful secret!"

INSPECTOR GHOTE AND THE
NOTED BRITISH AUTHOR

H. R. F. Keating

PERCHED UP ON a creaking wobbly chair in the office of the Deputy Commissioner (Crime), the peon put one broken-nailed finger against Inspector Ghote's name on the painted board behind the D.C.C.'s desk. He swayed topplingly to one side, scraped hold of the fat white pin which indicated "Bandobast Duties", brought it back across in one swooping rush and pressed it firmly into place.

Watching him, Ghote gave an inward sigh. Bandobast duties. Someone, of course, had to deal with the thousand and one matters necessary for the smooth running of Crime Branch, but nevertheless bandobast duty was not tracking down breakers of the law and it did seem to fall to him more often than to other officers. Yet, after all, it would be absurd to waste a man of the calibre of, say, Inspector Dandekar on mere administration.

"Yes, Dandekar, yes?"

The D.C.C. had been interrupted by his internal telephone and there on the other end, as if conjured up by merely having been thought of, was Dandekar himself.

"Yes, yes, of course," the D.C.C. said in answer to the forcefully plaintive sound that had been just audible from the other end. "Certainly you must. I'll see what I can do, ek dum."

He replaced the receiver and turned back to Ghote, the eyes in his sharply commanding face still considering whatever it was that he had promised Dandekar.

And then, as if a god-given solution to his problem had appeared in front of him, his expression changed in an instant to happy alertness. He swung round to the peon, who was carefully carrying away his aged chair.

"No," he said. "Put the bandobast pin against—er—Inspector Sawant. I have a task I need Inspector Ghote for."

The peon turned back with his chair to the big painted hierarchy of crime-fighters ranging from the Deputy Commissioner himself down to the branch's three dogs, Akbar, Moti and Caesar. Ghote, in front of the D.C.C.'s wide baize-covered desk, glowed now with pure joy.

"It's this Shivaji Park case," the D.C.C. said.

"Oh yes, D.C.C. Multiple-stabbing double murder, isn't it? Discovered this morning by that fellow who was in the papers when he came to Bombay, that noted British author."

Ghote, hoping his grasp both of departmental problems and the flux of current affairs would earn him some hint of appreciativeness, was surprised instead to receive a look of almost suspicious surmise. But he got no time to wonder why.

"Yes, quite right," the D.C.C. said briskly. "Dandekar is handling the case, of course. With an influential fellow like this Englishman involved we must have a really quick result. But there is something he needs help with. Get down to his office straightaway, will you?"

"Yes, sir. Yes, D.C.C."

Clicking his heels together by way of salute, Ghote hurried out.

What would Dandekar have asked for assistance over? There would be a good many different lines to pursue in an affair of this sort. The murdered couple, an ice-cream manufacturer and his wife, had been, so office gup went, attacked in the middle of the night. The assailants had tied up their teenage son and only when he had at last roused the nearest neighbour, this visiting British author—of crime books, the paper had said, well-known crime books—had it been discovered that the two older people had been hacked to death. Goondas of that sort did not, of course, choose just any location. They sniffed around first. And left a trail. Which meant dozens of inquiries in the neighbourhood, usually by sub-inspectors from the local station. But with this influential fellow involved . . .

Emerging into the sunlight, Ghote made his way along to Dandekar's office which gave directly on to the tree-shaded compound. He pushed open one half of its batwing doors. And there, looking just like his photograph, large as life, or even larger, was the Noted British Author. He was crouching on a small chair in front of Dandekar's green leather-covered desk, covering it much like a big fluffed-up hen on one small precious egg. His hips, clad in trousers already the worse for the dust and stains of Bombay life, drooped on either side while a considerable belly projected equally far forward. Above was a beard, big and sprawling as the body beneath, and above the beard was hair, plentiful and inclined to shoot in all directions. Somewhere between beard and hair a pale British face wore a look of acute curiosity.

"Ah, Ghote, thank God," Dandekar, stocky, muscular, hook-nosed, greeted him immediately in sharp, T-spitting Marathi. "Listen, take this curd-face out of my sight. Fast."

Ghote felt a terrible abrupt inward sinking. So this was how he was to assist Dandekar, by keeping from under his feet a, no doubt, notable British nuisance. Even bandobast duties would be better.

But Dandekar could hardly produce that expected rapid result with such a burden. He squared his bony shoulders.

Dandekar had jumped up.

"Mr Peduncle," he said, in English now, "I would like you to—"

"It's not Peduncle actually," the Noted British Author broke in. "Important to get the little details right, you know. That's what the old shell-collector in my books—he's Mr Peduncle—is always telling his friend, Inspector Sugden. No, my name's Reymond, Henry Reymond, author of the Peduncle books."

The multitudinous beard split with a wide, clamorously ingratiating grin.

"Yes, yes," said Dandekar briskly. "But this is Inspector Ghote. He will be assisting me. Ghote, the domestic servant of the place has disappeared—a Goan known as John Louzado. They had no address at his native-place, but we might get it from a former employer. Will you see to that? And Mr Ped—Mr Reymond, who is expressing most keen interest in our methods, can attach himself to you while I talk with the young man who was tied up, the son, or rather adopted son. I think somehow he could tell a good deal more."

Ghote put out his hand for Mr Reymond to shake. He did

not look forward to dealing with the numerous questions likely to arise from that keen interest in Bombay C.I.D. methods.

As Ghote drove the Noted British Author in one of the branch's big battered cars down Dr D.N. Road towards Colaba where the fleeing servant's former employer lived, he found his worst forebodings justified. His companion wanted to know everything—what was that building, what this, was that man happy lying on the pavement, where else could he go?

Jockeying for place in the traffic, swerving for cyclists, nipping past great lumbering red articulated buses, Ghote did his best to provide pleasing answers. But the fellow was never content. Nothing seemed to delight him more than hitting on some small discrepancy and relentlessly pursuing it, comparing himself all the while to his Mr Peduncle and his "The significant variation: in that lies all secrets". If Ghote heard the phrase once in the course of their twenty-minute drive, he seemed to hear it a dozen times.

At last, when they were waiting at the lights to get into Colaba Road, he was reduced to putting a question of his own. How did it come about, he interrupted, that Mr Reymond was living in a flat up at Shivaji Park? Would not the Taj Hotel just down there be more suitable for a distinguished visitor?

"Ah yes, I know what you mean," the author answered with an enthusiasm that gave Ghote considerable inward pleasure. "But, you see, I am here by courtesy of Air India, on their new Swap-a-Country Plan. They match various people with their Indian equivalents and exchange homes. Most far-sighted. So I am at Shivaji Park and the writer who lives there—well, he has written some short stories, though I gather he's actually a Deputy Inspector of Smoke Nuisances and a relation of your State Minister for Police Affairs and the Arts, as it happens—well, he at the present moment is installed in my cottage in Wiltshire, and no doubt getting as much out of going down to the pub as I get from being in a flat lucky enough to have a telephone so that people are always popping in and, while they're looking up a number in the little red book, talking away like one o'clock."

The Noted British Author's eyes shone.

"Yes," Ghote said.

Certain queries had occurred to him. Could there, for instance, be an exchange between a police inspector in Bombay and one in, say, New York? But somehow he could not see himself getting several months Casual Leave, and he doubted whether many other similar Bombayites would find it easy.

But he felt that to voice such doubts aloud would be impolite. And his hesitation was fatal.

"Tell me," Mr Reymond said, "that sign saying 'De Luxe Ding Dong Nylon Suiting' . . ." And, in a moment, they had struck full on another "significant variation".

Desperately Ghote pulled one more question out of the small stock he had put together.

"Please, what is your opinion of the books of Mr Erle Stanley Gardner? To me Perry Mason is seeming an extremely clever individual altogether."

"Yes," said the Noted British Author, and he was silent right until they reached their destination in Second Pasta Lane.

Mrs Patel, wife of a civil servant and former employer of John Louzado, was a lady of forty or so dressed in a cotton sari of a reddish pattern at once assertive and entirely without grace.

"You are lucky to find me, Inspector," she said when Ghote had explained their business. "At the Family Planning office where I undertake voluntary work Clinic begins at ten sharp."

Ghote could not stop himself glancing at his watch though he well knew it was at least half-past ten already.

"Well, well," Mrs Patel said sharply, "already I am behind schedule. But there is so much to be done. So much to be done."

She darted across the sitting-room, a place almost as littered with piles of papers as any office at Crime Branch, and plumped up a cushion.

"Just if you have the address of John's native-place," Ghote said.

"Of course, of course. I am bound to have it. I always inquire most particularly after a servant's personal affairs. You are getting an altogether better loyalty factor then. Don't you find that, Mr—I'm afraid I am not hearing your name?"

She had turned her by no means negligible gaze full on the Noted British Author. Ghote, who had hoped not to explain his companion, introduced him with a brief "Mr Reymond, from UK."

"Yes," said Mrs Patel. "Well, don't you find—Ah, but you are the Mr Reymond, the noted British author, isn't it? Most pleased to meet you, my dear sir. Most pleased. What I always find with criminological works is the basic fact emerging, common to many sociological studies, a pattern of fundamental human carelessness, isn't it? You see—"

But, river-spate rapid though she was, she had met her match.

"One moment—I am sorry to interrupt—but there is a slight discrepancy here. You see, there are two different sorts of crime books involved. You are talking about sociological works, but what I write are more crime novels. Indeed, it's just the sort of mistake my detective, Mr Peduncle the old collector of sea shells, is always pointing out. 'The significant variation: in that lies all secrets.'"

"Ah, most interesting," Mrs Patel came back, recovering fast. "Of course I have read a good deal of Erle Stanley Gardner and so forth, and I must say . . ."

She gave them her views at such length that Ghote at last, politeness or not, felt forced to break in.

"Madam, madam. If you will excuse. There is the matter of John's native-place address."

"Yes, yes. I am getting it."

Mrs Patel plunged towards a bureau and opened its flap-down front. A considerable confusion of documents was revealed, together with what looked like the wrappings for a present bought but never handed to its intended recipient.

Prolonged searching located, first, an address-book, then "a list of things like this which I jot down" and finally the back of a notebook devoted to household hints clipped from magazines. But no address.

"Madam," Ghote ventured at last, "is it possible you did not in fact take it down?"

"Well, well, one cannot make a note of everything. That is one of my principles: keep the paperwork down to the minimum."

She gave the British author some examples of Indian bureaucracy. Once or twice Ghote tried to edge him away, but even a tug at the distinguished shirtsleeve was unsuccessful. Only when he himself began explaining how British bureaucracy was a crutch that fatally hampered people like Inspector Sugden in his own books, did Ghote act.

"Madam, I regret. Mr Reymond, sir. We are conducting investigation. It is a matter of urgency."

And with that he did get the author out on to the landing outside. But as Mrs Patel was shutting the door with many "Goodbye then" and "So interesting, and I must try to find one of your books", Mr Reymond broke in in his turn:

"Inspector, there is a small lacuna."

Ghote stared.

"Please, what is lacuna?"

"Something missing, a loose end. You haven't asked where Louzado worked before he came here. Mr Peduncle would have a word to say to you. If there's one thing he always seizes on it is the little lacuna."

The bursting-out beard parted to reveal a roguish smile.

"Yes," said Ghote. "You are perfectly correct. Madam, do you have the address of John's former employer?"

"Why, yes, of course," Mrs Patel replied, with a note of sharpness. "I can tell you that out of my head. John was recommended to me by my friends, the Dutt-Dastars."

And, mercifully, she came straight out with the address—it was somewhat south of the Racecourse—and Ghote was even able to prevent her giving them a detailed account of the posh-sounding Dutt-Dastars.

Since their route took them past Crime Branch H.Q., Ghote decided to risk the Noted British Author re-attaching himself to Inspector Dandekar and to report progress. Besides, if he could install Mr Reymond in his own office for ten minutes only it would give him a marvellous respite from relentlessly pursued questions.

So, a peon summoned and Coca-Cola thrust on the distinguished visitor, Ghote went down to Dandekar.

"Well, Inspector," he asked, "did the son have more to tell?"

"More to tell he has," Dandekar answered, sipping tea and dabbing his face with a towel. "But speak he will not."

"He is not one hundred per cent above-board then?"

"He is not. I was up there at Shivaji Park within half an hour of the time he freed himself from those ropes, and I could see at a glance the marks were not right at all."

"Too high up the wrists, was it?"

"Exactly, Inspector. That young man tied himself up. And that must mean he was in collusion with the fellows who killed the old couple. How else did they get in, if he did not open to them? No, three of them were in it together and the Goan and a notorious bad hat from the vicinity called Budhoo have gone off with the jewellery. You can bet your boots on that."

"But the young man will not talk?" Ghote asked.

"He will not talk. College-educated, you know, and thinks he has all the answers."

Ghote nodded agreement. It was a common type and the bane of a police officer's life. His determination to push forward the case by getting hold of John Louzado's address redoubled.

"Well," he said, "I must be getting back to Mr Reymond, or he will come looking for us."

In answer Dandekar grinned at him like an exulting film villain.

But, when he got back to his office, he found the Noted British Author doing something more ominous than looking for Dandekar. He was furiously making notes on a little pad.

"Ah," he said the moment Ghote came in, "just one or two points that occurred to me in connection with the case."

Ghote felt this last straw thump down.

"Oh yes," he answered, waggishly as he could. "We would be very delighted to have the assistance of the great Mr Peduncle and his magical shell collection."

"No, no," the noted author said quickly. "Mr Peduncle's shells are by no means magical. There's a slight discrepancy there. You see, Mr Peduncle examines shells to detect their little variations and equally he examines the facts of a case and hits on significant variations there."

"The significant variation in which are lying all secrets," Ghote quoted.

Mr Reymond laughed with great heartiness. But in the car,

heading north up Sir J.J. Road, he nevertheless explained in detail every single discrepancy he had noted in his little pad.

It seemed that, in the comparatively short time between the apparently distraught son coming to say he had been set upon and Inspector Dandekar bringing him to Crime Branch H.Q., he had accumulated a great many facts and bits of hearsay. All of them must have been boiling away in his fertile mind. Now to spume out.

Most were trivialities arising from the domestic routine of the dead couple, or of his own flat or the flats nearby. To them Ghote succeeded in finding answers. But what he could not always sort out were the queries these answers produced. "Significant variations" seemed to spring up like buzzing whining insects in the first flush of the monsoon.

Only one point, to Ghote's mind, could be said to have any real connection with the killing, and that was so slight that in any other circumstances he would have thrust it off.

But it was a fact, apparently, that Mr Reymond's servant, an old Muslim called Fariqua, or more precisely the servant of the absent Indian author of some short stories, had been discovered on the morning of the murder asleep inside the flat when he ought to have been in the distant suburb of Andheri where since the author's arrival he had been boarded out—"Well, I mean, the chap actually seemed to sleep on the couch in the sitting-room, and I thought that was a bit much really"—and he had provided no explanation.

"Now," Mr Reymond said, turning in his seat and wagging his finger very close to Ghote's face, "he must have hidden himself away in the kitchen till I'd gone to bed. And isn't that just exactly the sort of variation from the normal which my Mr Peduncle would seize upon, and which my Inspector Sugden would try to shrug off. Eh, Inspector?"

Ghote felt the honour of the Bombay force at stake.

"Certainly I do not shrug off this at all, Mr Reymond," he said. "After we have seen the Dutt-Dastars I will have a word with Fariqua. But then, since you would be at home, perhaps you would care to rest yourself for the afternoon. I know this humid weather makes visitors most extremely fatigued."

He held his breath in anxiety. To his delight Mr Reymond, after consideration, acquiesced.

And if at the Dutt-Dastars' he got Louzado's address . . .

The Dutt-Dastars, it appeared, were a couple entirely devoted
to art. Their house was crammed with Mrs Dutt-Dastar's oil-
paintings, sprawling shapes in bus-red and sky-blue, and Mr
Dutt-Dastar's metal sculptures, jagged iron masses, inclined to
rust and a considerable menace, Ghote found, to trouser
bottom and shirtsleeve. And in the Bengali way their devotion
was expressed as much in words as in acts.

Mr Reymond they seized on as a fellow artist, blithely
ignoring any occasion when he tried to point out a discrepancy,
lacuna or significant variation. And equally ignored, time and
again, were Ghote's attempts to get an answer to the one
question he still saw, despite the somewhat odd behaviour of
Mr Reymond's Fariqua, as the plain and simple way to get
their evidence, "Do you have the address in Goa of your
former servant John Louzado?"

At last, when he had established to his complete satisfaction
that a couple as utterly vague could not possibly have recorded,
much less retained, a servant's address, he planted himself
abruptly full in front of Mrs Dutt-Dastar just as she was
explaining the full similarity between her painting "Eagle
Figure with Two Blue Shapes" and Mr Reymond's book "Mr
Peduncle Caught in Meshes," which she had yet actually to
read.

"Madam, kindly to tell: who was the previous employer of
John Louzado?"

"John Louzado?" Mrs Dutt-Dastar asked, seemingly totally
mystified.

"The servant you recommended to Mrs Patel, of Second
Pasta Lane."

"Ah, John. Yes, what to do about John? He did not suit,
not at all—it was sheer madness to have taken him on from
someone like Shirin Kothawala, a dear person but with no
understanding of the artist—but I could not sack the fellow
just like that. And then I remembered that funny Mrs Patel.
Well, she would never notice what a servant was like, would
she?"

"Madam, the address of Mrs Shirin Kothawala?"

"Well, but of course. In one of those divine but madly

expensive flats in Nepean Sea Road. A block called Gulmarg.
Anybody will tell you."

"Mr Reymond, I am departing to proceed with enquiries."

"Oh, yes. Yes. My dear fellow. Coming, coming."

On the way back, thanks to Ghote's unequivocal assurance
that he would immediately interrogate Fariqua, for all that he
privately knew nothing would come of it, the author's questions
were at least confined to the sociological. But before they
arrived Ghote decided to issue a warning.

"Mr Reymond, in India—I do not know how it is in
UK—servants often have matters they are wishing to conceal
from their masters, like for instance the true cost of vegetables
in the bazaar. So, you see, it would perhaps be better if you
yourself were not present when I question Fariqua."

He regarded the author with apprehension. But it seemed
he need not have worried.

"Excellent idea, Inspector," Mr Reymond replied. But then
he added: "Though there is one small discrepancy."

Ghote knew it had been too good to be true.

"Please?" he asked resignedly.

"Oh, just that we don't have servants in England now. It's
why I find it difficult to know how to behave with them."

"Well, you behave with them as if they were servants,"
Ghote said. "But if you do not wish to be present at the
interview, perhaps that would be best."

So he had the pleasure of tackling the Muslim unimpeded by
any bulky British shadow. It was a good thing too, because
Fariqua proved every bit as evasive as he had told Mr Reymond
servants could be. He needed, when it came down to it, to use
a little tough treatment. And he had a notion that cuffs and
threatened kicks would not be the way Mr Peduncle conducted
an interrogation.

But, after ten minutes in which Fariqua noisily maintained
he had not been in the author's flat at all the previous night, he
caved in quite satisfactorily and produced a story that might
well be true. He had been playing cards with "some friends"
and it had got too late to catch a train to Andheri. So he had
bided his time, sneaked back into the author's flat before the
door was locked and had hidden down between the stove and

the wall till he had been able to take what, he implied, was his rightful place on the sitting-room couch.

Ghote gave him another couple of slaps for impudence.

"Now, what are the names of your card-playing friends?"

"Inspector, I do not know."

But this time Ghote had hardly so much as to growl to get a better answer.

"Oh, Inspector, Inspector. One only am I knowing. It is Kuldip Singh, sir, the driver of Rajinder Sahib at Flat No 6, Building No 2."

"Achchha."

Ghote let him go. He ought to walk round to Building No 2 of the flats and check with the Punjabi gentleman's driver, but that must wait. The Noted British Author might change his mind and want to come with him. And he would get that address, the simple key to having a solid case against the three of them, much more quickly unencumbered.

It turned out, however, that the Parsi lady's "divine but madly expensive" flat was not, as Mrs Dutt-Dastar had said, in a block called Gulmarg in Nepean Sea Road but in a block of that name in Warden Road on the twin prominence of Cumballa Hill. But at least Mrs Kothawala, sixty, exquisitely dressed, precise as a crane-bird, was helpful. She knew to a week just how long she had employed Louzado. She knew to an anna just how much he had cheated her by. She remembered having warned Mrs Dutt-Dastar about him, and that Mrs Dutt-Dastar had clearly forgotten before the telephone conversation was half-way through. And she knew for a fact that she had never had John's address in Goa. But, of course, she was able to tell Ghote where he had worked before he had come to her.

But sorting out Mrs Dutt-Dastar's error had taken a long time and Ghote found that having dutifully telephoned Inspector Dandekar and made sure there was no sign of the Noted British Author—their suspect was still unshaken too, he heard—he had time that evening to make only this one inquiry. And that proved as exasperating as the others, worse even, since instead of getting at least the name of Louzado's next earlier employer he had to be content with the name only of a lady who would be "sure to remember".

Before trying her next morning he gritted his teeth and put in a call to Mr Reymond, who, of course, was only too keen to come with him—"I had been thinking of looking in on Inspector Dandekar actually"—and only by wantonly altering the geography of Bombay did he persuade him that it would be more economical for him to stay at Shivaji Park until after he had made this one inquiry, which he promised would be rapid. But in fact the task proved immensely troublesome since the possibly helpful lady had moved house and no one nearby seemed to know where to. Application to the postal-wallahs met with a certain amount of bureaucratic delay and it was not until the very end of the morning that he had an address to go to. So he telephoned Mr Reymond once more and dolefully arranged to collect him after lunch.

"No sleep for me this afternoon, Inspector," the cheerful voice had assured him. "I've a lot I want to ask you."

"Yes," said Ghote.

The first thing the Noted British Author wanted to know was why Fariqua had not been arrested. Ghote produced the fellow's explanation for the "significant variation" in his behaviour.

"Ah, so that accounts for it," Mr Reymond said, for once apparently happy. "I'm glad to hear it. I wouldn't like to think I was getting my breakfast scrambled eggs from the hands of a murderer."

Ghote gave a jolly laugh. It came to him all the more easily because he had felt sure there would be some lacuna or loose-end to pursue. But the journey passed with no more than questions about the peculiarities of passers-by—until they were almost at their destination, a house just inland from Back Bay in Marine Lines.

Then the author, after a silence that had prolonged itself wonderfully, suddenly spoke.

"Inspector Ghote, I can no longer conceal it from myself. There is a lacuna."

"Yes?" Ghote asked, misery swiftly descending.

"Inspector, you did not, did you, check Fariqua's alibi with Mr Rajinder's chauffeur? And I think—I am almost sure—Mr Rajinder is the man who left on holiday by car three days ago."

"Then I will have to make further inquiries," Ghote said glumly.

But he forced himself to brighten up.

"In any case," he said, "perhaps we shall learn here just where John Louzado is to be found in Goa, and then, who knows, a single telephone call to the police there and they would have the fellow behind bars and we would have evidence in plenty, even some of the stolen jewellery, if we are lucky."

"Yes," Mr Reymond said, "but Fariqua's invented story still leaves a loose-end."

Yet the interview at the Marine Lines flat looked from the start as if it was going to be all that Ghote and Inspector Dandekar had been counting on.

"Oh, John, yes," said the deliciously beautiful occupier, Mrs Akhtar Hazari. "Yes, we should have an address in Goa. Not for John himself but for a priest—John was a Christian—who was to provide a reference. In fact, it was when we heard that John had a criminal record that we decided he must go. My husband imports watches and we often have valuable stock in the flat."

Ghote was possessed of a sudden feeling that everything in the world was simple. Confidence bubbled in his veins. It would not be as direct a way of wrapping up the case as he had spoken of to Mr Reymond but the whole business might still be dealt with inside a few days.

"Of course it was two or three years ago now," Mrs Hazari said. "But I always seem to keep letters. I will look. Will you take tea?"

So they sat in her big cool sitting-room, Ghote on a fat pile of cushions, the Noted British Author swinging rather apprehensively in a basket chair suspended by a chain from the ceiling.

Time passed.

The servant came back and inquired whether they would like more tea. Mr Reymond hurriedly refused for both of them. Ghote would in fact have liked more tea, but even better he would have liked to see that letter. He asked Mr Reymond, who seemed to feel it necessary to speak in swift hushed tones, a few questions about his books. But the answers were not very satisfactory.

And then at last Mrs Hazari returned.

"Inspector," she said, "I must tell you that after all I have not got that letter. I had thought it was in an almirah where I put old papers like that. I even knew exactly the box it should be in. But my memory played me false. I threw out a lot of junk about a year ago, and it must have been in that."

Ghote felt like a child robbed of a sweetmeat. And now, he realised, with gritty dismay, he would solemnly have to pursue Mr Reymond's theory about Fariqua.

"And John came straight to you from Goa?" he asked Mrs Hazari desolately.

"No," she said. "He did have one short job first. He went to a family where at once the wife died and the man no longer needed so many servants. That was why we took him without a reference. It was a business acquaintance of my husband, I think. And unfortunately he's in Delhi. But if you would give me a ring tonight, I could perhaps tell you then."

With that Ghote had to be content. That, and the dubious gain to be had from dealing with Fariqua's final lie.

Happily by the time they got back to Shivaji Park Fariqua had left for Andheri, earlier than he should have done but not so much so that there was any reason to suppose he had run off like John Louzado. To placate Mr Reymond Ghote sadly confirmed that the Kuldip Singh with whom Fariqua had claimed to be playing cards on the night of the murders had indeed already left Bombay by then.

Perhaps, Ghote thought as he turned from saying a last goodnight, down at H.Q. the boy would have broken his obstinate silence and admitted the truth and then there would be no need to pursue next morning this surely—surely? —unsatisfactory loose-end. Or was it a lacuna?

But Inspector Dandekar had no good news. Indeed he seemed considerably worried.

"I had the damned boy in the interrogation room today for eight solid hours," he said. "I have kept him standing up. I have been drinking tea and smoking cigarettes in front of him. I have had a trestle set up and Head Constable Kadam standing there swinging a lathi. But nothing has moved him one inch."

"Inspector," Ghote said with some hesitation, "is it possible that those ropes on his wrists had been altogether badly tied by the real miscreants and not faked only?"

Dandekar sat in silence glaring down hook-nosed at his desk.

"Well, yes, anything is possible," he said at last. "But damn it, I cannot believe it. I just cannot believe it."

So Ghote was up at Shivaji Park before eight next morning, waiting for the tricky Fariqua and telling himself that there was no reason why the fellow would not come to work as usual.

But the surge of relief he felt when the Muslim did appear made him realise how much he was now expecting everything about the affair to go wrong. He pounced like a kite dropping down on a tree-rat.

It did not take long to reduce the fellow to a state of abject fear. And then he talked.

"Aiee, Inspector. No. No, Inspectorsahib. I swear to God I had nothing to do with it. Inspector, I just got to know those fellows. We used to sit and talk when I was sleeping here. Inspector, I did not know they were bad-mash fellows. Inspector, I am swearing to you. And then that night, that one Budhoo—Inspector, he is a really bad one that one, a devil, Inspector—Inspector, he said more than he was meaning. He said something was going to happen that night. We were in the kitchen of their flat, Inspector. All of them were out, Sahib, Memsahib and the boy. I did not know it was going to be murder, Inspector. I thought they had a plan only to take the jewellery, Inspector. They were saying she had jewellery worth one lakh, Inspector. They would hide under a bed. But no more were they telling me. And then they threatened that I should stay with them. But after they said I could go, Inspector. Then it was too late to go to Andheri. But Reymond Sahib had his door open still and I was able to creep in. I swear to you, honest to God, Inspector, I am never knowing anything about killing. But they said also that they would kill me if I spoke. Inspector, will you be saving me, is it? Is it, Inspector? Is it?"

Ghote stood looking down at the shrunken cringing figure. Was he letting the fellow trick him again? It did not really seem likely. What he had said this time had been more than simply logical, like the story of card-playing with the Punjabi's driver. This account of inconclusive talk with two of the murderers in the kitchen of the dead couple's flat had rung true through and through. No wonder the fellow had tried to set up an alibi if that had happened. Of course, there had been no mention of any involvement by the son. But then the other two would have kept quiet about that. Yes, what he had learnt would scarcely help Dandekar.

"You will be safe enough from your friends," he growled at Fariqua. "In the lock-up."

Without the rest of them there would not be a case worth bringing as an accessory before the fact. But no harm to have the fellow to hand.

He marched him off.

He gave the Noted British Author the news by telephone. A witness who had heard and not properly heard the criminals' plans: hardly the sort of thing for the pages of "Mr Peduncle Plays a Joker". A man induced by threats to join a robbery and then let go before it had begun: not exactly the sort of event for "Mr Peduncle Hunts the Peacock."

And indeed questions and doubts poured out so fast that he was reduced at last to pointing out sharply that Mr Reymond was now without a servant. At that the Noted British Author betrayed signs of disquiet. So Ghote explained he could get a replacement by talking to his neighbours and was rewarded by the author quite hastily ringing off.

Encouraged by this, he hurriedly set out for the address he had got from Mrs Hazari late the night before. It was, her husband had said, a Mr Dass whose wife, now dead, had first briefly employed John when he had come to Bombay. He lived in a block of flats in B Road behind Churchgate.

Climbing up the tiled stairway of the building, Ghote found he was retaining, despite the rather shabby air of the place, all his optimism. Louzado's trail had been long, but now it must be near its end. This was, after all, where the fellow had had his first Bombay job. They could go no further back. But it was equally the most likely place for an employer to have noted that Goa address.

On the door of the flat a small tree-slice nameboard had painted on it in much-faded script "Mr and Mrs Gopal Dass." It must, Ghote reflected, have been a long while since there had been a Mrs Dass if it was her demise that had brought Louzado's first Bombay job to its abrupt end. And certainly the little irregularly-shaped board had a strong look of dusty neglect.

He rang the door bell.

There was such a long silence that he almost became convinced he was to experience yet another defeat. He was even turning towards the next-door flat to make inquiries when the door opened by just a crack.

He swung round.

"Is it Mr Gopal Dass?"

The door opened a little more. Ghote saw in the bright light from the room beyond a man who had once been fat.

Afterwards he was able to account in detail for the instantly stamped impression. It had come in part from the old European-style suit, its jacket drooping from the shoulders in deep encrusted folds, the trousers hanging in baggy rucks from the hips. But even the face had shown the same signs: flesh seemed to sag from it.

"What is it you are wanting?"

The voice, too, appeared to be coming from someone no longer there, hollow and without force.

Rapidly Ghote introduced himself and stated his problem. He felt that the slightest chance might cause the tall empty man to close the door so barely opened.

Mr Dass heard him out however. Then he sighed, driftingly, like a puff of night breeze with hardly the strength to ruffle lonely waters.

"Oh, no, no," he said. "No addresses. Everything like that went when my wife left me for another life. Everything."

He turned slowly and looked into the room behind him. Ghote saw over his shoulder that it was almost completely bare. No curtains, no carpet, no pictures of the gods. Just a small table with a brass bowl, a brass tumbler and a packet of Mohun's cornflakes on it, and in a corner a bed-roll.

"Yes," Mr Dass said. "I got rid of everything. My life is at an end, you know. At an end."

And very slowly, and without any sense of discourtesy, he turned and closed the door.

And I too, Ghote thought in the thick sadness he felt

billowing from the shut door with its once gay tree-slice nameboard, I too have reached an end. The end of my hunt for John Louzado.

But one part of the affair certainly was not over. The Noted British Author would undoubtedly be out pursuing his loose-ends before much longer. He might be doing so already. One conversation could well have found a new servant.

He ran clatteringly down the empty echoing stairway, drove full-out back to H.Q., glancing wildly at Dandekar's office as he came to a gravel-squirming halt, and ran for his telephone.

"Ah, Inspector Ghote."

The British author's enveloping smile seemed to come all the way down the line. "Ah, good. I was just setting out to see you. You're speaking from your office?"

"Yes," Ghote answered. "That is—no. That is . . ."

"There seems to be a bit of a discrepancy," the plummy voice said.

"Not at all," Ghote answered with sharpness. "I am at office, and I shall be here all morning."

But when the Noted British Author arrived he was magnificently insulated from him. Within two minutes of his call Inspector Dandekar had asked him to take over his interrogation. It had been something of an admission of defeat for Dandekar. He had told Ghote he felt he dared no longer leave unexplored the possible trails in the Bombay underworld. If the boy was innocent despite everything, then enquiries through the usual network of touts and informers must be pursued now with extra vigour.

"Mind you," he had concluded, "I still swear young Raju is guilty as hell. I hope you can break him."

So, with Dandekar gossiping to thief acquaintances in such places as the stolen goods mart of the Chor Bazar and thus safe from any British botheration, Ghote felt perfectly justified in leaving the author to cool his heels.

And in the meanwhile he faced young Raju, cocksure graduate of Bombay University, adopted son of the murdered ice-cream manufacturer, and, as Dandekar had discovered at Shivaji Park, openly mutinous at having been given the fairly humble job in his new father's firm of going round to shops and restaurants instead of having a fat sum given him to start up on his own.

It was with this point that Ghote began.

"Sit down, sit down," he said. "I have been going over your answers to Inspector Dandekar, and there is one small thing I cannot understand. You wanted a sum to start up a business. But it is not at all clear what is the business."

The boy sat down on the hard chair in front of Ghote's table and with deliberate casualness put one leg over the other.

"You are not catching me that way, bhai," he said. "All along I am denying and denying I asked for money."

Ghote sighed.

"But we have a statement from a neighbour to whom you yourself complained," he said. "Two others also heard loud quarrelling."

"Lies," Raju answered contemptuously.

Ghote did not let himself be discomposed. But for all the calmness with which he went back to the point and for all the reasonableness of every other question he asked in the next two hours, he got, it seemed, nowhere. Some of the hard and shiny contempt left the boy's voice and the two of them eventually might have been friendly acquaintances, but the answers, though different in tone, were never one whit helpful.

So when a constable came in with a chit saying Inspector Dandekar had returned Ghote felt decidedly relieved. He had not really hoped for success where Dandekar had failed, but a small gleam in him had licked at the possibility. And now he knew it would not be.

Dandekar he found equally gloomy.

"Nothing," he said in answer to a query about his luck with the informers. "Not a whisper. Of course there may be something still, you know. When the newspapers get on to a case people hold out. But I did not get one word."

And if you did not, Ghote thought, no one else could.

"The boy is also the same as ever," he said. "I talked and cajoled and urged but he did not give one thing, except to stop back-answering."

"That little rat. I am going to have him, Ghote. I am going to get him talking if it is the last thing I do. I am going now."

And, all solidly compact determination, he marched out.

Ghote sat where he was on the small chair beside Dandekar's desk. He felt he could not face the waiting British author. He had used every atom of his patience with young Raju. He leant forward, banged the brass bell on the desk and when the peon came ordered tea.

He took his time sipping at the hot milky liquid and had not quite finished when suddenly the batwing doors clapped back with a noise like a pair of quick-following pistol shots and Dandekar came striding in again.

But now his face was alight with a dark joy.

"Got him," he said. "Got him. I knew I would, and by God I did."

Ghote's first feeling—he tried to overcome it—was chagrin. He had had Raju all morning and had ended up where he began: Dandekar had had him for scarcely twenty minutes and had broken him. But, never mind who had done it, the boy had talked.

"He confessed everything?" he asked Dandekar. "Faking the ropes, planning it all with Louzado and that Budhoo?"

"Everything. Thanks to you, Ghote."

"To me?"

"Oh yes. When I heard you had taken that soft line I thought that perhaps now one good hard push would do it. And it did. They did not set out to murder, of course. But when that Budhoo found not one lakh of jewellery but four or five rings only he went mad. That accounts for all those wounds."

"Shabash, Inspector, shabash," Ghote said, a rush of warmth swirling through him.

But Dandekar, slumping down into his chair, opening a drawer and pulling out a towel to dab his sweaty face, had begun to look less triumphant.

"It is all right, Ghote," he said. "But you know as well as I do that when it comes to court, as likely as not, young Raju will shamelessly deny every word."

"Yes," Ghote said. "We need Budhoo, though we would be lucky ever to find that one. Or we need John Louzado."

He began recounting how that trail had ended. But in a minute a look of wide-eyed staring came on Dandekar's hook-nosed face. Slowly Ghote turned, though he knew almost for a certainty what he would see.

And there it was, looming over the top of the doors like a bristling hairy moon, the face of the Noted British Author.

Resignedly Ghote pushed himself to his feet.

"Mr Reymond," he said, his voice ringing with brightness. "I was just coming to tell you. We have broken the case."

But congratulations did not come as freely as he felt they should. Indeed, as out in the sunshine his story progressed, the bushy beard gaped wide more than once with hardly restrained interjections.

Loose-ends, Ghote thought. Lacunas. Significant variations. Surely there could not be more.

And at last he ran out of words and had to face the author's objections.

"Inspector, I feel bound to point out a few things. You and Inspector Dandekar have been most kind to me. I can see that as soon as I get home I shall write a story called 'Mr Peduncle and the Indian Inspector'. And it would be nothing short of a betrayal if I kept silent."

"Most kind. But I assure—"

"No, Inspector, it is the least I can do. First then, let me say that I know young Raju well. He and I often had long, long talks when he came to phone friends in Delhi and other places. And I promise you, Inspector, he is not the chap to set criminals on to rob his own benefactors. There's a simple discrepancy between what the boy is and what you say he did. But that's not all."

"No?" Ghote said.

"No. You see, there's one piece of the puzzle which still doesn't fit. And time and again my Mr Peduncle has said to Inspector Sugden 'You've got to fit in every bit, my dear fellow, every bit of the puzzle'."

"But—"

"No, Inspector, hear me out. I know this can't be easy to take, but you can't get away from pure logic. What you heard from Fariqua this morning simply didn't add up. You've only to think about it. And if he's lying there can be only one reason. Young Raju wasn't the third man: Fariqua was."

Ghote stood there fuming. Who was this detective-story writer to come telling them what was and was not so? Him and his logic and his lacunas.

But, even as he encouraged the rage to squirt and bubble inside him, he also felt a streak of cold doubt.

Logic. Well, logic was logic. And suspects had been known to confess under pressure to crimes they had not committed, even to murder. And Dandekar, first-class though he was, certainly could put pressure on.

Was it possible that, despite what seemed plain facts, that story of Fariqua's, seemingly unlikely but perfectly in accord with the way things happened, was just a story?

One thing was certain. The shame, the ridiculousness, of having an author of detective books get to the right answer first must not make them ignore that answer. If only they were not relying wholly on that confession but had Louzado and Budhoo in a cell too. If only the trail of addresses had not—

And then, like a last monsoon storm coming winding rapidly in across the sea long after the monsoon ought to have ended, bringing a last welcome sudden coolness, an idea came winding and leaping into his mind.

"Sir, sir," he said. "Come with me straightaway, sir, if you please."

And without giving the author a chance to reply he bundled him into the car and set off into the darting traffic.

They made it to the Shivaji Park flat in record time. There, still begging for patience, Ghote took one fast look round the sitting-room—couches spread with cotton counterpanes, bookshelves, two tables, and, yes, the telephone.

And next to it "the little book" in which, so the Noted British Author had told him soon after they met, people from nearby looked things up. His mention just now of Raju telephoning distant friends had at last brought it to the front of his mind. He flicked at the indexed pages with sweat-slippery fingers. L for Louzado. And yes. Yes, yes, yes. There it was. The address.

He seized the phone, dialled furiously, shouted instructions for a Lightning Call and miraculously was speaking to the Goa police in Panjim in minutes. And got splendid co-operation. They knew the place, they would find the man, no doubt they would find his share of the missing rings. The fellow would be behind bars in half an hour.

It was almost as if he was putting a hand on his shoulder himself.

He turned from the telephone and looked the bursting-bearded British author full in the face.

"Let me tell one thing, sir," he said, savouring the irony to the last drop. "Let me tell one thing: never to neglect a loose-end."

BUSINESS LUNCH

Celia Dale

HERE WE ARE. After you, old chap. It's a simple little place,
nothing fancy, but they do a good bolognaise. Bon giorno,
Maria, comay sta? That's the extent of my knowledge of the
lingo, I'm afraid. We'll have the corner table . . . Reserved?
Ah. No, it's just the two. D'you mind being in the middle, old
chap? It's a bit cramped, but . . . You're sure? Okay, then.
They get very full at lunchtime, regulars, you know. I prefer a
nice little place like this where they know you to one of those
smart places where they charge the earth for nothing but a bit
of show.

Grazie, Maria. Now, what'll you have?

A gin and tonic for my friend and I'll have a medium
sherry—I have to keep off the hard stuff, the old insides, you
know. And what'll you eat? Right. Two prawn cocktails, one
escalope, and I'll have the rump steak and spaghetti. No,
vegetables come with. And a carafe of the red? A carafe of the
red, Maria. Great.

Well now, I've brought along the draft programme. It's only
rough, but you can take it it's pretty well the best procedure,
stood the test of time, you know. We've followed it the last
few years. Yes, these get-togethers were Bruce's baby, his
idea—public relations, personal contacts and all that. But of
course I do all the donkey work. It was my structure actually,
basically, right from the start.

Well, the seminar proper kicks off with a reception on the
Friday evening—informal, you know, short dresses for the
ladies. Yes, in the Dolphin Room at the Grand. Most of them
stay at the Grand, but some of us prefer the Royal Victoria
just round the corner. It's not as grand as the Grand, ha ha,
but it's more homely—and half the price, if one's got one's
good lady with one, as I always do. Bruce always stayed at the

Grand, of course, but his wife never came with him. And the Managing Director can always swing his expenses, can't he, ha ha.

Ah thanks, Maria. Cheers!

Well, after the reception we're what the Yanks call "at leisure". Usually we make up small parties for a meal somewhere and some of the boys get together later for a bit of a booze-up. Bruce was a great one for that, always one of the boys, don't you know—must've had a head like iron for he was always bright-eyed and bushy-tailed first thing next morning. Booze-ups aren't my style, alas—the old insides, you know. And anyway, there's always a lot of preliminary work to do the night before, checking everything out, the programmes, timing, seating, mikes—these seminars don't run themselves, you know, and I can pretty well say there's no one knows more about running them than I do. Although, of course, it was always Bruce's show.

Ah thanks, Maria. Everything okay, old chap? Worcester sauce? Roll? We'll have the wine now, Maria.

The seminar starts sharp at 9.30 Saturday morning—yes, in the Dolphin Room again. I'll have checked it's all shipshape and Bristol fashion after the previous evening's shindig. You wouldn't believe the things that have to be checked—hotel staff are just no good these days, can't rely on any of them, foreigners who couldn't care less, even at posh places like the Grand. I tell my wife we get far better service round the corner where we are. Last year I found the platform wasn't even prepared—no carafes, no glasses, no ash trays, shocking. The year before that the schedules were late, I had to go round in a taxi and collect them from the printers. I tell you, it's a hell of a lot of hard work, running a seminar for a front man.

You've got the draft programme there? Fine. Well, the Managing Director kicks off, speaks for about fifteen minutes, welcomes everyone and all that. Outlines the theme for the seminar—we all know it, of course, The Impact of Sales Promotions on Sales Productivity. Then the Production Manager speaks. That takes us to eleven and the coffee break. Eleven thirty, the Sales Manager speaks, then questions from the floor—that's you and your chappies, customers from all over—and break about twelve thirty. Buffet lunch, in the Old

Tars' Tavern Room this time, one to two thirty. Two thirty, the Area Managers speak, each for ten minutes. Then the floor's open again for you and your colleagues. Fire in questions, anything you like. Six o'clock, Managing Director winds up.

Seven thirty, assemble in the Neptune Ballroom, black tie, and glad rags for the ladies, for the banquet and dinner-dance.

It's hard graft for yours truly, I can tell you, but rewarding, rewarding . . . One doesn't expect credit or any special thanks —that was never Bruce's way. But it's satisfying to know the job's been well done and everyone had a good time.

Ah thank you, Maria. Molto bene. Got everything you want, salt, pepper? Let me fill you up. No, I have to go slow, acid in the old insides. Well, bon appeteet.

Well, Sunday morning, strictly speaking, the seminar's over. I'm pretty well bushed by then, I can tell you. The whole responsibility for the smooth running of it all is on my shoulders right from the start. All behind the scenes, of course, it looks like Bruce's show from out front. I'm whacked by Sunday morning, but Bruce was a great one for informal get-togethers, small groups chatting ad hoc, bringing up points there hadn't been time for in the sessions, especially with individual customers like your goodself. There's a fair amount of drinking and I daresay the chats are useful, personal contacts, like you and me now, ha ha. Bruce would be breezing about in the bar doing his all-boys-together-act—or sometimes he liked to hold court up in his room at the Grand, just one favoured person perhaps, tête-à-tête . . . He reckoned more business was done at his informal drinking and chatting meetings than at the whole of the seminar. Naturally I don't agree. Couldn't expect me to, could you, ha ha, since the whole shebang was on the road entirely due to yours truly, old muggins here. Still, I never argued. One didn't argue with Bruce.

Yes, it was sad. Tragic. It shook us all, I can tell you. The prime of life, hardly that really, only forty-nine. Tragic. I'm sorry for his wife. Yes, two children. A great loss.

You never met him, did you? No, that's right, you took up the contract four, five months ago and Bruce went—what, well, a year ago, almost to the week, the last seminar, of course. Who should remember it better than me? Extraordinary chap he was. Dynamic. What he said, went. Ride roughshod over anyone, yet everyone seemed to like him. Especially the ladies. You could see them eyeing each other at the dinner-dance to see who he took out on the floor most often. I used to pull my wife's leg about it. How far it went I wouldn't know. His wife never came with him, and those Sunday morning chats in his room weren't all for the customers, I can tell you. Charisma, I think they call it. He certainly believed in himself. That's the secret, eh? Believe in yourself and others will do likewise.

Mind you, he was brilliant. No denying that. He had drive. He knew exactly what he wanted and he saw that he got it, never mind what other people felt. There's no doubt he worked wonders for the Company, no doubt at all. A real go-getter. Brilliant.

No, he'd not had much business experience. Not like most of us in the firm. Take me, for instance. I went into it almost straight from school, junior clerk, worked my way up. There's no one knows the Company better than I do, every aspect of it—stands to reason, after all these years. I could run any department you care to name, inside out I know it. I didn't do National Service, my old insides, you know. I just went into the Company and slogged my way up like none of the young ones bother to do nowadays. Always after new jobs, new experiences. Where will they be when they're sixty, I ask myself? On Social Security, you mark my words . . .

Take Bruce, for instance. Typical. Did his National Service in the Parachute Regiment and stayed on. Got to Major, served all over the place, saw plenty of action here and there. Must have enjoyed that. Came out, did a course in Business Studies—I ask you, Business Studies!—and straightaway got offered a plum job by the Company. Personnel he was at first—had the knack of handling men, we were told. Then up to Sales Manager. Then Managing Director. Up like a rocket, with no experience at all. And down like a rocket too, of course. Tragic.

Now, what'll you have for afters? Nothing? You're sure? Ice cream, cheese? They do a good gâteau. Well, if you're sure. Just coffee, Maria—black for my friend, white for me. Grazie.

Yes, I was with him. He had this habit of having people up in his room on the Sunday morning. They'd be the favoured few, special customers he was out to catch. And, between you and me, women. I've a shrewd suspicion he had lady friends up there for a quiet session before getting into his Jaguar and heading home to his wife. A dynamic fellow, our Bruce.

Thanks, Maria. Sugar? A liqueur? Sure?

Yes, I was with him. It was just before lunch and me and the wife were just getting ready to leave for home. I'd been run off my feet all morning, paying bills, keeping contacts, tidying up all round after everyone while my wife took herself off for a walk along the front. I seldom have time to spend with my wife at these seminars, I'm at everyone's beck and call and she has to find her own amusements, I tell her. She's good at that. So she'd been out on her own and just got back and we'd got our bags packed and just when I thought I was off the hook a summons comes from his lordship to go up to his room.

He had this habit of summoning one to his room and tearing a strip off one. That's if he hadn't got better fish to fry, of course. He'd want to go over the whole thing, query and criticise, that sort of thing. Things that could perfectly well have waited to sort out in the office next morning, but well, that was Bruce's way. Like being sent for by the headmaster. One didn't argue.

The chambermaid hadn't been in yet. The room was a mess, suitcase open, the bed all tumbled, ashtrays stinking, and a couple of glasses and a bottle on the bedside table. The room was one of the best, naturally, on the top floor with a lovely view of the sea. Bruce was standing in the french windows, they were open on to the little balcony, more like a window-sill really with just a low rail, and the net curtains were blowing to and fro round him. He was in his shirt-sleeves and had a drink in his hand. I could tell he'd had a few by his voice, and he was sort of flushed and bright-eyed—you know, like he'd just had a good workout or something to set him up. You had to have seen him in similar situations to know he was really half-seas over. He had this rough way of speaking to you, never gave you time to answer, as though he was back in the guardroom or somewhere and this was a court martial. He'd just fire questions and criticisms at you, "No excuses!" if you opened your mouth. The room was a pigsty, all those bed-clothes tumbled about and the ashtrays and the smell of stale smoke and drink, and that small snap-purse women keep their makeup in in their handbags lying there on the floor by the bed, just like my wife's got . . .

More coffee? Sure?

Well, he started the usual criticisms about the way the seminar had gone, with his back half turned to me and the glass in his hand. Didn't even look at me, just stood there criticising. And then—well, I simply don't know what happened. It must have been some kind of heart attack—although the inquest brought in Misadventure. My own view is that he was drunker than I thought and just blacked out. Anyway, as we all know, he fell over the balcony—twelve storeys down and crashed through the hotel canopy. My God, it was frightful! I saw him go and just couldn't do a thing to stop him—I rushed over and tried to catch hold of him but he'd gone . . . I'll never forget it. I stood there in that pigsty of a room and thought "He's gone. Bruce is gone."

Well, these things happen. Life goes on. But what a tragedy, eh? A brilliant chap, charismatic. Put the Company on its feet, no doubt of that. Mind you, it was always a real going concern, as I'm sure you fully appreciate. This seminar next week will show you just how effective we are as a team that can supply just the kind of commodity you're looking for. Bruce's sad passing won't affect that. So me and my wife look forward to seeing you there and we'll do our best to see you have a really worthwhile experience.

La conto, Maria, please. Grazie molto. I'll just give you our latest brochures. And the programme for the seminar. Any queries you have, don't hesitate to give me a buzz. Or any problems with the hotel—the Grand? Should be okay. We're round the corner, of course, as usual. Most of the guests will be at the Grand but we find the Victoria more homely. Tommy Mulgrave, Mr Mulgrave, our new Managing Director, he's at the Grand, of course. Yes, he was appointed last month. Quite a surprise. We'd thought perhaps the Board would promote someone from inside the Company, someone who knows it all inside out . . . But they say he's a brilliant chap, in his mid-forties. Been in advertising somewhere, open up new horizons and all that. I'm still in charge of the seminar, naturally. Yes, I'm still plugging away, like always. I know the ropes, you see, inside out. It could none of it happen but for old Muggins here.

What became of the purse? What purse? You must've misheard me, old chap. There was nothing found in the room that didn't belong to Bruce himself, poor fellow. I'll always remember that room and the curtains blowing and the way he just pitched over the rail . . .

Thank you, Maria. A riverderchi. After you, old chap . . .

TIME TO LAUGH

Joan Aiken

WHEN MATT CLIMBED in at the open window of The Croft, it had been raining steadily for three days—August rain, flattening the bronze-green plains of wheat, making dim green jungles of the little woods round Wentby, turning the motorway which cut across the small town's southern tip into a greasy nightmare on which traffic skidded and piled into crunching heaps; all the county police were desperately busy trying to clear up one disaster after another.

If there had been a river at Wentby, Matt might have gone fishing instead, on that Saturday afternoon . . . but the town's full name was Wentby Waterless, the nearest brook was twenty miles away, the rain lay about in scummy pools on the clay, or sank into the lighter soil and vanished. And if the police had not been so manifestly engaged and distracted by the motorway chaos, it might never have occurred to Matt that now would be the perfect time to explore The Croft; after all, by the end of three days' rain, what else was there to do? It had been ten years since the Regent Cinema closed its doors for the last time and went into liquidation.

A Grammar School duffel coat would be too conspicuous and recognisable; Matt wore his black plastic jacket, although it was not particularly rainproof. But it was at least some protection against the brambles which barred his way.

He had long ago worked out an entry into the Croft grounds, having noticed that they ended in a little triangle of land which bit into the corner of a builder's yard where his father had once briefly worked; Matt had a keen visual memory, never forgot anything he had once observed and, after a single visit two years ago to tell his father that Mum had been taken off to hospital, was able to pick his way without hesitation through cement-mixers, stacks of two-by-two and concrete slabs, to the exact corner, the wattle palings and tangle of elderberry bushes. Kelly never troubled to lock his yard and, in any case, on a Saturday afternoon, no one was about; they were all snug at home, watching telly.

He bored his way through the wet greenery and, as he had reckoned, came to the weed-smothered terrace at the foot of a flight of steps; overgrown shoots of rambler rose half blocked them, but it was just possible to battle upwards, and at the top he was rewarded by a dusky, triangular vista of lawn stretching away on the left towards the house, on the right towards untended vegetable gardens. Amazingly—in the very middle of Wentby—there were rabbits feeding on the lawn, who scattered at his appearance. And between him and the house, two aged, enormous apple-trees towered, massive against the murky sky, loaded down with fruit. He had seen them in the aerial photograph of the town, recently exhibited on a school notice-board: that was what had given him the notion of exploring The Croft; you could find out a few things at school if you kept your eyes open and used your wits. He had heard of The Croft before that, of course, but it was nowhere to be seen from any of the town streets: a big house, built in the mid-nineteenth century on an inaccessible plot of land, bought subsequently, after World War Two, by a rich old retired actress and her company-director husband, Lieutenant-Colonel and Mrs Jordan. They were hardly ever seen; never came out, or went anywhere; Matt had a vague idea that one of them—maybe both?—had died. There was a general belief that the house was haunted; also full of treasures; also defended by any number of burglar-alarms inside the building, gongs that would start clanging, bells that would ring up at the police-station, not to mention man-traps, spring-guns, and savage alsatians outside in the grounds.

However, the alsatians did not seem to be in evidence—if they had been, surely the rabbits would not have been feeding so peacefully? So, beginning to disbelieve these tales, Matt picked his way, quietly but with some confidence, over the sodden tussocky grass to the apple-trees. The fruit, to his chagrin, was far from ripe. Also they were wretched little apples, codlins possibly, lumpy and misshapen, not worth the bother of scrumping. Even the birds appeared to have neglected them; numbers of undersized windfalls lay rotting already on the ground. Angrily, Matt flung a couple against the wall of the house, taking some satisfaction from the squashy thump with which they spattered the stone. The house had not been built of local brick like the rest of Wentby, but from massive chunks of sombre, liver-coloured rock, imported, no doubt at great expense, from father north. The effect was powerful and ugly; dark as blood, many-gabled and frowning, the building kept guard over its tangled ground. It seemed deserted; all the windows were lightless, even on such a pouring-wet afternoon; and, prowling round to the front of the house, over a carriage-sweep pocked with grass and weeds, Matt found that the front doorstep had a thin skin of moss over it, as if no foot had trodden there for months. Perhaps the back—? But that was some distance away, and behind a screen of trellis-work and yellow-flecked ornamental laurels. Working on towards it, Matt came to a stop, badly startled at the sight of a half-open window, which, until he reached it, had been concealed from him by a great sagging swatch of untrimmed winter jasmine, whose tiny dark-green leaves were almost black with wet. The coffin-shaped oblong of the open window was black too; Matt stared at it, hypnotised, for almost five minutes, unable to decide whether to go in or not.

Was there somebody inside, there, in the dark? Or had the house been burgled, maybe weeks ago, and the burglar had left the window like that, not troubling to conceal evidence of his entry, because nobody ever came to the place? Or—unnerving thought—was there a burglar inside now, at this minute?

Revolving all these different possibilities, Matt found that he had been moving slowly nearer and nearer to the wall with the window in it; the window was about six feet above ground, but so thickly sleeved around with creeper that climbing in would present no problem at all. The creeper seemed untouched; showed no sign of damage.

Almost without realising that he had come to a decision, Matt found himself digging his toes into the wet mass and pulling himself up—showers of drops flew into his face—until he was able to lean across the window-sill, bracing his elbows against the inner edge of the frame. As might have been expected, the sill inside was swimming with rainwater, the paint starting to crack; evidently the window had been open for hours, maybe days.

Matt stared into the dusky interior, waiting for his eyes to adjust to the dimness. At first, all he could see was vague masses of furniture. Slowly these began to resolve into recognisable forms: tapestried chairs with high backs and bulbous curving legs, side-tables covered in ornaments, a standard lamp with an elaborate pleated shade, dripping tassels, a huge china pot, a flower-patterned carpet, a black shaggy hearthrug, a gold-framed portrait over the mantel. The hearth was fireless, the chair beside it empty, the room sunk in silence. Listening with all his concentration, Matt could hear no sound from anywhere about the house. Encouraged, he swung a knee over the sill, ducked his head and shoulders under the sash, and levered himself in; then, with instinctive caution, he slid down the sash behind him, so that, in the unlikely event of another intruder visiting the garden, the way indoors would not be so enticingly visible.

Matt did not intend to close the window completely, but the sash cord had perished and the heavy frame, once in motion, shot right down before he could stop it; somewhat to his consternation, a little catch clicked across; evidently it was a burglar-proof lock, for he was unable to pull it open again; there was a keyhole in the catch, and he guessed that it could not now be opened again without the key.

Swearing under his breath, Matt turned to survey the room. How would it ever be possible to find the right key in this cluttered, dusky place? It might be in a bowl of odds and ends on the mantelpiece—or in a desk drawer—or hanging on a nail—or in a box—no casual intruder could hope to come across it. Nor—he turned back to inspect the window again—could he hope to smash his way out. The window-panes were too small, the bars too thick. Still, there would be other ways of leaving the house, perhaps he could simply unlock an outside door. He decided that before exploring any farther he had better establish his means of exit, and so took a couple of steps towards a doorway that he could now see on his right. This led through to a large chilly dining-room where a cobwebbed chandelier hung over a massive mahogany dining-table, corralled by eight chairs, and reflecting ghostly grey light from a window beyond. The dining-room window, to Matt's relief, was a casement; easy enough to break out of that, he thought, his spirits rising. But perhaps there would be no need, perhaps the burglar-catch was not fastened; and he was about to cross the dining-room and examine it closely when the sound of silvery laughter behind him nearly shocked him out of his wits.

"Aha! Aha! Ha-ha-ha-ha-ha-ha!" trilled the mocking voice, not six feet away. Matt spun round, his heart almost bursting out through his rib-cage. He would have been ready to swear there wasn't a soul in the house. Was it a ghost? Were the stories true, after all?

The room he had first entered still seemed empty, but the laughter had certainly come from that direction, and as he stood in the doorway, staring frantically about him, he heard it again, a long mocking trill, repeated in exactly the same cadence.

"Jesus!" whispered Matt.

And then, as he honestly thought he was on the point of fainting from fright, the explanation was supplied. At exactly the same point from which the laughter had come, a clock began to chime in a thin silvery note obviously intended to match the laughter: *ting, tong, ting, tong.* Four o'clock.

"Jesus," breathed Matt again. "How about that? A laughing clock!"

He moved over to inspect the clock. It was a large, elaborate affair, stood on a kind of bureau with brass handles, under a glass dome. The structure of the clock, outworks, whatever you call it, was all gilded and ornamented with gold cherubs who were falling about laughing, throwing their fat little heads back, or doubled up with amusement.

"Very funny," muttered Matt sourly. "Almost had me dead of heart-failure, you can laugh!"

Over the clock, he now saw, a big tapestry hung on the wall, which echoed the theme of laughter: girls in frilly tunics this time, and a fat old man sitting on a barrel squashing grapes into his mouth while he hugged a girl to him with the other arm; all of them, too, splitting themselves over some joke, probably a rude one to judge from the old chap's appearance.

Matt wished very much that the clock would strike again, but presumably it would not do that till five o'clock—unless it chimed the quarters; he had better case the rest of the house in the meantime, and reckon to be back in this room by five. Would it be possible to pinch the clock? he wondered. But it looked dauntingly heavy—and probably its mechanism was complicated and delicate, might go wrong if shifted; how could he ever hope to carry it through all those bushes and over the paling fence? And then there would be the problem of explaining its appearance in his father's council flat; he could hardly say that he found it lying on a rubbish dump. Still he longed to possess it—think what the other guys in the gang would say when they heard it! Maybe he could keep it in Kip Butterworth's house—old Kip, lucky fellow, had a room of his own and such a lot of electronic junk all over it that one clock more or less would never be noticed.

But first he would bring Kip here, at a time just before the clock was due to strike, and let *him* have the fright of his life . . .

Sniggering to himself at this agreeable thought, Matt turned back towards the dining-room, intending to carry out his original plan of unfastening one of the casement windows, when for the second time he was stopped dead by terror.

A voice behind him said, "Since you are here, you may as well wind the clock." And added drily, "Saturday is its day for winding, so it is just as well you came."

This time the voice was unmistakably human; trembling like a leaf, Matt was obliged to admit to himself that there was no chance of its being some kind of electronic device—or even a ghost. It was an old woman's voice, harsh, dry, a little shaky, but resonant; only, where the devil *was* she?

Then he saw that what he had taken for a wall beyond the fireplace was, in fact, one of those dangling bamboo curtains, and beyond it—another bad moment for Matt—was this motionless figure sitting on a chair, watching him; had been watching him—must have—all the time, ever since he had climbed in, for the part of the room beyond the curtain was just a kind of alcove, a big bay window really, leading nowhere. She must have been there all the time . . .

"Go on," she repeated, watching Matt steadily from out of her black triangles of eyes, "wind the clock."

He found his voice and said hoarsely, "Where's the key, then?"

"In the round bowl on the left side."

His heart leapt; perhaps the window key would be there too. But it was not; there was only one key: a long heavy brass shaft with a cross-piece at one end and a lot of fluting at the other.

"Lift the dome off; carefully," she said. "You'll find two keyholes in the face. Wind them both. One's for the clock, the other for the chime."

And, as he lifted off the dome and began winding, she added thoughtfully, "My husband made that clock for me, on my thirtieth birthday. It's a recording of my own voice—the laugh. Uncommon, isn't it? He was an electrical engineer, you see. Clocks were his hobby. All kinds of unusual ones he invented —there was a Shakespearean clock, and a barking dog, and one that sang hymns—my voice again. I had a beautiful singing voice in those days—and my laugh was famous of course. 'Miss Langdale's crystalline laugh,' the critics used to call it . . . My husband was making a skull clock just before he died. There's the skull."

There it was, to be sure, a real skull, perched on top of the big china jar to the right of the clock.

Vaguely now, Matt remembered reports of her husband's death; wasn't there something a bit odd about it? Found dead of heart-failure in the underpass below the motorway, at least a mile from his house; what had he been *doing* there, in the middle of the night? Why walk through the underpass, which was not intended for pedestrians anyway?

"He was going to get some cigarettes when he died," she went on, and Matt jumped; had she read his thoughts? How could she know so uncannily what was going through his head?

"I've given up smoking since then," she went on. "Had to, really . . . They won't deliver, you see. Some things you can get delivered, so I make do with what I can get. I don't like people coming to the house too often, because they scare the birds. I'm a great bird person, you know—"

Unless she has a servant, then, she's alone in the house, Matt thought, as she talked on, in her sharp, dry old voice. He began to feel less terrified—perhaps he could just scare her into letting him leave. Perhaps, anyway, she was mad?

"Are you going to phone the police?" he asked boldly. "I wasn't going to pinch anything, you know—just came in to have a look-see."

"My dear boy, I don't care *why* you came in. As you *are* here, you might as well make yourself useful. Go into the dining-room, will you, and bring back some of those bottles."

The rain had abated, just a little, and the dining-room was some degrees lighter when he walked through into it. All along the window wall Matt was amazed to see wooden wine-racks filled with bottles and half-bottles of champagne. There must be hundreds. There were also, in two large log baskets beside the empty grate, dozens of empties. An armchair was drawn close to an electric bar-fire, not switched on; a half-empty glass and bottle stood on a silver tray on the floor beside the armchair.

"Bring a glass, too," Miss Jordan called.

And, when he returned with the glass, the tray, and several bottles under his arm, she said, "Now, open one of them. You know how to, I hope?"

He had seen it done on TV; he managed it without difficulty.

"Ought to be chilled, of course," she remarked, receiving the glass from him. One of her hands lay limply on the arm of the chair—she hitched it up from time to time with the other hand when it slipped off; and, now that he came near to her for the first time, he noticed that she smelt very bad; a strange, fetid smell of dry unwashed old age and something worse. He began to suspect that perhaps she was *unable* to move from her chair. Curiously enough, instead of this making him fear her less, it made him fear her more. Although she seemed a skinny, frail old creature, her face was quite full in shape, pale and puffy like underdone pastry. It must have been handsome once—long ago—like a wicked fairy pretending to be a princess in a kid's book illustration; now she just looked spiteful and secretive, grinning down at her glass of bubbly. Her hair, the colour of old dry straw, was done very fancy, piled up on top of her head. Perhaps it was a wig?

"Get a glass for yourself, if you want," she said. "There are some more in the dining-room cupboard."

He half thought of zipping out through the dining-room window while he was in there; but still, he was curious to try the fizz, and there didn't seem to be any hurry, really. It was pretty plain the old girl wasn't going anywhere, couldn't be any actual danger to him, although she did rather give him the gooeys. Also he did want to hear that chime again.

As he was taking a glass out from the shimmering ranks in the cupboard, a marvellous thought struck him: Why not bring all the gang here for a banquet? Look at those hundreds and hundreds of bottles of champagne—what a waste, not to make use of them! Plainly *she* was never going to get through them all—not in the state she was in. Maybe he could find some tinned stuff in the house too—but anyway, they could bring their own grub with them, hamburgers and crisps or stuff from the Chinese Takeaway—if the old girl was actually paralysed in her chair, she couldn't stop them . . . In fact it would add to the fun, the excitement, having her there. They could fetch her in from the next room, drink her health in her own bubbly; better not leave it too long, though, didn't seem likely she could last more than a few more days.

Candles, he thought, we'd have to bring candles; and at that point her voice cut into his thoughts, calling, "Bring the two candles that are standing on the cupboard."

He started violently—but it was only a coincidence, after all—picked up the candles in their tall cut-glass sticks and carried them next door with a tumbler for himself.

"Matches on the mantel," she said.

The matches were in a fancy enamel box. He lit the candles and put them on the little table beside her. Now he could see more plainly that there was something extremely queer about her: her face was all drawn down one side, and half of it didn't seem to work very well.

"Electricity cut off," she said. "Forgot to pay the bill."

Her left hand was still working all right, and she had swallowed down two glasses in quick succession, refilling them herself each time from the opened bottle at her elbow. "Fill your glass," she said, slurring the words a little.

He was very thirsty—kippers and baked beans they always had for Saturday midday dinner, and the fright had dried up his mouth too—like Mrs Jordan he tossed down two glasses one after the other. They fizzed a bit—otherwise they didn't have much taste.

"Better open another bottle," she said. "One doesn't go anywhere between two. Fetch in a few more while you're up, why don't you."

"She's planning," he thought to himself; knows she can't move from that chair, so she wants to be stocked up for when I've gone. He wondered if in fact there was a phone in the house? Ought he to ring for a doctor, the police, an ambulance? But then he would have to account for his presence. And he and the gang would never get to have their banquet; the windows would be boarded up for sure, she'd be carted off to the Royal West Midland geriatric ward, like Auntie Glad after her stroke.

"There isn't a phone in the house," said Mrs Jordan calmly. "I had it taken out after Jock died; the bell disturbed the birds. —That's right, put them all down by my chair, where I can reach them."

He opened another bottle, filled both their glasses, then went back to the other room for a third load.

"You like the clock, don't you," she said, as he paused by it, coming back.

"Yeah. It's uncommon."

"It'll strike the quarter in a minute," she said, and soon it did—a low, rather malicious chuckle, just a brief spurt of sound. It made the hair prickle on the back of Matt's neck, but he thought again, Just wait till the rest of the gang hear that! A really spooky sound.

"I don't want you making off with it, though," she said. "No, no, that would never do. I like to sit here and listen to it."

"I wasn't going to take it!"

"No, well, that's as maybe." Her triangular black eyes in their hollows laughed down at him—he was squatting on the carpet near her chair, easing out a particularly obstinate cork. "I'm not taking any chances. Eight days—that clock goes for eight days. Did you wind up the chime too?"

"Yeah, yeah," he said impatiently, tipping more straw-coloured fizz into their glasses. Through the pale liquid in the tumbler he still seemed to see her eyes staring at him shrewdly.

"Put your glass down a moment," she said. "On the floor—that will do. Now, just look here a moment." She was holding up her skinny forefinger. Past it he could see those two dark triangles. "That's right. Now—watch my finger—you are very tired, aren't you? You are going to lie down on the floor and go to sleep. You will sleep—very comfortably—for ten minutes. When you wake, you will walk over to that door and lock it. The key is in the lock. Then you will take out the key and push it under the door with one of the knitting-needles that are lying on the small table by the door. Ahhh! You are so sleepy." She yawned, deeply. Matt was yawning too. His head flopped sideways on to the carpet and he lay motionless, deep asleep.

While he slept it was very quiet in the room. The house was too secluded in its own grounds among the builder's yards for any sound from the town to reach it; only faintly from far away came the throb of the motorway. Mrs Jordan sat impassively listening to it. She did not sleep; she had done enough sleeping and soon would sleep even deeper. She sat listening, and thinking about her husband; sometimes the lopsided smile crooked down one corner of her mouth.

After ten minutes the sleeping boy woke up. Drowsily he staggered to his feet, walked over to the door, locked it, removed the key, and, with a long wooden knitting-needle, thrust it far underneath and out across the polished dining-room floor.

Returning to the old lady he stared at her in a vaguely bewildered manner, rubbing one hand up over his forehead.

"My head aches," he said in a grumbling tone.

"You need a drink. Open another bottle," she said. "Listen: the clock is going to strike the half-hour."

On the other side of the room the clock gave its silvery chuckle.

TO HAVE AND TO HOLD

Clare Dawson

HAVING HAD TO face up to the heart-rending decision to sell the eighteenth-century manor house where she was born and had lived all her twenty-four years, Laura Cresswell-Stevens was desolated.

It had been a shattering discovery to learn that her father had left no money, making it quite impossible for her to keep the home she loved so dearly.

Watching the chauffeur-driven Daimler leaving, with the latest prospective buyer, Ken Halstead, her large blue eyes were hot with tears, knowing that soon now she must leave. She was sure Halstead had been impressed enough to want to buy the place.

She knew too that he had shown a more than casual interest in *her*, and this was borne out when she saw him turn to look at her through the rear window of the big car, in a speculative way. Not that she was unaccustomed to male interest, she thought smugly. Plenty of men had told her how beautiful she was, had ogled her perfect figure and admired the long fair hair which fell in smooth curtains around her oval-shaped face.

When the car had passed from sight, she saw Lambert locking the big wrought iron gates and watched as he made his way bent-backed and with a slow dejected gait back towards the house.

Poor Lambert. He was as sad as she was. All the other servants had gone now, but Lambert would never leave. He'd been with the Cresswell-Stevens for as long as she could remember, rising from odd-job man to chief gardener and now, in his sixtieth year, a caretaker too.

A bachelor, he had been the family's most loyal servant. The salt of the earth, her late father had often called him.

Thoughts of her father brought renewed tears. His sudden

death had shattered her, but discovering that he'd lived a double life and gambled away the entire family fortune was a shock which had left her numb.

Chalmers, the family solicitor, had faced her gravely on the day of the will-reading but had tried to be kind.

"I can't tell you how deeply sorry I am, my dear. I had no notion he had been gambling to such an extent. No one had, it seems. It was horses, of course. Then the gambling tables, not only here but in the South of France. He even gambled recklessly on the Stock Exchange. All this, coupled with his extravagant lifestyle, well . . ." He had paused to assess her reactions before going on to worse things. "His debts, I'm afraid, have run into thousands of pounds. The final figure shows they topped two million!"

She still couldn't believe it. Her father had had a distinguished career in the army and, later, in merchant banking. It was inconceivable he should have been so foolhardy. Now, all she had was the manor house, its gardens and land, all of which she was obliged to sell to pay off his huge debts. There would be precious little left over for her to live on, and the future looked bleak.

The prospect of having to work for her living was abhorrent. She'd never worked in her life. She had no training, no work experience.

Anyway, why should she? Her natural, inborn arrogance fuelled her anger and now she silently cursed her father for leaving her in such dire circumstances. Why should she have to find another home? Sink to the level of having to work for a paymaster? It was all too much. Her whole being rebelled against it. She just couldn't face that sort of life! It was unthinkable.

Lambert, stocky, balding and dressed in his working clothes, stopped beside her. She read the unspoken question in his eyes.

"Yes, Lambert. He *is* interested. He made no attempt to conceal it. And he didn't quibble over the price either. He's quite willing to pay a million for the house and gardens and a further two million for the land. Chalmers will advise me to sell. I know he will."

"S'pose it's better than having to part with the old place to one of them Arabs," muttered Lambert gloomily. "It's not hard to see why he wants to buy. This is one of the most beautiful houses in the whole of England."

They turned to gaze at the superb landscaped gardens and beyond them, stretching away from the neatly trimmed perimeter hedges, an expanse of lush green meadows dotted with magnificent oaks and tiny coppices.

Laura sighed softly. "Halstead marched around the grounds like a conquering hero. Fat, ugly and quite repulsive. I hated him!"

"Don't reckon he found *you* repulsive, Miss Laura."

She looked at Lambert sharply. She knew he'd been snooping again.

"I might have guessed you'd been keeping a wary eye on the proceedings. Well . . . maybe you're right, but that doesn't alter my opinion of him."

Lambert prodded the gravel with his shoe and said softly: "Sometimes it pays to turn a blind eye to unpleasant things. Concentrate on what might benefit you . . . if you follow my meaning."

Laura understood him fully, shocked by the idea he was slyly mooting.

"You're not serious, Lambert. I mean . . . *me* and that odious little man? And what about Tony—"

"No need to worry about Tony, Miss Laura. He and I have already talked this over. Fact is—he suggested it. This Halstead man knows all about your circumstances, thanks to the gossipy newspapers. It may sound a bit mercenary but you don't really want to leave the manor, do you? It could be one way to ensure you stay."

"Halstead may be married already!"

"He isn't. Tony's been making some discreet enquiries, and our multi-millionaire is a confirmed bachelor. Keeps himself amused, of course. Got a couple of dolly birds installed in separate flats in London, according to rumour."

"Dolly birds!"

Lambert laughed out loud at her outraged expression.

"Exactly! So just you make sure he weds you before he beds you, or you won't get him near a church."

"I don't think he was *that* taken with me—"

"He couldn't take his eyes off you today and I reckon he'll be an easy conquest. It's up to you to encourage him. A man chases a woman until she catches him, that's what they say."

With mixed feelings, she said: "I'm not in the market for marriage. You know that, Lambert. I'm in love with your son and—"

"I'm not forgetting that. Neither is Tony. But you've waited two years already."

"Yes." Discernible bitterness crept into her voice now. "With me naively believing that next May I'd get the twenty-five thousand my father promised me on my twenty-fifth birthday."

"Don't dwell on it, Miss Laura. Point is, you're both young. You can afford to wait a bit longer. Say about a year?"

Beginning to see how the man's mind was working, she gradually found herself coming round to the idea, much as Halstead had revolted her. Pensively she said: "A year married to Halstead then a divorce with generous settlement. I'd end up free and a rich divorcee. I doubt if he'd want a legal battle through the courts. It'd mean adverse publicity and excessive costs."

"How easy it'll be will depend on what kind of man this Halstead is. It's up to you to assess him and decide for yourself. You might even demand Cresswell Manor as part of the divorce settlement. After all, if you were leaving him, he'd probably not want to stay on here anyway."

A familiar deep voice hailed them and she turned to see a tall, handsome young man about her own age, coming through the gate in the perimeter hedge and heading their way. Laura greeted him with a kiss and wrapped an arm around his waist.

"Okay, so how did things go?" Tony asked, squeezing her waist gently. "Was this millionaire bloke interested?"

She told him about the man's visit, then mentioned what she and Lambert had been discussing before he arrived. Tony smiled and kissed her cheek playfully.

"Let's go indoors. I want to talk to you about that."

Lambert watched them disappear into the house and set off home with a broad, satisfied grin on his weather-beaten features.

The wedding was in mid-August and Laura looked stunning as she emerged from the fashionable Mayfair church on the arm of her husband, Ken Halstead. He looked almost elegant, despite his obscene paunch, and the reception was a lavish affair with hundreds of guests.

They spent their honeymoon cruising around the Greek Islands in Halstead's luxury yacht and returned to Cresswell Manor in mid-September.

A welcome home party had been arranged by Halstead's friends, one of whom had carried out the tycoon's instructions to engage new staff for the manor. Laura had asked Ken to keep Lambert on, in view of his long service to her family. To please her, Halstead had agreed, although he made no secret of the fact that he disliked the man.

"I don't mind Lambert staying on provided he sticks to his gardening," he had told her firmly. "I'm not putting up with him wandering all over the house and especially snooping around the garages. Those cars are worth thousands and I only allow people who know about cars to go near them."

Laura had quickly learned that her husband's one passion in life was motor-racing. One of their large garages already housed a couple of his sports cars and the other, his most recently acquired Porsche, the pride of his collection. The Daimler and Laura's Alfa Romeo were kept on the drive, under canvas covers, until the third garage had been built.

"I'll speak to him about it at once, darling," she had promised and then promptly put the matter out of her mind.

Three days after their return to the manor, Halstead went up to London on business and Laura at once arranged a meeting with Tony, through Lambert.

They met where they always met—in Tinker's Coppice—the place where, two years before, Tony had been on hand to help her after a tumble from her horse. From the moment she had set eyes on him, she knew he was the only man in the world for her.

When she left him, almost two hours later, she felt as she always did—elated and blissfully happy. Tony had missed her as desperately as she had missed him.

In the weeks and months that followed, Laura found married life tolerable only because Halstead was away a lot on business and much of his spare time was taken up with his obsession with cars. Three months later, just before Christmas, Laura discovered that she was pregnant. Ken, always astute, noticed her quieter mood and asked if anything was wrong.

"No, of course not, darling. I'm fine. It's this dreary winter weather. Gets me down a bit."

He said no more then, but she could see he wasn't convinced. The following evening, he dropped a bombshell.

"Why didn't you tell me you were pregnant, Laura?" he asked calmly as they relaxed in the drawing room after dinner.

She was unable to disguise her shock.

"How—how did you find out?"

"The wife of one of my business colleagues went to see a Harley Street gynaecologist three days ago and recognised you. She was in the waiting room when you were there. She said you stayed with the doctor for quite some time."

Laura was suddenly frightened. There was no doubt in her mind that the child was Tony's, for she had forgotten to take precautions before their blissful reunion in Tinker's Coppice. Where her husband was concerned, she never failed to ensure she was "safe" before slipping into bed beside him.

"And I suppose you got on to the doctor in question and bullied the information out of him?" she said curtly.

"Don't I have a right? I *am* your husband."

Ken looked hurt. His smile had faded and she noticed a furrowing of his brow. Recognising suspicion in his eyes, she moved quickly across to his chair, sank easily into his lap and wrapped an arm around his neck.

"Of course you do, darling. But you really *are* a bad boy, you know. I didn't want you to know! It was to be a special surprise and I was planning to announce the news during our first Christmas Party here. I knew how thrilled you'd be with all our friends there to congratulate us . . . and—"

Ken's smile returned. He reached up and kissed her and later, as they celebrated with champagne, Laura kept up her pretended happiness, secretly thanking God for her presence of mind and quick thinking.

That night, however, her thoughts were in turmoil. The pregnancy altered everything. Now she couldn't afford to wait the year she and Tony had agreed upon, before she left her husband.

She had to talk to Tony. To amend their plans. She would drive over to Lambert's cottage early the next morning, even though he had been reported ill and had been off work for three days. She couldn't wait until he was fit again.

The next day when Ken left for London, she drove to Lambert's cottage in a remote corner of the village. She didn't want to be seen by any of the villagers. When she arrived, Lambert welcomed her warmly but laughed when she apologised for calling when he was ill.

"There's nowt wrong with me, Miss Laura," he confessed with a grin. "I just felt like a few days off. That new staff you've got up at the manor are a right snobby lot. They all treat me as if I was a leper and I reckon Halstead's behind it. Anything to discourage me from roaming around the place. I belong in the garden, he says, as if I were a bloody vegetable or something. A right pain, he is!"

Despite the wry smile, Laura could sense the intense loathing he had come to feel for Ken Halstead. When she told him about the baby, Lambert pondered on the unexpected news and agreed they had a problem.

He left her with a strong cup of tea and walked back into the village to fetch Tony who worked in the village garage.

Alone in the cottage, Laura reflected on her love for Tony. She knew that her father would never have approved of him as a son-in-law, so their affair had become a closely-guarded secret. With the invaluable help of Lambert, it had remained so for over two years. Even now she remembered her surprise when the gardener had revealed that Tony was his illegitimate son.

"Bachelor though I am, I've had my moments. And one of those moments was Tony's mother, if you follow my meaning. She was married at the time. When she died, ten years ago, I told Tony the truth and we've been good friends ever since."

When Lambert came back with Tony, the trio spent the next hour discussing the problem. Before she left, Tony promised he'd come up with a solution soon. Three days later he did, but her relief turned to shock when he gave her details of his plan. It involved murder.

For a while, she struggled with her fear and horror but eventually she had to accept that it was the only answer. With Ken dead, she would automatically inherit a fortune and the house. And playing the rôle of the grieving wife and expectant mother would gain her everybody's sympathy.

Lambert decided the death must be made to look like an accident and that Laura—who stood to gain the most from her husband's demise—must appear to be absolutely innocent.

Every detail was carefully planned and Laura mentally rehearsed her vital part in the scheme. The following Sunday, the plan was set in motion.

During breakfast, she asked Ken if he'd take her for a spin in his new Porsche.

"I thought you didn't like the Porsche, darling," he replied, slightly bemused.

"I don't, but I know you won't drive too fast. I just feel I'd like a run out somewhere."

Eager to please her every whim, Ken obliged and they stopped off at an olde-worlde pub for lunch.

Once home again, he found he had mislaid the garage key. Leaving the Porsche in the drive, he followed Laura into the house. Part of the plan was that Laura should delay his return to the car and she detained him with a warm display of affection which Ken, for all his preoccupation with finding the garage key, could not resist.

Having earlier slipped the garage key into her bag, Laura now casually suggested that it might be in the kitchen and when he went to look, she dropped it on to the hall table and called after him: "I've found it, Ken. It's out here on the hall table, half hidden by a vase of flowers."

Emerging once more from the house, Ken spotted Lambert hovering around the Porsche, dressed in his grubby working clothes.

"What the hell are you doing here on a Sunday?" he shouted, hurrying over to the car.

Lambert ignored his shout and, to Halstead's disbelief, opened the car door and slipped in behind the wheel. Laura, watching from the drawing room window, saw her husband rush to the Porsche and begin yelling. Lambert, equally incensed, yelled back.

She hurried outside, aware that some of the staff had come to the door to see what was going on. The vociferous exchange between the two angry men was frightening.

"What's the matter with you, you miserable devil!" bellowed Lambert. "I'm only looking at the thing. You don't think I'd be daft enough to try and drive it, do you? Me, who's never had a driving lesson in his life. What's wrong with just looking?"

Ken glared at the older man. The front car seat cover was smeared in mud and dirt from Lambert's overalls; his muddy boots had left cakes of mud on the pedals and floor and greasy finger-marks were visible on the fascia, wheel and door.

"Get out of that car!" Ken bawled, red in the face.

Laura halted beside her husband and, to his astonishment, turned her anger on Lambert. For the first time ever, she supported Ken in his outrage.

"Do as you're told, Lambert. Come out at once!" she demanded and when the gardener obeyed, went on: "You've really gone too far this time, Lambert. I've warned you enough times and I've tried to be fair in view of your long service to my family—"

"I'm sorry, Miss Laura," he began, doffing his cap and looking at her with large, sorrowful eyes.

"Sorry isn't enough any more. You're sacked! You can come and collect your wages tomorrow and then you're not to set foot on this property again. My husband won't sack you, for my sake. So I'm doing it!"

Ken Halstead relaxed, beamed a smile.

"You're showing some sense at last, Laura. I told you the man's a bloody nuisance." He paused to leer at the gardener. "All right, Lambert. You heard the lady. Get going!"

The gardener, clearly shattered, collected his cycle and rode off down the drive, hurling abuse over his shoulder as he went.

The rest of the day was a strain on Laura. Her husband talked ceaselessly about the incident; spent hours in the garage cleaning his precious car and polishing it till it gleamed. Even in bed that night, he kept up his string of complaints about Lambert till Laura turned out the light and said she wanted to sleep.

But she didn't sleep. She lay awake, thinking, waiting, going over in her mind every detail of the plan. The waiting seemed interminable but timing was essential; she knew she mustn't make a move until one-thirty in the morning.

Precisely on the half-hour, she got up and went to the window. There was a full moon, as Tony had said there would be that night, and the gardens were bathed in soft yellow light. She was grateful for it. Explanations later would sound less convincing if the garden had been cloaked in total darkness.

She went over to the bed and began shaking Ken vigorously.

"Darling, wake up. There's someone in the garden. Wake up!"

Halstead snorted into wakefulness and blinked in the light she had turned on.

"There's someone in the garden—with a shotgun."

Halstead stared at her incredulously, then his mouth began to tighten. "Lambert!"

Laura gasped. "It can't be. I know he was angry but—"

Ken wasn't listening. He was already out of bed, pulling on a dressing gown, taking a small revolver from the cabinet near the bed and loading it carefully. Laura felt sick with fear.

She followed her husband downstairs but when she mentioned ringing the police, he responded with characteristic contempt.

"No, you don't!" he roared. "I don't want those idiots tramping all over the house. I'll deal with this myself. Anybody trespassing on my property at night has got it coming. And I don't care if he *is* in his sixties. Now go back to bed!"

She ignored him and went into the kitchen. From the window, she watched as he stalked the unseen intruder in the soft moonlight, shouting Lambert's name and, once, even firing a shot into the air.

Laura could hear doors opening, shuffling feet, anxious whisperings. Suddenly, the housekeeper was in the kitchen, followed by the butler. She ordered them back to their rooms and they went out, but she knew they would linger out of sight at the top of the stairs.

At that moment, Ken joined her in the kitchen.

"I must have scared him off. There's no sign of him out there."

It was then she pointed through the window towards the

garage, housing his precious Porsche. The rear door was standing open. Predictably, her husband's face turned deep crimson and the rage in his eyes was frightening as he rushed out, gun in hand. She could hear him yelling Lambert's name in the garage, swearing to kill him if he had laid hands on the Porsche, his voice verging on the hysterical.

She went out and joined him in the garage. She shivered in the cold night air. There was no sign of Lambert.

"He's not here," breathed Ken, putting down the gun and moving towards the car, after switching on the garage light. "The bastard's gone but he's been up to something. I didn't leave the car jacked up last night. Nor was the bonnet raised. And I locked that garage door. I'd swear to it. If he's done any damage—"

"Surely not, darling," she protested. "He wouldn't be so stupid—"

"He *is* stupid! It's second nature to him. Somebody's been in here, Laura. I just know it. I'm going to see what he's been up to. You go back to bed!"

"Can't it wait till morning—"

"It *is* bloody morning." Ken's patience with his wife had come to an end and he was past caring about her feelings. "Go back to bed and stay there."

She went. Halstead was already crawling under the car. Seconds later, heart pounding, Laura returned on slippered feet and stood watching him under his beloved car. Then, wrapping a handkerchief around her fingers, she reached out with a trembling hand for the release button on the hydraulic jack.

In silent horror, she saw the Porsche begin to descend. She heard her husband's muffled exclamation of alarm, saw his feet moving in sudden agitation as he tried to wriggle out quickly. But he wasn't quick enough.

She fled, reaching the kitchen in a state of terror. But she struggled to get a grip on herself. She had to stay calm. So far, everything had gone to plan. She couldn't afford any slip-ups now. She filled the electric kettle, plugged it in and put two mugs on a tray with milk and sugar. Then, gritting her teeth, she returned to the garage.

At the door, she took a deep breath and let out an ear-splitting scream. When the butler and housekeeper appeared, Laura slumped forward. The butler caught her as she fainted.

"Proof, that's what I need, Butch. Proof!"

Detective Inspector Mike Rowberry paced his office at C.I.D. headquarters, hands thrust deep into his trouser pockets, his young face creased with worry. On the other side of the desk, Detective Sergeant Jim (Butch) Millington gazed at his senior officer, nonplussed. He was a patient man but Mike had been on about the Halstead case for weeks now and Butch was almost at the end of his tether.

"Proof of what, sir?" he asked wearily. "It was an accident."

"A mysterious death," corrected Rowberry, pausing briefly.

"An accident. The inquest decided it."

"I don't care what the blasted inquest decided. I'm saying it was murder. I'm convinced of it."

Butch fell silent. He knew better than to argue with Mike when he was in this sort of mood. And he wasn't without some sympathy with his views, for the mystery surrounding the death of the local multi-millionaire Ken Halstead had bothered him for a long time too. But now, after a thorough police investigation, he'd come to agree with the coroner's verdict of accidental death. Not so, his senior officer. Rowberry just wouldn't give up and gnawed away at the mystery like a dog at a bone.

"Look, let's recap what we know," said Butch with heavy patience. "An angry quarrel takes place between Halstead and this gardener bloke, Lambert; plenty of witnesses to that. In the early hours, Mrs Halstead is awakened by her husband saying he's spotted Lambert in the garden with a shotgun. Halstead rushes downstairs with his own gun, searches the rear garden, yelling the man's name in a very hysterical fashion and disturbing the servants."

"Then," Rowberry interrupted, "Halstead spots the garage door open, suspects Lambert is inside and goes after him. Again, no Lambert. What he does find is his Porsche jacked up and the bonnet raised. Halstead, according to his wife, now goes beserk, swearing Lambert's been at his car and that he'll kill the old man if he finds anything wrong with it. He screams at her to go away and he crawls under the car to inspect the thing."

"Then," went on Butch, "she tries to calm herself; puts the kettle on to make them both a hot drink; waits for her husband to join her and when he doesn't, she goes back to the garage to fetch him. She finds Halstead lying on the ground with the Porsche on top of him."

"Right. Now who released the button on that jack?"

"We've been over this a dozen times, sir. It was an accident. Halstead jacked the car up himself the previous evening. His wife confirmed it. He'd been working on the car, came in tired and said he'd call it a day. He didn't even bother to lock the garage door."

"Ah that's what's so wrong with her story, Butch. All the servants testified that he was obsessive about that damned car. Wouldn't let anybody go near the thing. He'd never have left that door unlocked."

"Then who unlocked it? It certainly wasn't Lambert. We established that. No one else had the opportunity. The answer's simple. He left it open the night before. Halstead's doctor testified that he was a very excitable man. After his row with Lambert, he'd talked of nothing else all day. The servants confirmed hearing him going on about it." He paused to look directly at Mike. "I agree with you that Laura Halstead might have had the opportunity to release that jack, but it was proved that she didn't even know how the thing worked. And where was her motive? They were happily married, according to everyone we interviewed including the servants; he was a generous man who denied her nothing; she was having his child. There was no motive."

"I didn't believe it then and I don't believe it now. They had a whirlwind romance. She was almost penniless. He was wealthy. What better motive for marriage than that?"

"Ah, you're a cynic, sir, that's your trouble. Look, you questioned her. Hour after hour you kept at it but she stuck to her story. There was no flaw in it. She and Halstead were very happy together. Everybody said so. And don't forget—Mrs Halstead even turned on her old friend and long-time employee when he upset her husband. It was she and not Halstead who sacked Lambert."

Inspector Rowberry stopped pacing.

"Lambert's alibi was water-tight, I'll admit that. He doesn't even own a shotgun. He was in bed by ten that night and three independent witnesses confirmed it. There's no way he could have been at the big house at that time in the morning.

"Bit of a surprise finding out he had a son, wasn't it? This Tony character certainly gave him a sound alibi, saying he got to Lambert's cottage around nine o'clock that evening with his two workmates and that they played cards long after his dad went to bed. The two friends confirmed they left for home around two in the morning and that Tony gave them a lift in his car."

"And by that time Halstead was already dead," said Butch. "And we know the gardener hadn't slipped out unnoticed around one in the morning, because one of the visitors popped into his bedroom to see if he was okay. Tony asked him to. That was about one-thirty-five. He was sound asleep."

"So we come back to the wife again and what I said at the beginning. Proof. I just don't believe her story, Butch, no matter how much she's convinced you and the coroner and everybody else. I've got a gut feeling she was responsible somehow."

"Even though she was found by the servants standing at the garage door in a dreadful state of shock and she fainted? Nobody felt she was putting on an act, did they? She had everybody's sympathy, especially when she complained of pains and was rushed to hospital after a miscarriage was feared. Fortunately, it was a false alarm." He paused to sigh, ponderously. "That child will be born lucky, though. All that money . . . one day that kid will be able to travel the world if he or she wants to, just like Halstead did."

Mike Rowberry nodded and then, suddenly, he froze.

"Travelled the world!" he repeated. "Yes, Halstead did, didn't he? Especially France. He spent a lot of time in France, according to our investigations."

"So—what's wrong with that?"

Butch got no reply for Rowberry was already heading for the door, saying he had an urgent job to do.

The sergeant went back to his desk and got through a load of paper work. It was twenty-four hours later when a triumphant Rowberry announced:

"Come on, sergeant. We're going to call on Mrs Halstead. I've got a bit of bad news for her."

All the way to Cresswell Manor, Rowberry kept silent and Butch quietly seethed with frustration, itching to know what was going on.

An attractive, smiling Laura Halstead admitted them, dressed in a pretty floral-design shift which covered her condition skilfully. She looked well and happy.

In the spacious luxury of the drawing-room, she invited the two men to sit down. Before Rowberry could speak there was a noise outside the door and Lambert came in. He looked startled, recognising the two plain-clothes policemen instantly.

"Surprised to see you here, Mr Lambert," said the inspector at once. "Thought you and Mrs Halstead had fallen out—"

"That's all water under the bridge," snapped Lambert. "I'm not a man to harbour petty grudges and Miss Laura needed a bit of moral support after her husband's terrible accident."

"Well, we've come to speak to Mrs Halstead. It's a private matter, if you don't mind."

The inspector's tone was brusque and Lambert went out with a shrug.

"I'm afraid we have some rather disturbing news, Mrs Halstead," Rowberry began quietly. "It concerns your late husband."

"Ken. What about him?"

"We understand that he lived in France for approximately three years, returning to this country in 1980?"

"Yes, that's right. Why do you ask?"

Noticing a measure of anxiety in the woman's face, Rowberry took his time.

"We've been informed by the French police that a certain lady, now living in Rouen and having read about your husband's tragic death in the newspapers, has come forward with certain claims."

"What sort of claims?" demanded Laura, anger as well as anxiety reflected in her blue eyes.

"That she and Mr Halstead were married in Paris on 10th June 1977."

"That's ridiculous! My husband was a bachelor when I married him. He told me so."

"I'm afraid he must have lied to you. The woman has produced a valid marriage certificate as well as birth certificates for her two sons, twins, born ten months after the wedding. Her husband, she claims, deserted her and the children in September 1980 and she hasn't heard from him since."

Laura stared at the inspector, disbelief in her face.

"You're saying my marriage to Ken was bigamous?"

"I'm afraid it looks that way, Mrs Halstead. He and his French wife were never divorced. She has a will too, which Halstead made a year after they were married, leaving all his estate to her and the children. Of course, he didn't have so much to leave her then as he did when he died, but I s'pose she can legally claim everything—including Cresswell Manor."

At a nod from his senior officer, Butch took several quick strides across the room and pulled open the door. Lambert almost fell into the room.

"Thought you'd be listening, Mr Lambert," said Rowberry.

The gardener said nothing as the two police officers left, returning to their car without a backward glance.

At the end of the long drive, however, Butch stopped, turned the car and drove back to the manor house. One of the servants let them in when Rowberry explained he'd left his hat behind. When they reached the drawing-room door, they heard an angry altercation going on.

"Oh my God, Laura. You stupid, stupid bitch! How could you have failed to find out a thing like that?"

"*You* were supposed to have checked him out. *You* should have known." Laura Halstead sounded hysterical.

"For God's sake, keep your voices down!" pleaded Lambert in vain.

"But *you* married him! You should have made sure first."

Rowberry and Butch exchanged glances as Tony's voice rose in a pathetic wail: "You've lost everything. *We've* lost everything. All of it was for nothing . . . the planning, his death, the lot!"

Several months later, driving back to the station from the Old Bailey after the much-publicised murder trial in which the three conspirators were found guilty and sentenced to long terms of imprisonment, Butch commented:

"They say the simplest ideas are the best, don't they? It never occurred to any of us that Lambert could have slipped out of his cottage at any time between ten, when he went to bed, and one-thirty when he was seen back in bed and fast asleep. Laura had provided him with a duplicate key; Tony had explained what he had to do to raise the car and it was Tony who gave Laura her instructions."

"Hm," said Rowberry at his side. "But it isn't only the criminals who make use of simple ideas, is it Butch?"

"No, inspector," said Butch with a big grin. "Still, I feel honour bound to remind you of something I learned at my mother's knee."

Rowberry frowned. "And what was that?"

"Detective inspectors who go around telling bare-faced lies about non-existent wives—never get to heaven."

JOE

Penelope Wallace

I DIDN'T SEE Lady Fate's hand as I opened the pub door at ten past nine that Friday evening—I always went into The Dog and Duck at ten past nine on Friday evenings, business permitting.

Marie, the barmaid, was resting her boobs on the bar counter same as usual, and same as usual I wasn't going to get anywhere with her.

"Evenin', Marie."

"Evening, Joe. The usual?"

I nodded and she heaved her equipment off the bar and headed for the pump. Her strong right arm pulled the lever twice and the foaming pint was on the counter.

"What are you havin', love?" I asked her.

"Campari, please, Joe."

It used to be port and lemon but times change. All this bloody telly.

I looked round and nodded to the regulars I knew. Then I saw Ted. He was sitting at a lonely table under the dimmest light. He saw me, left his beer on the table, and came over.

"'ullo, Joe, join me?" He jerked his head towards the table. Always furtive was Ted.

I followed him with misgivings and sat opposite him. As something to look at, he didn't measure up to Marie. He looked right, left, and under the ashtray, then he spoke in a harsh whisper. "I got a good job for you, Joe."

"Last job you got me they had a bloody great Alsatian. I had to sleep on my face for a fortnight."

"No dogs, no trouble—it's an 'ouse in 'ampstead."

"That's bad news for a start. Hampstead's swarmin' with the Old Bill."

"But you got the van—and this 'ouse, it's on the corner, so

you park down the side street under the laurels, Bob's yer uncle, and the ground floor loo 'as an ordinary catch. Snick with a knife, up with the winder, and up the stairs. Everyone's away. First door on the left—on the windersill be'ind the curtain all in a cardboard box. Good antique stuff wot your friend—"

"No names."

"Well, 'e'd give you a good price. Are you on?"

Instinct and experience told me to say no, but the bookie was pressing and the girl friend was expensive. "All right, you're on."

Ted fished out a dirty piece of paper and handed it over.

An ill-drawn map showed the house on the corner of Allington Avenue and Rayne Road with the entrance in Allington.

"The 'ouse is called The Cedars," said Ted hoarsely. "You'll burn the map, won't you?"

"You bin watchin' too much spy stuff on the telly."

"Don't burn it too soon or you'll forget it, with your memory."

"Come off it. Now how do I get there?"

He dipped a finger in his beer and mapped it on the table.

"'ere's The Royal Tree, then you turn left, left, right—" The beer trail wound on to Rayne Road. "You can park there, then over the wall. Lav's 'ere. Through the window, up the stairs, turn left—"

Four hours later I was cruising along Allington Avenue. No lights in the corner house and, happy sight on the doorstep, one pint of milk and the paper in the letter box. I hoped that didn't mean the owners planned a late return. I took the back streets to Rayne Road, parked the van away from the light, and proceeded—as the Old Bill says—to the house on the corner. No lights anywhere. Over the wall—there's the loo. In easy, up the stairs, then left into the room, over to the window, and—

That's when it started to go wrong.

Suddenly there was a flood of light and a sweet voice said, "Turn around slowly."

I turned. There was a flash of light. She was sitting up in bed—young and attractive—and holding a camera.

"You've got me bang to rights," I obliged.

You might wonder why I didn't smack her one there and then; but I'd never done anything violent in my life and I didn't intend to start now. Besides, she'd have come round in time and described me to the Old Bill, who've a nice photo of me in their album.

"'You've got me bang to rights'," she repeated with a touch of sarcasm. "Is that the best you can do?"

"All right, I thought I saw smoke coming from the window and I broke in to effect a rescue."

"Come here," she said.

Aye, aye, I said to myself and moved towards the bed.

"I've taken your photo and I'll hand it to the police if you don't do what I ask you."

Aye, aye. So she was one of those. I started to loosen my tie.

"No," she snapped. "Sit on the end of the bed."

I did as she said and thought it was a pity she wasn't one of those. A very nifty little number she was with her fair hair and blue eyes. She leaned across and picked up a tape recorder.

"You're not recording my voice," I told her. "It'd be as bad as being in your bloody camera."

She looked uncertain.

"Suppose you tell me what it's all about," I said. "Are you going to scream for the police? They might tell you not to leave the paper in the door and the milk on the step."

"Did it fool you?"

"Yes, it did."

"It was part of the plan—that and getting the news through to the right quarters."

I wondered if Ted ever got anything right and how she'd gotten the info to him. "So you wanted to be burgled. Insurance?"

"No," she said. "I'm a reporter, freelance. I'm doing a crime series and I want to get the view—if you'll forgive the expression—of the little man."

I didn't like that, but I let it pass.

"Of course," she went on, "I could talk to a dozen men in

pubs who'd tell me they pulled this blag and that blag when the most they've thieved is a free ride on the bus. Of course, you'll probably tell me a pack of lies too but at least I'll know you're the genuine article."

"So you just want to talk to me?"

"Yes. Sorry. Are you disappointed?"

"Well, you can't shoot all the ducks at the fair. What do you want to know—and what happens if I tell you?"

"If you give me an interview, I'll give you the photo—and the camera. It's quite a good one and you might find it useful. Then I'll say goodbye and thank you and that'll be the end—unless you want to buy the Sundays and see who offers the most. My name's Jill." She stuck out her hand and I leaned across and shook it. She was wearing pajamas—the top, at least—and a very fetching perfume.

She picked up a notebook and pencil. "My shorthand's pretty good. Let's start with your upbringing. You're better educated than I'd expected."

"So-so. Not your fallen public-school boy."

"Right. Start with your first crime."

So I told her my life story, from nicking spares from the garage. I even told her about some of my birds, but I was careful not to be too detailed about jobs I'd got away with. Even the Old Bill sometimes reads the Sunday newspapers.

It was six in the ayem when I left, but still December dark, and I climbed back over the wall with the camera in my pocket, reckoning I was ruining my reputation if anyone saw me. But they didn't and I was in the van and away before the milkman added another pint to the doorstep.

I hadn't gone far up Allington Avenue when I was flagged down by two coppers in a Rover. Well, for once I felt no sweat about them looking under the floorboards—I was clean as a whistle. Well, a fairly grubby whistle when they found the camera.

"Just been visiting a bird and she took a photo of me," I explained.

"And gave you the camera."

"Yes—a kind of anniversary present."

The copper looked at it carefully.

"Eleven photos taken. All of you?"

"No," I said, wondering what the hell the other ten were.

The second rozzer got out of the car then and strolled up. "Evening, Joe," he said.

So it wasn't surprising when I ended up in the nick.

Eventually they let me go and kept the camera. It hadn't been too bad, but you don't get treated like royalty when you've got a record.

I trundled home in the old van, faced a bad reception from Karen, who was just off to work. "You said late, but you never said bloody morning," she complained. It was too long a story and I didn't think she'd believe the part about the blonde, so I said I was sorry and agreed to buy her a new coat and turned in for a kip.

I was still dreaming about the blonde when there was a thunderous knocking at the front door. Wondering if the blonde had a disbelieving husband or if the bookie had sent his boys, I staggered to the front door, wrapping a dressing gown around myself.

Suave is the word I'd have used—suave and cold as a volunteer virgin. I didn't invite them in but they stepped by me. *Very* hard-nosed Gestapo? Hit men?

"Special Branch," said the largest.

So I was right. Christ, what now?

"About the film in your camera, which was a present from your girl friend. Name?"

"Well—"

"Right." He read the caution and advised me I was being done for espionage.

I thought I'd be safer standing trial for attempted burglary so I gave him the S.P. He didn't believe a word of it. "And the name and address of your contact?"

"She's not my contact. All I know is her name's Jean or Jill and the house is on the corner of—" Damn, Ted was right about my memory. "It's Allington Avenue, that I do remember, and it's the name of a tree—bloody great big one in the front garden. Pine! That's it, The Pines."

So off we go with the big one sitting in the back with me and the other by the driver.

There's The Pines on the corner and we march past the tree and up to the front door. There's a tinkling bell and the door's opened by a tinkling little brunette. Quite an eyeful but not the right girl.

The leader announced his identity, the girl announced hers, and—reluctantly—invited us to follow her to the library.

"Have you seen this man before?" he asked her.

She glanced distastefully at my unshaven face and said she hadn't.

"No," I agreed, "she's not the one who was here last night."

She looked even more distasteful and said she'd returned an hour ago from Paris, and she could prove it.

"Someone else was here," I said.

SB glared down at me. "Are you sure it's the right house?"

"Of course I'm sure—I can describe the downstairs loo – blue-striped wallpaper and a catch a baby could open."

So the girl led us through and there was the loo—yellow with green flowers and a couple of highly efficient locks on the window.

I don't remember much of the journey to the nick. You could say I was stunned. Twenty-four hours of questioning, a brief appearance before the beak, remanded in custody.

Ted would remember the right house, but how to get hold of Ted without landing him in it? Well, I'd have visitors—Karen, someone who could pass on the message.

But all I had was a visit from my brief and that not in private. I did ask him if he could check the corner houses for girls named Jean or Jill, but he didn't like espionage and he obviously thought I was mixed up in it or how did I have a camera with one picture of myself guiltily starting and ten excellent pictures of Britain's latest and most secret weapon?

After twelve years of thieving, I was prepared for the odd spot of bird, but this was something else. I'm as patriotic as the next man and my feelings were hurt—particularly by the prospect of a long, long spell in maximum—maybe even a swap and an everlasting winter in Russia.

Time passed slowly.

No visitors—not even Karen, though I'd written her a couple of times, and not even the brief.

Not even the bastards from Special Branch.

Then the miracle happened.

Someone saved me a copy of the *Sunday World*—and there she was, blonde little Jill and banner headlines on her series of articles. And guess who figured in this one?

No names and a few unflattering comments on the waste of my mediocre abilities. I started to yell for my brief, for Special Branch. It took them a time, but they checked Jill, checked her story that the film contained photos taken at Wimbledon, checked the boy who sat beside her there and confirmed what she said, checked the number on her insurance policy and the one on the camera they held—and found that somewhere along the line the cameras had been exchanged. Someone had seen a fat man. Me, I was free to go—Jill said she wouldn't bring charges—and when the Old Bill heard how she'd laid the bait they agreed.

The Special Branch boys drifted away without even an apology and I was back for a tearful reunion with Karen.

The next Friday at ten past nine I went to The Dog and Duck.

"Evenin', Marie."

"Evening, Joe. You been away?"

"Just a short holiday."

"The usual?"

"Please—and for you?"

"Campari, thanks. Ted's been asking for you."

Well, you don't tempt fate twice. I'd been a fool to come here and I would have to find another drinking place.

"No, Ted," I told him. "It's not on."

"Sorry, Joe. Just thought you'd like to hear about the fat man."

Reluctantly, I followed him to his corner table.

"What fat man?"

"The one you was in a spot of bovver over. The one 'oo swapped the camera."

"So?"

"So 'e give 'imself up, said 'e was sick of them foreign bastards askin' 'im if the weapon was in the ball or in the racquet."

LOVE AFFAIR

Julian Symons

FROM THE BEGINNING of their marriage it had always been Don who made the decisions and, as Moira told their friends, this was not because he was aggressive or domineering, it was just that both of them thought it right and natural for things to be that way. When, after a year of marriage, he suggested that it was time they moved from the little flat in Kilburn to a district where you could see a bit more of God's green earth and sky, she agreed at once.

He ticked off on his fingers just what they wanted: a three- or four-bedroomed house, central heating, a garden big enough to sit in, and of course the whole thing set in a nice place with neighbours who were their own sort.

She agreed with it all. But wouldn't a garden mean a lot of work?

"I'll look after it. Always fancied myself with the old spade and trowel." Tamping down the tobacco in his pipe, not looking at her, Don said, "And you need a bit of garden for the kids."

"But you said we ought to wait."

"Got a bit of news. MacGillivray's retiring. I get a step up next month."

"Oh, Don! Why didn't you tell me?"

"Best not to say anything till you're sure. What you don't know won't hurt you, that's my motto." He had got his pipe going. "I've been in touch with a few estate agents already."

It proved more difficult than they had expected to find exactly what they wanted, but when they saw the house at Gainham Woods they knew it was just the thing. It was a new development—you didn't call it an estate any more—but the thing that made this particular house a snip, as Don said, was its position on a corner, so that you faced two ways, had more windows than your neighbours, and a bigger garden as well.

There was an attached garage, which Don said would come in handy as a workshop or playroom since they had no car. Gainham Woods was half an hour from central London by train, but Don worked out that the cost of extra fares would be balanced by the fact that living would be less expensive. And, of course, the house would run itself, so that Moira could keep her secretarial job.

"For the time being," Don said with a smile. "Later on you'll have your hands full."

She did stay in the job until she was nearly three months pregnant. After that she had rather a bad time, with a good deal of morning sickness, so she gave up the job. At six months she had a miscarriage. She was disturbed, partly because she felt it showed her incompetence, but Don was very sympathetic and told her to look on the bright side. Perhaps it would have been a bit soon anyway, and they were still young, they would try again.

When she had her second miscarriage he said that perhaps they weren't meant to have children. She had not gone back to her job because it hardly seemed worthwhile, and after the second miscarriage she found that she didn't really want to work again.

It was at this point that Tess arrived. She was a nice little black sedan, three years old but for that reason a real bargain. Don lifted the hood and expatiated on the cleanliness of what lay inside.

"It's lovely." Then Moira added doubtfully, "But can we afford it?"

"Have I ever bought anything we couldn't afford?" Don asked, and it was perfectly true that he never had. It turned out that he had received another minor promotion and was now an Assistant Personnel Officer in the large corporation for which he worked. He proudly showed her the name "Tess" which he had stuck on to the side of the car with plastic letters. It was one of several names they had talked about for the baby.

There could be no doubt that Tess was a boon and a blessing. They took her occasionally on trips to the seaside, and were able to visit Don's family at weekends. His father was a retired bank manager and lived with his wife in a semi-detached house at Elmers End, a pleasant enough house but, as Don said every time they left, you couldn't compare Elmers End with Gainham Woods.

Sometimes Don's brother and sister also came to Elmers End. They were both married, and it was a real family party. Moira had no family, or none that was ever mentioned. Her father, a grocer, had gone off with another woman when Moira was in her teens, and after his departure her mother had taken gas. Of course, Moira could not be held responsible for any of this, but she always felt that the Bradburys thought their son had married beneath him.

Don had already passed his driving test—one of the things Moira had admired about him from their first meeting at the Conservative Club dance was his competence in practical matters; but she couldn't drive. As he said, there was no point in wasting money going to a school when he could easily teach her how. It would be a pleasure, he said, and on the first day that she sat in the driver's seat, with Don beside her explaining the gears and saying that there was nothing to it, not really, but it was just a bit tricky going from third down to second gear, she thought it might be a pleasure too, but this did not prove to be the case.

Don was immensely patient—that was another of the things she had always admired in him—but it took her a long time to understand just when and how to shift gears. First gear was close to reverse, and she frequently engaged one when she meant to use the other. And somehow Don's habit of treating every drive as an adventure didn't help.

"You see that Austin up ahead there," he would say. "Just crawling along. We're going to pass that fellow. Get ready now. Up into top, arm out to show you're passing, and away we go! No, steady now, something coming the other way, tuck yourself in behind him—right. Now, road's clear, give her all you've got." And as they passed the car he would beam. "Managed that all right though you went out too far, nearly had us in the ditch."

"I'm sorry."

"Nothing to worry about. Turn down this side road—no, left, not right. And you didn't give an arm signal."

"I shall never be able to do it! There's so *much* to remember."

"Don't worry. If at first you don't succeed, try, try again—as Confucius says. Now, this road takes us back into town and when we're back we'll try some low-gear practice."

After six weeks of lessons he said she was ready to take her test. A day or two before it was due, however, she misinterpreted something he told her, turned left instead of right, and then stalled the engine. When she started up again, she confused reverse with first and drove straight into a tree. While Don got out to look at the damage she sat over the steering wheel and wept.

"Poor old girl." He was addressing the car. "She's had a nasty knock. Buckled her bumper." He came back and patted Moira's shoulder. "Never mind. Worse things happen at sea. Shall I drive back?"

She got out. "I never want to drive that bloody car again!"

"Now, now, it's not her fault." He patted the hood, got in, and turned on the ignition. The motor hummed. "She's a good old girl, Tess is."

It proved possible to beat out the buckled bumper, and when it was resprayed you couldn't tell that anything had happened. At least, that was what Don said, but she caught him occasionally giving comparative glances at the bumpers, and she knew that for him the repaired one didn't look *quite* the same as the rest of the car. When he mentioned her taking the test she shook her head. "No, I won't take it. I don't want to drive that car, ever—I hate it!"

"You're being hysterical." It was his severest term of condemnation. "But perhaps it would be a good thing to delay taking the test for the time being."

"I shall never drive it again."

Four years had passed since then and Moira had kept her word. They still had Tess—who was getting, as Don said, a bit long in the tooth but was a gallant old girl. He spent a good deal of time with the car, cleaning it inside and out every week, making adjustments in the carburettor, checking the spark plugs. She was in beautiful condition, except that the gears had become a little dicky. They had a tendency to slip, and there were even a couple of occasions when Don himself had shifted into reverse instead of into first, although he always caught himself in time. He was shocked when she suggested that they should buy another car.

"Get rid of Tess, you wouldn't want to do that! There's a lot of life in her yet, before she's ready to be put on the junk heap."

But although Moira had not driven Tess again, she had passed her driving test. She saved a pound a week of the money Don gave her every month for household expenses, took lessons at a local driving school, and passed the test the first time. She never told him about this, partly because he would have been upset, partly because—well, she couldn't have said exactly why, but it was a thing she had done entirely on her own and she wanted to nurse her feeling of achievement.

It was after this small achievement that she found herself looking at her husband with a more critical eye. She became conscious of the fact that his sandy hair was rapidly thinning, and what had once appeared to her as profound or witty remarks now seemed obvious clichés. Also his devotion to doing everything in a certain way ("there's one right way and a thousand wrong ones") which she used to admire so much now seemed to her a childish insistence on routine. Why, for example, did he always come home on the six-fifteen train, she asked, why not sometimes take an earlier one? He assumed what she regarded as his wounded expression.

"There's work to be done, my dear. A.H. himself never leaves before five thirty."

"Just sometimes—say, once a month. You can't tell me A.H. would mind that?" A.H. was Head of Personnel.

"I daresay not. But it wouldn't be quite the thing."

"Or catch a later one then—have a drink with the boys."

"I don't see the point. The next one's the six forty-seven, and the six-fifteen's a better train. Mind you, if there's a reason why I should get off earlier one day I can manage it—no problem there. Did you have something in mind?"

"No, no, nothing at all. It doesn't matter."

You've become middle-aged at thirty, she thought, and I'm still young at twenty-seven. The mirror, which showed a neat little figure and a pretty, slightly discontented, and somehow unused face, did not contradict her. She had hair which Don had called Titian when they first met, and a white milky skin.

In Gainham Woods, where she saw nobody except the neighbours, most of whom had children, these things were being wasted, but when she suggested that they might move nearer to London he was astounded. It was healthy out here, the neighbourhood was pleasant, you could see green things growing. They would never get a place with such a good garden. He had become devoted to gardening and had recently bought a whole set of gleaming new chromium-headed tools, including a special hoe and a rake whose sharp tines shone like silver. These tools hung neatly on the rear wall of the garage, just behind the car. What was the point of moving? he asked. Besides, they couldn't afford it.

"What about when you get moved up to become A.H.'s deputy?" Two years earlier he had told her that this was likely.

"Yes, well." He hesitated.

"You'll get more money then." He said nothing. "You mean you won't get the job?"

"Salisbury's had a step up."

Salisbury was another Assistant Personnel Officer, and Don's deadly rival.

"He's been made Deputy?" she persisted.

"In a way. There's been a reorganization."

"But he's moved up and you stay where you are."

"At the moment. I think A.H. may have something special in mind for me. In any position you're really dealing with people, man to man. That's my strength, as A.H. says. Salisbury's really just an administrator."

"But he gets more money?"

"I tell you, there may be something special ahead for me. In a year or two."

He looked away as he spoke and she knew that there was nothing special ahead for him, that he was a nonentity who had climbed the short way he would ever go up the ladder of success. When he added that he would get his yearly increase and that the corporation had a wonderful pension scheme, she saw a vision of herself in Gainham Woods forever, seeing the same people, being driven in Tess every other Sunday to see

Don's father and mother, going to the pictures once a week, having sex once a month, going in Tess to an English seaside resort for a holiday once a year. The car seemed the symbol of this terrible routine.

"When shall we get rid of that car?"

"Tess? She may need a new battery soon, but she's running beautifully now I've tuned up the engine."

"Shall we still have her when you're pensioned off? Perhaps she'll outlive us and come to the funeral." She began to laugh on a high note.

"If that's meant to be funny, I think it's a very poor joke."

A few weeks later Moira had a letter from a solicitor telling her that her father had died out in New Zealand. It seemed that he had done rather well out there, and although he had married the woman he went off with and she got most of his money, he had remembered Moira in his will to the tune of several thousands.

She spoke to Don again about moving, saying that they could use her money as deposit on a new house. He positively refused. It was her money, and he wouldn't think of using it for any such purpose.

"After all, I'm the breadwinner, my dear, and that's how it should be. I'm quite able to support us both."

He had taken to calling her "my dear" lately, but she did not say how middle-aged it made her feel, or how much it irritated her.

"Couldn't we at least use the money, some of the money, to get another car? A new one."

His mouth turned down in the expression that she had once thought conveyed strength of character. Now it just seemed to her to show weak, pouting obstinacy.

"I shouldn't think of getting rid of Tess."

"I could buy a car of my own."

He looked at her in astonishment. "Where should we keep it? I couldn't turn Tess out of the garage. And anyway, my dear, your driving—"

He did not finish the sentence. It was on the tip of her tongue to say that she had passed the test with flying colours, but what was the use? It was true they only had a one-car garage, and if she bought a car it would not be allowed to stand in the road.

So she said nothing further. Don read all the financial columns to discover the safest forms of investment, and consulted Mr Bradbury who advised putting the inheritance into National Savings. It stayed on deposit in the bank.

Twice a year Don went away on group study courses to which the corporation sent their personnel officers. The courses lasted five days, and it was during one of his absences that she went to Marjorie Allenden's party. Marjorie had been to school with Moira, and they had met in a department store when Moira went up to London to do some shopping. Marjorie worked on a fashion magazine and was married to Clive, who worked in some editorial capacity on a glossy weekly.

The Allendens had a flat just off Earl's Court Road. It was furnished with brightly coloured sofas and eccentrically shaped chairs. There were lots of paintings on the walls, most of them abstracts. Moira was very impressed. It was just the kind of place she would have liked, although she did not say so. The mantelpiece was quite bare except for a large Victorian teapot, and Marjorie drew the attention of all her visitors to this.

"Clive picked it up in the Portobello Road for thirty bob," she said in the high emphatic voice she seemed to have acquired. "Don't you think it's too fascinatingly hideous?"

"Just hideous," a voice behind Moira murmured. It belonged to a dark young man of about her own age who wore narrow light-blue trousers, a dark-blue jersey, and the small gold-rimmed spectacles that she knew were the latest thing. When he smiled at her she smiled back.

His name was Louis and he was a partner in a photographic agency. While they drank some kind of rather potent reddish liquid they talked—rather, he talked and she listened. Through the hum of noise she heard that he was an American who had been in London for two years now, and wasn't going back.

"I've always wanted to go to New York," she said.

"Beside London it's just dead, baby."

"It's not your scene," she ventured. It was a word she had often heard used by young people on television; but perhaps she used it wrongly, because he laughed.

"You're wonderful." He looked at her through those fascinating little gold-rimmed glasses. "Look, this is strictly from Deadsville. What do you say we get out of here and eat? I know a nice little place."

His car was parked just outside the house, ignoring the forbidding double yellow lines, and she gasped when she saw it. It was long, sleek, low and immensely wide, and seemed to be totally enclosed in glass. When she ducked down into the passenger seat she had the double feeling of being almost on the ground because the car was so low, and of being on the bridge of a ship with total visibility all round her. He dropped into the seat beside her, gunned the engine, and she felt the exciting surge of power as they drove away.

She asked what make of car it was and he said casually it was Italian, a Ghiani-Lucia, a make she had never heard of. "Felix Ghiani's a friend of mine, asked me to try it out."

They reached the restaurant and she felt that people were looking at her as they got out of the gleaming monster. Louis was known, a doorman rushed forward to greet him, and inside the restaurant everybody knew him; the head waiter left another table to come over and shake hands.

Afterwards she tried to remember what they ate and drank, but although she clearly recalled the long menu and could even see the mauve ink in which it was written, she had not the faintest recollection of any of the dishes or the wines. But she could afterwards remember talking about herself, about Don and the boredom of life in Gainham Woods, and possibly—she was not quite sure of this—about her hatred of Tess.

Once or twice she had caught him looking at her through his gold rims with a speculative gaze, as though she were a creature of some new species to whom he was giving coolly sympathetic consideration. At the end of the meal he said, "Coffee at my pad, as you cool young hipsters put it."

"You're laughing at me," she said happily. She longed to be back inside the Ghiani-Lucia, to feel the exhilarating movement of it beneath her.

The drive was all that she had expected and when they reached his flat she was a little drunk, just enough to make the outlines of everything seem faintly hazy—but not so drunk that she failed to look forward with excitement to the prospect of making love. Yet in the end the exciting prospect turned into something rather dismayingly practical and even disappointing when he said that he thought every woman should remember the Boy Scouts' motto, "Be Prepared", before going to a party, and then seemed to take for granted a great deal that was strange and uncongenial to her. Afterwards she looked at his dark hairy body, thought of the clean metallic power within the Ghiani-Lucia, and shuddered slightly. At the same time it occurred to her that Don might phone home, and she was suddenly eager to be back.

"Okay, I'll ring for a taxi." She had hoped he would take her in the car, but did not say so. "I'd take you myself, but it's been a hard day."

"It's not very far." She wanted very much to ride in the car again.

His gaze was mocking. "Gainham Woods? Baby, I've never been that far in my life."

On the way back she cried, although she could not have said exactly why. The taxi took her home and she paid the man off at the end of the road. In the house she looked at everything as though it belonged to a stranger, then went out into the garage, turned on the light, and stared at the dull black car. Don did not phone.

She telephoned Louis the next day, not because she particularly wanted to see him, but because she wanted to experience again the excitement she had felt in the car. He said that he was going out of town and wasn't sure when he would be back. "Don't call me, baby, I'll call you," he said. She put down the phone without saying goodbye.

Two days later, on Friday night, Don returned. The group study course had been pretty exhausting, he said, had anything happened in his absence? Yes, she said, she had something to tell him. She showed him her driver's licence and he was as surprised as she had expected. He agreed that she could drive Tess, but she sensed his lack of enthusiasm.

On Saturday morning she sat in the driver's seat. But Tess would not start.

Don had the hood up in a flash, but soon closed it. "Battery's almost dead. Perhaps if I push her out she might start. You guide her."

She nodded. It was a small garage and he had to squeeze round to get between the car and the rear wall. The gleaming row of garden instruments was directly behind him. He levered himself against the wall and pushed the car ahead of him two or three yards, then indicated that she should try again to start it. She turned the ignition and the motor came to life.

Don raised a thumb. "Good old girl. Now back her out."

She put the car into reverse (as she explained to a sympathetic coroner at the inquest) and released the clutch. But it moved forward instead of back. She lost her head, tried to brake, instead pushed the accelerator harder, and then . . .

The sympathetic coroner spared her the necessity of going on. Don was standing directly in front of the rake. He was transfixed by the sharp new tines like a piece of bread on a toasting fork. But if the rake had not been there, the coroner said consolingly, he would undoubtedly have been crushed to death against the wall.

An expert motor-car engineer gave evidence. He said that the car was very old and badly needed new gears. You hardly needed to depress the clutch to move from one gear to another. It was the easiest thing in the world to slip into first instead of reverse.

Friends and neighbours were very sympathetic, like the coroner. Don Bradbury had made himself known and respected in Gainham Woods, and indeed they were a most devoted couple. "He was a real member of our community," the vicar said to Moira at the funeral.

Afterwards she got rid of Tess. As she explained to Marjorie Allenden, she couldn't keep a car that had killed her husband. It was Marjorie who helped her to find a nice little flat in Camden Town, which at least wasn't in the heart of deadly exurbia like Gainham Woods.

A week after moving in she bought a Ghiani-Lucia.

DETECTIVE'S WIFE

Herbert Harris

THERE WAS AN air of quiet menace about the house that afternoon.

Linda could not quite put a finger on it, but she knew it was there, that feeling of menace that seemed to crawl insidiously under the skin.

The baby in the next room kept on crying, sometimes in pettish whimpers, at other times exploding into loud sobs.

Linda was not sure which was worse, the vocal outbursts of the baby or that terrible silence when the crying stopped.

She was not usually as jumpy as this. A premonition of something perhaps? But a premonition of what?

The afternoon was dragging on. Soon the daylight would be fading into dusk. It would be worse then . . .

She went to the street door and slipped the safety-chain into its slot. She had got out of the habit of actually using the safety-chain, but this afternoon . . .

The baby became vociferous again and she called out, "Yes, all right, all right, my precious, I'm coming!"

She picked up the baby, and the crying turned to plaintive gurgles as she dispensed comfort. "My goodness, you are a big cry-baby today, aren't you? What is it, then?"

Maybe the baby, too, felt the crawling menace—like a dog whose hackles rise in the presence of an unknown terror . . .

She ought to have a dog really in this isolated empty house. Perhaps she ought to speak to Geoff about it . . .

As she put the baby down, the doorbell rang suddenly, the shrill sound scything unnervingly through the silence.

Linda went to the street door.

"Who is it?" she shouted, an irritable edge to her voice.

"It's all right, Linda, it's only me—Janet!" The comforting familiar voice of a woman friend.

She released the safety-chain and opened the door.

Her visitor had noticed the rough edge to Linda's voice. "Oh, hello, Linda—am I being an awful nuisance?"

"No, no, of course not, Janet! Only . . . well, Baby was being a bit vocal . . . and then I thought you might be the laundryman . . . and I haven't got the laundry ready yet . . . and . . . oh, you know, just one of those days when things never seem to go smoothly . . ."

"Well, I'm not stopping," Janet said. "I just looked in for a minute, as I happened to be passing your place in the car. The infant seems to have quietened down for a moment . . . ?"

"Yes, a bit of peace at last. Not for long, though. Can't you stay for a cup of tea?"

"No, I won't stay, Linda. As I was out this way, I thought I would give you these tickets for the Hospital Dance on Saturday. Will you be able to get a baby-sitter?"

Linda shrugged ruefully. "I'm hoping to persuade Geoff's mother to come over and sit for us."

"What about the girl who usually comes—Mary, isn't it?"

Linda said, "I don't like to ask her now. She's a bit nervous about being left in the cottage on her own."

"Well, I can't say I blame her," Janet replied. "After all, you're a bit isolated out here, aren't you?"

"Yes, that's why we bought the place cheap," Linda told her. "One gets used to it after a while."

Janet frowned. "But do you feel *safe*?"

Linda thought: perhaps today I *don't* feel safe. But she was not going to admit it. Instead, she laughed. "Of course! Why not?"

Her friend said, "I mean, Geoff does leave you on your own quite a lot. And then . . . his job makes you a bit of a target, doesn't it?"

"Target?" Linda laughed again. "Really, Janet, you've been watching too many police thrillers on television. Just because Geoff is a detective sergeant, it doesn't mean that we have gangsters shooting it out across the flower-beds every five minutes!"

This time Janet laughed with her hostess. "No, I suppose not. But if *I* was a detective's wife all alone in an isolated cottage, I should start thinking about all the thugs coming out of jail with a grudge against my husband."

"You would get used to it—like me," Linda told her.

Janet looked at her watch. "Will Geoff be home soon?"

Linda said, "About six o'clock, I expect—that is, if something doesn't turn up to delay him."

The baby in the next room began crying again, and Linda went on, "Oh dear, here we go again! The joys of motherhood!"

"Oh well, you go and do your duty, darling," Janet said. "I *would* have stayed for tea, but I've got to rush off because I promised to pick somebody up at the station. 'Bye, darling. See you on Saturday at the dance. Give my love to Geoff."

"All right, Janet . . . 'Bye!"

Linda closed the door and heard Janet's car whirr away into the distance.

A deep silence again except for the child's whimpering.

Once again she comforted the baby. "There, there, my pet . . . What's the matter with my silly cry-baby, then?"

The fretful whimpering ceased, and the silence—the complete silence—folded itself around her again.

Suddenly the doorbell rang again. The sound was more strident and unnerving than before.

She went to the door. "Is that the laundry?"

No answer. Only the silence. She called out again, "Is that the laundry?"

A man's voice answered "Yes!"

Linda opened the door.

She said fearfully, in a choked whisper, "But you're not . . . !"

He stepped quickly into the hall, and she let out a small scream. He smothered the scream with a hand clamped over her mouth.

She struggled ineffectually against the grip of strong young arms, her eyes wild as she watched him shut the door with a backward kick.

He released her, and stood with his back against the door in a queer lounging posture, insolent and challenging.

Breathlessly, jerking the words out aggressively to hide the tremble in her voice, she demanded, "What do you want?"

A smile flickered briefly on his face, then was snuffed out, and she saw only the cruel mouth and the pale menacing eyes.

He was quite young, she decided, a youthful delinquent with, already, a lengthy record of lawlessness. His eyes roamed over her body. Perhaps, she thought, he would rape her. The trouble was, as Geoff said, rapists all too often killed their victims . . .

"It's all right, kid," he said in a crude mixture of London cockney and Chicago hoodlum, "you'll be okay if you don't try any funny business."

Her heartbeats were thundering in her ears. She stood as still as a statue, looking at him, hiding her terror behind a façade of forced calmness.

"But . . . what is it? . . . what do you want?" she managed to say.

"I've a bit of business to settle with your husband, kid," he said.

"Oh . . ."—a pause, then she called out to an empty house: "Geoff! Geoff! Can you come downstairs for a minute, darling!"

There was a long silence, taut as stretched elastic. Then, faintly, the renewed whimpering of the baby in the next room.

He smiled crookedly at her. "That kind of bluff won't work, Mrs Mason. I've been watching and listening . . . and I know he isn't at home, see?"

There was a tiny convulsive movement in her throat. She said, "I'm afraid I've got to go and see to Baby . . ."

He moved towards her threateningly. "Stay where you are! Don't move!" A pause. "Now then, when do you expect him home, kid—soon?"

"Yes," she answered automatically.

"That's fine," he said.

Linda added desperately, "No . . . no . . . I don't know."

"You're a liar," he said. "You're expecting him soon."

"He . . . he may be late."

"How late?"

"I . . . I don't know. I'm never sure. He . . . he may be delayed. When he expects to be late, he usually rings and tells me."

"In that case, I'll wait," he said.

"It won't be worth your waiting!"

"I'll wait just the same," he told her.

Linda and the man stood eyeing each other. Then, backing away from him almost imperceptibly, she turned with a sudden movement and snatched wildly at the telephone.

He was on her in a flash, wrenching the receiver from her hands and slamming it back home in its cradle.

"I wouldn't try that again, kid, if I was you," he said. "If you do, I might be tempted to use *this* . . ."

She looked at the black automatic which had suddenly appeared in his hand.

"You won't need a gun," she told him. "I haven't got one."

"Then you'll have to get your 'old man' to fix you up with one, won't you?" he sneered at her.

Linda said, "I don't scare easily, you know. I've seen guns before. They don't make me faint with fright."

"So you won't mind if I keep it in my hand, kid, will you? That's where it belongs. It makes me feel good. Puts me on top, see?"

"Yes," she said wearily. "I'm sure it does."

He said, "Turn around and walk into the sitting-room."

She hesitated. "Look, I . . ."

"Do as I tell you!" he barked at her brutally. "Get into the sitting-room, and quick!"

Linda said, "I ought to see to Baby . . ." The baby had started whimpering again.

He rapped out, "When I say so—not before! Go on . . . get moving."

She walked into the sitting-room, the young intruder close behind her.

"Now then . . . sit down!" She hesitated, and he scowled. "I said *sit down*!" She sat. He said, "Right. Now we'll wait. And if you get any fancy ideas, kid . . . Don't forget I've got this! And it ain't no water-pistol. It's the real thing. And I shoot to kill—you got that, baby?"

Linda said, "How did you get to talk like that—from going to the movies?"

"Yeah, maybe." Thick dark eyebrows met in the centre of his low brow. "But I like scaring the pants off people, because I'm bad. I get a real kick out of being bad. Everyone says so."

"And you think you're going to scare my husband?" Linda asked.

"Oh, no, I ain't going to scare him," he said, "I'm going to kill him."

Linda said flatly, numbly, "No . . ."

The eyebrows met above his nose again. "I wonder what's the best way of doing it. If he's got a key, he comes straight in . . . I could shoot him as he walks through the door . . .

"Or maybe I could shoot him as he gets out of his car . . . from this window?

"Either way, kid, he's not going to get a chance . . . That'll be the beauty of it . . . He won't have a cat-in-hell's chance."

She felt the blood drain out of her face, but asked him almost calmly, "Why do you want to kill my husband? Just because he's a detective?"

"You don't recognise me, do you?" he said.

She shook her head.

"The name's Terry Hagan. That mean anything to you?"

She shook her head again.

"I had a kid brother," he told her. "Paddy Hagan. We always worked together—ever since we were kids. We did that big warehouse job together. The one that was in all the papers. Remember?"

Linda made no reply.

"The bloody cops tried to trap us . . . up there on the roof. And that's when we had to let 'em have it, see? Paddy got shot. My kid brother. They took him to hospital. He died there with a bullet in his guts. And do you know the cop who shot him? I'll give you three guesses, kid . . . It was your 'old man' . . . Detective Sergeant Bloody Mason. Did you know?"

"No, I didn't know."

"You know now, don't you?"

She said, "I suppose he was only doing his job."

"But he killed my kid brother!"

"You were shooting too," she argued. "You shot a policeman."

He scowled. "That was just an accident. They shot my kid brother in cold blood."

"I don't believe that."

"They shot him in cold blood, I tell you. He didn't have a chance! But me . . . me they didn't get, see?"

"If you kill my husband," she said, her face paper-white, "you'll spend the rest of your life in prison."

"I'll do that anyway if they get me," he said. "But Geoff Mason's going first. One more don't make no difference!"

Linda sat staring at him, saying nothing.

"It's now or never," he said. "I've been waiting my chance for weeks, waiting to do to *him* what he did to Paddy. I've taken a big risk coming here, kid . . . and there won't be another chance!"

The baby's whimpering suddenly burst into an explosion of sobbing.

He said, "What the hell's wrong with that brat of yours? It's getting on my nerves!"

"You can go if you don't like it," she answered.

"Is it sick or something?"

"Yes," she told him, "sick."

"Well, go and see to it, then, for God's sake. Stop it yelling!"

"I shall have to go in the bedroom," Linda said quietly.

"Okay . . . get cracking. And don't try anything. I'll be right behind you. No . . . wait! . . . listen!"

There was the distant sound of a car. He said, "Is that him?"

Linda said tensely, "I don't know."

The sound of the car died away as it passed on down the lane. He said, "Okay . . . go and see to the brat."

The telephone started ringing. He said, "Wait! Don't move!" It went on ringing. "That's him, isn't it?"

"I expect so," Linda answered.

He bit his lip. "You'd better answer it, then. He'll think something is wrong if you don't answer it. Get into the hall."

She walked slowly into the hall, the young man at her heels.

"Now then . . . answer it . . . Act normal. One word out of place, and *you* go first . . . got that?"

Linda picked up the receiver. She found herself speaking surprisingly levelly. "Bushmill 47 . . ."

Her husband's voice said, "Hello . . . Linda?"

"Yes, darling, this is Linda."

"You were rather a long time answering," Geoff Mason said.

"I know, Geoff," she said, "but I was seeing to your Simon!"

"Simon?"

"Well, you know young Simon was poorly when you left here this morning. He doesn't seem to be any better."

"But, darling, I don't . . ."

"Geoff, dear, I know you think I'm making an unnecessary fuss about Simon, but the medicine he's been having doesn't seem to have done any good, and I'm really worried about him. I think the time has come to call in Doctor Carter . . ."

"Not the usual doctor, then?" Mason asked.

"No," she replied, "Carter. The other man seems to be past it. He doesn't seem to understand that Simon is in a bad way, and I think Dr Carter may be able to help us . . . Everybody speaks very highly of him."

"Yes, love, they do . . ."

"Could you call on him on the way home, then?"

"And fetch him, you mean?"

"Yes, darling."

"All right, Linda, I'll do that."

"He does nothing but cry. Get here as soon as you can, won't you, darling?"

"Sure . . . Don't worry. Simon will be okay. 'Bye for now, dear."

"'Bye, Geoff."

She replaced the receiver, and stood for a moment with her eyes closed. The baby had quietened down again.

"That was nice," the man with the gun told her. "You did that fine. Only fetching the doctor home with him won't help him, kid. He'll be too far gone for any doctor when I've finished with him."

He took hold of her arm, but she tugged it roughly away from him. He said, "Look, kid, don't try and get tough. Nobody gets tough with Terry Hagan, especially dames."

She asked in a tired voice, "What do you want me to do now?"

"The brat's stopped crying, so we can go back to the sitting-room and make ourselves comfortable." He prodded her back into the sitting-room. "Right. Now sit down. All we got to do now is wait . . . just wait . . .

"I've got nothing against you personally, kid, so if you behave yourself and do as I say, nothing will happen to you . . . It's your 'old man' I want . . . just him. It isn't your fault you're married to a stinking copper . . .

"We'll hear his car arrive . . . Then his key in the door . . . That's how it will be, isn't it? But you won't do anything, kid. You won't yell out or throw anything, see? You won't try and warn him. You'll keep perfectly still and quiet, like you are now . . .

"If you don't, I'll blast a hole clean through that pretty bosom of yours. You first . . . and then him as he comes in . . . But you won't want to kick the bucket as well, will you, on account of the baby . . .

"I remember my kid brother looking like your little brat in there . . . That was way back . . . A dozen years ago . . . My Mum got knocked down by a lorry crossing the road, and killed . . . Not that she knew anything about it at the time . . . She was lousy drunk, see. I never knew my father. I was only about seven at the time . . ."

He stopped talking, and looked at her. She sat very still, staring down at the long delicate fingers interlaced in her lap.

He said gruffly, "Aren't you going to say something? I don't like talking to myself, and this bloody silence is getting on my nerves . . . worse than your brat yelling . . ."

Linda neither spoke nor looked at him.

"I must say you're a pretty cool chick," he told her. "I mean you haven't gone crazy or screamed or anything. That's pretty good, kid, considering that I'm going to kill your 'old man' the moment he steps through that door . . ."

She remained doggedly silent.

"Okay . . . if you don't want to talk . . . don't!" he snarled at her.

In the deadly hush all they could hear was the distant ticking of the grandfather clock in the hall, its measured sounds like the heartbeats of eternity.

She imagined that the first intimation of Geoff's arrival would be the crunching sound of his car on the gravel. Then the scuffling of his feet on the porch. After that the click of his key in the lock . . .

But there was none of those sounds.

The first noise, only faintly audible, was a rustle near the window in front of the house, as if somebody had shouldered a path between two of the shrubs.

She glanced swiftly at Terry Hagan. Their eyes met as if by appointment. She knew that he had heard the sound too, and now his whole face was alert, like a hunted animal's, his body stiff with tense vigilance.

Linda looked at the gun. It was levelled at the door that led in from the hall. Her knuckles were milk-white as she gripped the arms of her chair. Her lungs stretched to bursting point as she held her breath.

"What was that noise?" he hissed.

She said, "I didn't hear anything."

"Yes, you did," Hagan said tensely. "I saw your face change. You heard it. Sit still . . . Don't move!" He cocked his ears. "That's it again!"

"It's the wind," she said.

"There's no wind," Hagan answered. "A rustling sound . . . Outside the window . . . Shhh . . . Listen . . . Somebody moving outside . . . Keep still . . . Don't make a sound . . ."

She found her voice, and shrieked out suddenly, "WATCH OUT, GEOFF!"

His eyes, dark and glinting, darted towards her. "Shut up, you bitch, or I'll let you have it!"

But the automatic stayed pointing towards the door through which Geoff Mason would walk.

She ignored his warning. After all, if he fired at her, Geoff would hear the shot, would be warned in time . . .

"DON'T COME IN, GEOFF! DON'T COME IN! DON'T COME IN!" she screamed at the top of her lungs.

The crash of glass was like a bomb-explosion in the silence of the room.

Terry Hagan screamed like a wounded animal as a bullet tore through the flesh and bone of his wrist. She saw his arm jerk upwards in a swift reflex action. The gun leapt from his fingers and thudded to the floor.

"Christ!" Hagan said, whimpering like the baby in the next

room, swaying, staring at his wrist. Blood trickled from it, running in bright red rivulets between his knuckles, staining his cuff.

"Lousy stinking cops!" He moaned in agony. "Lousy stinking goddam cops!"

There was a much louder crash of glass, and the tearing sound of splintered wood as a heavy foot battered open the french doors from the garden.

As the gunman made a wild rush towards the french doors, Geoff Mason ran in from the direction of the hall.

"Okay, Tony, grab him!" Mason shouted.

The strong right arm of Mason's companion wrapped itself around Hagan's neck, jerking his body backwards, making the young gunman cry out with pain.

Mason said, "It's all right, he hasn't got a gun, it's on the floor."

The other detective said, "Yes, I got him clean through the wrist. Not bad shooting, was it?"

Geoff Mason turned to his wife solicitously. "You're all right, sweetheart?"

She nodded. "I'm okay."

"And Baby?"

"Yes. He didn't harm either of us."

"Thank God!"

The other detective said, "He's passed out, Geoff."

"It's Terry Hagan, isn't it?" Mason asked.

"Yes."

"Better rush him to the hospital, Tony. I'll ring Inspector Brooker."

"You needn't bother, Geoff—he's already here."

"Good God, that was quick work," Mason whistled. "You're quite sure you're okay, Linda?"

"Yes, Geoff, quite okay."

Detective Inspector Brooker came bustling into the room.

"Good evening, sir," Mason greeted him. "This is my wife."

The Inspector acknowledged Linda with a polite smile.

"Young Terry Hagan has been holding her as hostage. We've really got my wife to thank for the way things have turned out."

"So it would seem, Sergeant." He frowned in puzzlement.

"But how did you *know* that there was something wrong at the cottage?"

Geoff smiled fondly at his wife, then turned back to his superior.

"Well, sir, it was when I telephoned Linda, you see . . . I thought at first it might be a wrong number I'd got hold of . . . But, then, it couldn't be, because she'd announced the number . . . Bushmill 47 . . . And it was Linda's voice all right . . . No mistaking it . . . And she called me Geoff all the time . . . But, then, her other conversation about the baby—was completely crazy, sir, as if she'd gone off her head . . .

"You see, Inspector, in the first place she spoke about Baby being ill in the morning, which wasn't true . . . And she was calling the baby Simon, which is my *own* second christian name, one I never use, and isn't Baby's name either . . .

"And then she asked me to bring a Doctor Carter—a doctor who doesn't exist, sir . . . And we know only one person called Carter . . . That's Detective Sergeant Tony Carter . . . And he's not only a very good friend of ours, *but also the best pistol shot at headquarters* . . ."

Inspector Brooker nodded approvingly. "So you took the hint and brought Carter with you?"

"Yes, sir. He fired through the window, and, as usual, was absolutely bang on target."

The Inspector smiled. "That sounds like your youngster now, Mason. And if he isn't Simon, what *is* his name?"

Geoff Mason smiled back. "You tell him, Linda."

Linda said, "It's a girl, Inspector. Her name is Hope."

LITTLE KNIVES

Madelaine Duke

RUPERT AND I still sleep in the same room. Between his bed and mine stands the rectangular rosewood table which I made when I consigned our double divan to my studio. Switching to single beds, combined with the new table, was meant to save his pride. It was not that his wife had migrated from his bed—not at all. He'd tell his sister that Elsa had carried out one of her artistic ideas—said with undertones of contempt for all the arts—and re-designed the master bedroom. As a matter of fact it didn't look too bad. When Elsa put her mind to making something practical, like a table, instead of carving these lumps of stone, she usually made a reasonable job of it.

When I got into my new bed it felt wonderful. Better still, the rosewood table put a whole metre between Rupert and me. But he soon killed that little pleasure.

I am half asleep when he comes in from the bathroom, glass of water in hand—as usual. As he sips and then puts it down, asserting his domination of the waxed table-top, I have a vision of the ugly stain he is making. Well, I'll do something about that. Much as I like the feel of natural wood, I'll put glass over the top. Better than letting Rupert irritate me night after night. I know, I know; foolish of me, but I can't help my dislike of seeing finely crafted objects marked and maltreated.

Perhaps it's something to do with being a sculptor. The years have increased the sense that the stone or the wood I'm working is living matter—so much alive that it dictates how I am to treat and shape it. Whenever Rupert sees me pick up a bottle he's put on a polished surface, and surreptitiously slip a mat under it, he gets angry.

"That's all you care about," he niggles. "Never mind that I've been working bloody hard . . . operating on people all day long . . ."

"What's that got to do with putting down a table-mat?" I ask.

"It's your way of nagging," he says. "I come home tired. I want to pour myself a drink and relax, and you . . ."

I escape by contemplating the rose I've put into the Venetian specimen vase until his voice sounds no worse than the whine of my power-drill.

But back to that first night in my new bed. Rupert comes in, sips water, puts down his glass—as he has for the past thirty years. He looks at his watch, takes it off, puts it under his pillow. Then the routine unexpectedly changes.

When we'd had the double bed he'd sat down on it, facing away from me. Now he sits facing me. He slides his feet out of his slippers and then slowly peels off his socks. He always takes off his socks in the last moment before he lies down and puts them on again first thing in the morning before changing into a clean pair.

I feel like asking him whether he'd mind taking off the socks on the far side of the bed, where the dust won't fly in my face. But I don't, because he'd accuse me of being nasty to him. I accuse myself of being an intolerant bitch. Rupert can't help his upbringing; in a London slum, so poorly heated that any bright boy would have kept his socks on until he got into bed. Doesn't everyone suffer from childhood hangovers? Isn't my obsession with neatness and order a childhood hangover?

I can see me arrive home after a typical business day in London. (A client, who'd commissioned marble twin pillars for his house in Hampstead, wants a second pair to make his entrance hall more *important*—for a reduced price, of course.) Right. I walk into our drawing room.

"I didn't hear you come in," complains Rupert.

Is it my fault that he's been glued to the little screen, letting Starsky and Hutch thunder their car into a Chinese laundry?

"Sorry," I say.

He points to a heap of cherries. "Got these for you."

"How nice," I say, but not exuberantly enough.

"What have I done now?" he pounces.

"Nothing . . . nothing." But he's bought me white cherries,

knowing that I like black ones only, and he's put them into the dog-bowl which he won in the hospital raffle.

"Eat," says Rupert, "I bought the cherries for you."

I eat, wandering around the room, straightening the paintings, rearranging the chairs. I hate myself for irritating him, but I can't let well alone. God knows how often I've tried to justify this habit. "Look darling—the way furniture is grouped can be beautiful or ugly. Angles are important. Peggy is great at polishing floors, but she has no feeling for the overall design of rooms."

"What the hell does it matter whether the couch stands at twenty or forty-five degrees to the wall? Your obsession with what you call *order* seems to be more important to you than my comfort."

"Won't you allow me one or two stupidities, Rupert? I've tried to explain . . ."

"Okay, okay . . . You need harmony in your own home— beauty, pleasing shapes and angles. What do you call it—a still centre?—because you feel the cruelties and chaos of the outside world so much—delicate creature that you are—the fighting in Afghanistan, the executions in Iran, all the nasty things you read in the papers . . ."

"Rupert, these things are happening to *people*."

"But not in your drawing-room. Oh no. As long as your cherries are in the right bowl, on the right table, cruelty to your husband is of no account."

Here we go. The wrong cherries in the wrong bowl. He knows. But keep your mouth shut, Elsa. Think—if you must—of Afghanistan, stop throwing the furniture about and don't be cruel to Rupert.

On the revolutionary first night my new bed is no great improvement on the old. In the double Rupert had usually driven me to the edge, sooner or later. I'd wakened, clinging to the mattress as if it were a life-raft, got up, padded around the bed, and climbed back in on the free side—a performance repeated several times a night. In the single bed Rupert has no one to chase. He therefore takes to sprawling on his back, which makes him snore. His roars keep me awake.

Eventually I make myself go to the bathroom. Might go to

sleep on an empty bladder. His dressing-room, which I don't normally see until I clear it up in the morning, is littered with the clothes he's taken off—minus his socks, of course. How does he manage to make these pathetic little heaps so ugly? In the small hours, at my lowest ebb, I'm convinced that his continuing sluttishness is due to a subconscious desire to prove that he's my master.

In the bathroom his towel is lying damp on the carpet. I pick it up, of course. How many soggy towels have I picked up in the past thirty years? The lavatory seat is speckled with yellow drops. It doesn't really matter whether he's remembered to put up the seat or not; his aim's always been casual. I wipe the seat. The washbasin next. Rupert hasn't used the scouring glove beside it. So, before washing my hands, I wipe off the rough rim of scum.

Why, why does he persist in so many unpleasant little habits? He knows how I feel about some of them. Why must he go on twisting his little knives into me? Have I not tried from the beginning to avoid doing things that irritate him? On the whole I've succeeded to the extent that I never cook a dish he doesn't like, never clear up a room in his presence, never ask when he'll be home for dinner, never mention that he's drinking too much. Surely he wouldn't do things I dislike if he cared for me—not to say, if he loved me. Can he help it if he's never loved anyone but himself; not even you, our daughter?

Don't ask me why I've stayed with your father, my darling Janet. It's something I don't understand myself, not even with hindsight. It isn't as if the relationship between Rupert and me had begun as a great passion.

When we met at the concert in Vienna, in that improbable hall of fat-bottomed baroque cherubs, we were a couple of English-speaking people among foreigners. I'd been in Vienna longer than Rupert, so I could give him the information he wanted—about the all-night drinking places in Grinzing. After the Eroica, which was noisy enough to keep him awake, he took me out for a meal at Sacher's. I knew that he wanted me, and I wanted to be wanted. Vienna had made me feel lonelier than ever. Back in London I slept with Rupert.

Our first night together was excruciating. He didn't satisfy me. Worse, he failed in satisfying himself. He just managed to bruise my legs and my pubic bone. I felt nothing but sympathy for his joylessness. And I thought a surgeon was bound to get it right in the end. After all he had to know some anatomy, something about erotic areas.

After our marriage, when the physical position hadn't improved, I tried to analyse the trouble. I came to a few conclusions and tried to discuss them with Rupert. Wouldn't it work better if he gentled me for a while, instead of pouncing on me like a rapist the moment I got into bed. Wouldn't he do better if he cut down the whisky? Wouldn't he be more successful if he made love to me in the morning, when he was rested and relaxed, instead of flogging himself to sleep at night? His reaction to my suggestions? He was offended and said I didn't know what I was talking about. I never had the heart to tell him that the man who'd been my first lover had made sex a delight and that he, Rupert, made it—unnecessarily—a joyless wifely chore. After that, just once or twice, I did try to change his agonizing night habits. It was love's labour lost.

I needn't have gone on living with him. It wasn't his money that kept me tied. By the time we married I had made a name as a sculptor. My commissions included the big *bas-relief* on the city bank, the *Playing Children* in the forecourt of a New York college, and enough lesser works to keep me and my daughter in civilized comfort.

So why did I stay? The answer that served in the past—it doesn't seem true now—is that Rupert needed me. He was so poverty-stricken emotionally; he had many acquaintances and colleagues, but no real friends; his life would be so bleak and shadowy if I didn't make friends for us both, if I didn't give parties and create an attractive background for him.

He has never mentioned to me that he likes this background of a well-known artist-wife and a beautiful home. But people have told me that he talks with pride of my professional successes or the new studio *we* have built or the garden *we* have made. Yet, whenever I suggested improvements like the studio or the garden he bitterly opposed my ideas, until I went ahead and carried them out without his blessing.

Did I stay with him because I pitied his bleakness and

loneliness? or did I stay because I feared my own innate loneliness? One should, perhaps, take into account that I have no family of my own, apart from you, Janet. All my relations were killed in the war.

My female friends almost envy me my helpful husband, who has allowed me to have a *career*, who's put up with the inconvenience of my working away from home now and again. It hasn't occurred to any of them that we might welcome the occasional break.

When I do work at home there are incidents—like when Mr Ferguson, the museum curator, came to dinner. We were to discuss the *bas-relief* for the new library wing. We talked about details of the design in my studio. Rupert came in and served drinks. He said my design, if Ferguson wanted his opinion, wasn't quite in keeping with the building, was it? He explained at length how he would tackle the job—remarkably eloquent with ignorance. He said the *protuberances* would soon get covered in birdshit. He said I was a talented little woman, but so unpractical.

By the time Peggy served dinner Mr Ferguson had lost all faith in my work. Oh yes, the *bas-relief* was commissioned because the committee had already approved the design. But nothing ever killed the story that I'd been given the job because I'd charged less than another sculptor who'd been in the running.

What had come over Rupert that evening? Just a bad mood? No, it's been a regular feature—his habit of publicly denigrating my work. Implication: I'd be incapable of making a living as a sculptor if he, the practical professional man, weren't providing me with the roof over my head.

I suppose there's no such thing as an ideal marriage. There are usually faults on both sides. A useful cliché, don't you think?

To return to the first night of the single beds. I've left the bathroom, around four in the morning. I am in the studio. I've taken the sheet off my half-finished sculpture of the Three Graces—a new, original concept of the classic theme. It'll go into the Summer Exhibition of the Royal Academy. I'm certain the committee will accept it, if for no other reason than that it's been commissioned by a famous patron of the arts for a London park. Examining the lines and angles of the figures drains the agitation out of me and makes me feel serene. The Three Graces are more real than Rupert's dusty socks or the bespattered lavatory seat.

Janet, I have admitted to myself that this will be my last big, important sculpture. (As you know I do my best work on large-scale projects.) Why? Well, I don't like talking about aches and pains—it's boring—but my spine is giving me a lot of trouble. Dr Brown—Rupert has made me consult him—says that the years of hard physical labour have so affected the spine that parts have worn out. The prognosis is gradual deterioration, but it's a mechanical problem—not an illness. The other nuisance is stomach cramps. Dr Brown sent me to hospital for investigation. No cause was discovered for my periodic stomach pains.

Dr Brown and I have agreed that the pains are due to stress. Me, I agreed reluctantly. My work certainly isn't stressful. I enjoy it even at its most demanding. You, dear Janet, give me no trouble. You seem fulfilled as a writer, satisfied with your husband and children. I say *seem* because no outsider can ever be certain, though I think you'd have told me by now if your marriage were as resounding a failure as mine.

That leaves stress due to Rupert. It's my fault if I let myself be affected by the trivial little knives he's stuck into me all these years. More self-control; that's what I need. I wish I had the strength I used to have though; my niggling spine and temperamental stomach are taking their toll.

Rupert, bless him, is doing his best. For the past two years he's walked the dog for me. (I'm rather stiff first thing in the morning.) And he makes his own breakfast. When I get up, after he's gone to the hospital, I find the cooker caked with coffee-grounds. I clean it. Shut up Elsa. Remember your stress-prone stomach and Rupert's new-found kindness.

Rupert is keeping up an end-of-day effort too; China tea, as I used to make it. Put tea into the perforated silver egg, dip it into the glasses of boiling water in their silver holders—a clean, fragrant night-cap. It used to be when I made it. Rupert doesn't clean the tea-egg or wash the glasses properly. He insists on doing these chores and is offended when Peggy or I clean the implements.

"Not good enough my way, is it Elsa? You make it quite impossible for anyone to look after you."

I say that I appreciate his tea. I'd hoped he wouldn't mind my cleaning the things occasionally, but in future I will leave it to him. So, the silver-egg has turned from brown to black and the tea tastes foul.

I don't remember when I first got the idea that Rupert was putting some drug into my tea. For a moment—as it occurred to me—I wondered whether I was losing my sanity. Certainly not. I've never been hysterical, let alone paranoic. Rupert wasn't treating me with any show of affection, but that was normal. Surely poor Rupert was being kinder than ever before, walking the dog, making tea. His way of acknowledging my aching back. But tea, made with a dirty egg in dirty glasses, was bound to taste a little peculiar. For that matter his glass is no cleaner than mine.

Routine established, I no longer clean *his* tea things. Every night I must go to bed first. He insists. Then he comes in with the two tumblers in their silver holders and puts them on the glass-topped table, one beside his bed, one beside mine. Then he goes to change into his pyjamas and to the bathroom. By the time he returns his tea is cold, which he blames on my stupid system of making it.

In the days of our double bed he'd have pulled off his socks, got in and sipped his tea, ruminating on his prospects for the night. Was he ready to drop off or would he sleep more soundly if he tired himself on my body? If the latter, he'd begin by grinding his unshaven face into mine. In the morning my skin would feel raw. I'd asked him once or twice to use his electric razor before turning in, but that had turned him off. He's never forgiven me for it. Now his unshaven state no longer matters. He hasn't once attempted his acrobatics on my bed. He'd said from the beginning that a single bed was not conducive to love-making. Thank heavens for that. Nowadays he wouldn't just bruise my pubic bone, he'd break my back.

Well, I have dismissed the silly notion that he's poisoning

my tea with drug samples provided by the endless stream of pharmaceutical company representatives who call on doctors. For one thing Rupert wouldn't have enough imagination to do such a thing; for another he'd probably have to combine the samples of half a dozen companies to produce something suitably lethal, and that would be too much trouble.

All the same—when he's put the tea glasses on the table and gone to his dressing-room I take his glass and put mine beside his bed. It's become a habit. When he returns he always drinks the tea. No hesitation. It makes me realize my foolishness. Other considerations apart, if Rupert were doctoring my glass of tea he would be the one to suffer. But he's keeping fit, very fit.

I'm writing all this down in the mornings, after Rupert's gone to work. For my benefit or for yours, Janet? Yes, writing down what is—in a way—the story of a marriage helps me let off steam. Yet I don't think I'd make the effort if it weren't for you. You've always been curious about human relationships, especially your parents'. If I had recognized your curiosity as a facet of a novelist's mind—if I'd understood that while you were still living with us—I would have answered your questions more truthfully. I'm making up for my evasions now.

My conclusions about marriage are that it is not the big spectacular injuries a couple inflict upon one another which spoil the relationship. It's the sum total of trivia—such as I've been telling you—that kill a marriage. Not just Rupert's and mine. A good many of my friends, who believe in my discretion, have told me about the little knives that cut into their marriages. The little knives come in many forms, but basically they all do similar damage. It's just a matter of degree—small lacerations that heal over quickly and cleanly, deep cuts that take time to heal, or ragged wounds that become festering sores.

I've been lucky in being given so much more in life than a marriage. I've had joy in you and joy in my sculpturing. Janet, the Three Graces are finished. I believe it's one of the best things I've done. I wish I had the strength to begin work on the piece of marble which arrived six months ago—your exciting birthday present. I have an idea for it. But I won't start until the summer. I've always had more energy in summer. It's not so much the warmth. It's the light I need—those wonderful balances of light and shade.

I wish I didn't feel so tired.

It's a funny thing. Rupert never used to call Dr Brown when I was ill in the past. Not that I was ever seriously ill—just the odd touch of flu. Now he calls the doctor every few days. Dr Brown tells me that Rupert is terribly concerned about my health.

I am concerned about my looks. I'm fifty-five, but all of a sudden I've come to look ten years older—thin, pale and lacklustre. So, I've taken to putting on make-up first thing in the morning. It helps, also, *vis-à-vis* Rupert. He'd been complaining of my pallor as if I'd accused him of causing it. He, who'd never told me that I looked good or otherwise, has actually asked me why I don't put some pink stuff on my cheeks. I really should appreciate it when he shows such concern. Yet, the more he's trying to do for me the more I keep asking myself why he is making such efforts.

Janet, I've got the answer. Back to our nightly tea-ceremony. Last night it took place as usual, except that your father returned to the bedroom unexpectedly—for no reason I could discern—before he'd changed into his pyjamas. I had just changed over the glasses and I was very conscious of the way he was gazing at his glass. As I had just put it down on his side the tea was still astir. He picked up the glass—he was actually smiling—and drained it.

"You're a funny one," he said, as if I'd done something that amused him.

"Why?" I asked him.

"How long have you been switching our glasses?"

"That's silly," I protested, rather weakly.

"Come on, tell me."

What was the point of denying it? I said, "For a couple of years, may be."

His eyes went as cold as Russian granite. You know, that dismal speckled stone. And then he laughed. He sat on his bed and laughed his head off. That's what thirty years of marriage have done for us; there really was no need for us to say anything to one another. It was totally unnecessary. Do you know, Janet, while my stomach knotted into a horribly painful ball I too laughed. I had to laugh.

I thought I wouldn't be able to get up this morning. But I made it. Not enough energy to have my bath though. I've unlocked the drawer in my desk and put the notes I've written for you in the right order. My nice italic handwriting's gone, but I expect you'll be able to decipher these squiggles. Dr Brown's pills have deadened the pains in my stomach, but even so they're getting the better of me. "I don't feel meself," as Peggy used to say before she had her hysterectomy.

Yet I can still see the funny side of it. I'd been feeling as guilty as hell for suspecting Rupert of poisoning me, and for suspecting him about getting Dr Brown to attend me regularly—which would make a post mortem seem unnecessary. But I'd kept switching the tea-glasses all the same. My subconscious reasoning: if Rupert hasn't drugged my tea the switch will do him no harm. If he has, then he will be the one who'll die, and it'll serve him right. What I didn't bargain for was—oh my God! the pain! Janet, night after night he put some lethal stuff into *his* glass. He knew me better than I thought. So, you see, he *hasn't* murdered me. I've committed suicide, haven't I?

You're to do nothing about it . . . nothing. But I will . . . will put this into an envelope . . . if it's the last thing I do . . . It will be . . . I feel empty . . . It's a floating feeling . . . Not unpleasant . . . Floating . . . Ah yes, envelope . . . stamp. Sure of one thing . . . Peggy will post this to you . . . Peggy never forgot to post my letters . . . Won't fail now . . . Peggy's as predictable as me . . . thank God. Janet . . . don't show this to . . . anyone. Understand? . . . No scandal . . . It would be absurd . . . for a doctor like Rupert to be . . . to be caught for . . . the murder of his wife . . . Let him go . . . He'll retire next year . . . I won't be around to irritate him . . . He'll die of boredom soon . . .

I feel now . . . I feel the days when he was away from home . . . long sunny . . . beautiful . . . time to watch a blade of grass in the wind . . . watch the light on your hair . . .

such peace . . . What a beautiful world when he's away from home . . .

Will I have to meet him again . . . somewhere . . . particles in a magnetic field . . . ? No more . . . No more little knives . . . If I meet him I'll cut him dead.

HIGH-VOLTAGE INTRIGUE!

WOLF TRAP by Frederick Nolan

Against the inner sanctums of Nazi intelligence, secret operation Wolf Trap ensnares a German double agent, an American spy, a beautiful Czech resistance fighter, and a ruthless Gestapo officer in a web of plots and counterplots. "Fast-paced and mesmerizing." —*The Grand Rapids Press*
___90395-6 $3.95 U.S.

THE WINDSOR PLOT by Pauline Glen Winslow

What if Hitler planned to kill Churchill and King George and put the Duke of Windsor on the throne? "A chilling plot...that leaves the reader breathless." —*Publishers Weekly*
___90389-8 $4.95 U.S. ___90390-1 $6.25 Can.

ATTACK THE LUSITANIA!
by Raymond Hitchcock

Suppose the *Lusitania* had really been attacked by a British submarine disguised as a German U-boat...
"Smartly done" —Kirkus *Reviews*
___90389-8 $4.95 U.S.